THE GUEST BOOK TRILOGY BOOK ONE

THE MAN IN CABIN NUMBER FIVE

*Donna
glad you
enjoyed the
Book!
Chrysteen*

CHRYSTEEN BRAUN

Design and distribution by Bublish, Inc.
Published by Marble Creek Press

ISBN: 978-1-647044-62-6 (paperback)
ISBN: 978-1-647044-64-0 (hardcover)
ISBN: 978-1-647044-63-3 (eBook)

For Larry;
Always the wind beneath my wings.

When you find this, time has stopped for me.

I am desperate and I can think of no other way to end this. I didn't mean to destroy their family. And now I'm destroying mine. I'm a terrible person. A monster. A fool. I'm so sorry. I can never forgive myself for what I've done.

Last thoughts, John Murphy, 1957

THE IDEA

A friend once told me I'd live until the ripe old age of eighty-six. When you hear this in your mid-twenties, it's almost impossible to imagine ever growing that old. *Old,* was your grandparents. It seems like there's plenty of time to do everything you want to do in your life. I've used that prediction as a gauge, a tool to measure the risks, and sometimes I was fearless. And whenever asked, I say, "I've done everything I wanted to." I've even thought about having that put on my gravestone.

I've survived two husbands, and I'm still working on my third. When you remarry after sixty, you look at relationships differently than you did in your youth. You tend to overlook a lot of the things that were so important when you were younger: dashing handsomeness, a muscular physique, hair. Body parts have shifted for us both; I have saggy breasts, and he has little breasts too. We both have gray hair *everywhere*. His legs have gotten slimmer over the years; mine have gotten thicker and have orange peeled more. We both have sagging upper arms; his from losing muscle mass, mine from being overweight. We both have crepey skin, but mine bothers me more than his does him.

He's a terrific guy, and while he's a little younger than I am, he has different issues than I do. His prostate gives him problems, and yet he has managed to live with the impact that's made on his life and ours. He's kept his diabetes under control. Not so surprisingly, I have diabetes, neuropathy in my feet, and in fact have lost part of my smallest right toe. I have high cholesterol, high blood pressure, and have had two stents put in my chest.

But other than that, I'm in good shape.

If I take it easy, I can do just about anything I want to.

You know how when people hear your life stories, they sometimes say, "You should write a book." I suppose that means over the years, some of my stories must have been interesting to others, and lately, I've been thinking about *writing* that book. While I can't always remember what I had for dinner last night, I *can* remember things that happened to me over my lifetime...and I've also been known to embellish a little here and there, so I'd be able to come up with stories to fill in any gaps.

I've just had my eightieth birthday, thank God, for I'm getting close. As much as I swore I hated the idea of a party, my family and friends had one for me anyway...and I ended up having the best time ever. People I hadn't seen for years surprised me by coming, and of course, talking with them brought back a lot of old memories. Some reminded me of unpleasantness, but I recalled most with fondness.

My husband's daughter, Sissy, had gone through my drawers of old photos, much to my dismay, for some of them could have been considered damning. She made up some poster boards showing my life at various ages. She meant well, but I couldn't help but feel that I was a spectator at my own funeral. Plus, I absolutely hated seeing photos of myself in *private*, much less on public display.

"Remember the old Helm's Bakery truck?" my husband asked us all.

"The moment we saw it stop down the street, we'd rush to our mother to ask for enough money to buy a doughnut or cookie," someone said.

We'd wait, almost jumping in anticipation, until that long wooden drawer rolled out, revealing all the goodies we had to choose from.

I said, "I can picture it all clearly. I always chose the brownie, for it was pre-cut into squares and covered in a thin chocolate glaze. Sometimes, if I had enough money in my pocket, I'd get two and hide the second one in a napkin for you, Sarah," I said, turning to my old friend.

"I've never had brownies like those since. Yum," she said.

Sarah had flown in from New York and when I saw her, more old memories flooded back to me; images of her slugging a young boy who constantly teased me, and me bringing her something nice to wear, and watching her change into it while my mother drove us to school.

One of my stepchildren from my first marriage was there; sweet William. He was an old man now too, only ten years younger than me, although he looked *much* younger. He reminded me so much of David, it shocked me when I first saw him; he had that 'forever youthful' look about him. I hadn't seen him in ages and we did a lot of catching up. His brother, who had no children, and his sister, who had two, had never married and still lived in the family home, whereas William had traveled and had married twice; he lost his first wife and divorced his second. His daughter had given him three grandchildren, who were all married with families of their own.

"This is for you, Annie," he said, handing me a clasped manila envelope. "It's not a gift, really. Save it for a quiet time."

I couldn't resist feeling the contents, and then I said, "Old photos, eh?" Suddenly I laughed.

"What?" he asked.

"Remember when I'd drive you kids somewhere, and I'd hit the brakes?" I laughed again. "We'd lurch forward and laugh our heads off. Then I'd do it again."

"Good God," William laughed too. "Don't tell me you did that on purpose? You used to scare the hell out of me. I always thought you were just a terrible driver."

"Oh, my." I wiped tears from my eyes. "I haven't giggled like this in years."

"You know, Annie, those were the best years we ever had with my dad. Before you married, we never saw him." He smiled. "And then we lost you. We were almost grown by then."

"Oh, sweet William," I said, taking his hands in mine. "Thank you."

"What do you think?" I asked my husband about a week after my party.

"About what?" He looked at me as though I'd been talking to him about something he hadn't heard.

"About me writing a book?" I asked, wrinkling my face in concentration. I was sitting in front of my computer losing at solitaire.

"Oh," he finally answered. "If that's what you want to do."

I looked over at him while he went back to his newspaper.

"Well, that doesn't sound too convincing," I said.

"Annie, I think you should do whatever it is you want to."

"Do you think my life has been that interesting?" I asked, knowing the answer I was hoping for.

"Of course I do. Just don't put in any sex scenes. They could be embarrassing." And he went back to his paper.

So there you have it. I've decided to write a book.

Now I'd have to figure out what I wanted to write about and then get started.

I pulled down a few of my favorite books to see how *they'd* started. I hadn't ever read with a critical eye before; like how a book started, I mean. I was sure there was a craft or art about writing, but I didn't have years to spend learning if I wanted to get anything written before I ran out of good summers.

So I started at the beginning...or where my mind took me.

I was never the prettiest or the most popular in school. Other students never gathered around me or joined me at lunch; I always felt that if I wanted to sit with someone, I had to seek them out. For you see, my father was Taiwanese, and my mother was German and Norwegian, therefore I had a distinct look about me.

Our house was at the end of the block, and the farthest from school, so I was always the one who knocked on my friend's doors to walk with them to school. Until I met Sarah, I was always the one who finished walking home alone.

*We'd gotten a record player for Christmas and my older sister Loni fina-
gled to set it up in her room, which, of course, was off limits to me. By the
time I got home from school, she was usually playing records, or giggling with
girlfriends behind closed doors. Outwardly, she made fun of our heritage by
either bowing to her friends or talking in a sing-song voice that made them
laugh even harder. She never shared with me how she truly felt inside.*

*Sometimes, after I'd gone to bed, I'd wake to my parent's laughter as they
danced to the music on the living room stereo. I'd stand in the hall doorway,
rubbing my eyes like I'd just awakened and watch them until they noticed
me. My father would stop and motion for me to join them, and he'd pick me
up in his arms and continue dancing with me and my mother.*

*"Why aren't I pretty like Loni?" I once asked him as I laid my head on
his shoulder.*

"My beautiful Annie, why would you ask such a question?"

*I remember my mother tilting her head in surprise, and then gently
touching my cheek.*

*"You're exquisite," my father said, giving me a kiss. "And as you grow
older, you'll see, you'll be even more so."*

*I got to dance with them a while longer before they both scooted me
off to bed.*

I was crestfallen at my first attempt at writing. This wasn't the beginning
of my story. These were just memories of how I felt as a small child.
I sat for the longest time, looking at my notepad, willing my pen to
write again.

"Pooh," I said to myself.

As it turned out, it came to me.

I blossomed in my early twenties, after I married David.

The stories came after I left him. There were three books right there,
about people I met who would never know the secrets my mountain
cabins guarded.

The Mountains

CHAPTER ONE

1960–1970

I remember a lot of things about the lake house and our first summer there.

"Let me know if you're going to toss your cookies," my sister Loni said.

I'd never had a history of having a sensitive stomach, but when she said that, I had terrible visions of getting car sick from all the turns the first time we drove up the winding road to the mountains.

"Thanks for that," I said.

It was also the first time my father had driven such a road, and my mother warned us to be quiet as he took the curves with a firm grip on the steering wheel. There were no seat belts then, and when he cut a turn too tightly, Loni and I slid from one side of the back seat to the other. The more Loni and I tried not to laugh, the more we did.

"Stop!" my mother scolded, turning to look at the two of us. All that did was make us laugh all over again.

It turned out I loved the drive up and down the mountain. On a clear day, you could pick out a small lake to the southeast, and the city below seemed to continue forever to the west. Sometimes the clouds would back up to the rim of the mountain, and they would be so thick, you couldn't see anything below. They looked like balls of cotton you could just step out on. We later learned that when moisture pushed the clouds higher against the mountain, a dense fog would cover the roads and it would often be impossible to see the road ahead.

My mother worked in the lunch program at the elementary school, so she was usually off during the summer. My father was a chemical engineer, and had taken some vacation time so he could spend a week with us.

"You two should have lots of fun up here," she said.

Loni's head was resting on the back window, but I could still see her roll her eyes. The times when Loni and I still had fun together were getting fewer; she was just enough older than me that we were in two separate worlds. I was ten and Loni had just turned thirteen. I wasn't included when she wanted to go places with her friends, and although she wasn't allowed to, I knew she wore make-up when she left the house.

"We're here," my mother finally said as we pulled into a circular driveway.

My father slowly stretched as he stood. He unclenched his hands and shook them, willing the circulation and color to return to them. He sighed.

"Now that wasn't so bad, was it?" she said, patting him on the shoulder. "Grab something," she called as Loni and I scrambled out of our station wagon. "Open the back."

I paused long enough to realize how quiet it was here. It was a warm day, and the wind whistled through the trees that circled our house, providing us with a cool breeze. And then I turned and saw it.

"I see the lake!" I shouted, pointing to the deep blue water. It was smooth as glass until a gust of wind ruffled its surface. I dropped whatever it was I'd carried, but my father gently turned me around and pointed me back in the right direction before I could run to see it...

"Not until we're unpacked," he said, grabbing some boxes. "Then we'll all go down together."

The Pinecone Lake House, as we called it, was large enough for at least two families to stay comfortably. There were fifteen rooms and twenty-nine doors and windows. Unlike most homes, lake houses had two fronts; one that you saw when you drove up to it, and the real front, the more architecturally interesting one, which you could only see if you were on the lake itself. There was a small grassy area on the lakeside which ended down at our dock and into the water.

We nicknamed our room the 'Bunkhouse' for it had two sets of built-in bunk beds and it was perfect for sleepovers; however, the term *sleepover* was inaccurate, for we never got much sleep when we were there with our friends.

There were three other bedrooms plus my parent's room, a gigantic living room, dining room and a large kitchen where at least three people could work at the same time. The walls were pine, even in the kitchen, and floors were covered in western style area rugs. The previous owner left their artwork and a deer's head, which hung over the fireplace mantel.

After our family tour of the front and the lake, I could hardly wait to roam the land around the house. Even though it was summer, mud and leaves clung to my shoes as I made my way further to the back of our property. Wooden planks ran along the ground, toward the weathered and splintered garden shed, which even then looked like it would fall down in a strong wind. While chipped and peeling, it was painted the same colors as the house. Thick brush kept me from going any further, which was disappointing, so I turned to make my way back to the house. One of the low-lying branches that covered part of the view of the lake clipped me on the forehead as I ran under it, and I immediately felt blood trickle down my face. Not to be outdone by a tree, I wiped my face with the back of my hand, and then wiped my hand on my pants. I'd be in trouble for doing that when I returned, but I continued on. The glimmer of the water in the sunlight called to me.

That was the year we bought our boat. Lake Arrowhead is a private lake, and in order to keep the water free from mussels, all boats had to be inspected and licensed before they could be put in the water.

At first, my mother wasn't interested in learning how to operate a boat, but at our insistence, she relented and got herself a permit too. Although it was superstitious to change the name of a boat, ours was named "Rum Runner" and my father wanted to name it "Destiny" after what he thought coming to America and marrying my mother meant for him.

I remember the first time we all went out in it, and when my mother took the wheel, she was timid and nervous. By the second time around the lake, she'd worked up the nerve to increase the speed enough, so that water sprayed on our faces. My father, who was the more conservative of the two, had to tell her to slow down, or we'd all get into trouble.

"Well, that was fun," she said breathlessly.

That was the summer Loni started her period and my mother learned how to start the fire in the pit so we could roast marshmallows; and, more importantly, how to put the fire out properly. It was the summer I twisted my ankle when I tripped on a tree branch as I ran back to our house for lunch, and it was the first time we saw wild animals. Deer leisurely searched our property, looking for something to eat, and a bobcat graced us with his presence. We were as quiet as we could be as it walked through the trees, getting closer to the house. When Loni went inside to grab our camera, he casually turned to see who we were before heading off back into the forest before she could get back. It turned out there was a postcard from the previous owner still stuck on the refrigerator with a photo of a bobcat, so he'd most likely visited them too. We nicknamed him "Bob."

It was the first time we learned you couldn't leave your trash cans outside the night before the trash truck came the next day, for hungry bears and other wild animals would come out during the night searching for something to eat. They'd not only damage your trash barrel, but remnants of whatever was not edible would end up scattered all over the ground.

It was the first time of many that I collected pinecones and greenery to put in a bowl that sat on the entry table, hoping to bring to the indoors the fragrances of being outdoors. And when we went into town, I bought a guest book with my own money so we could have everyone who stayed with us sign their names. Of course, I signed my name first.

It was also the first time I fell in love.

His name was Joe, and he cleared the tables at the local diner where we had Sunday breakfasts. Sundays were the only times we could splurge and order whatever we wanted, as long as we ate it all. I usually had the Belgian waffle with syrup, whipped cream, and bacon.

This one Sunday, I'd put too much syrup on my last bite and some had run down my chin. Joe was passing by and pointed it out by touching his chin and winking. I thought I'd die of embarrassment as I grabbed my napkin and quickly wiped my face. At the same time, Loni, who had witnessed it all, kicked me under the table.

"Ow," I said.

"What?" my mother asked, looking up from her magazine.

"Nothing," I answered, kicking Loni back.

Joe was probably sixteen, tall and lanky, but I thought he was the most handsome boy I'd ever seen. For the next few weeks, all I could do was think about him, and one day Loni caught me drawing a heart around our names in my diary.

"There's no way someone his age would be interested in *you*," she said, scoffing.

"Shut up."

"I heard that," my mother said from another room.

I was certain he liked me, for he'd winked at me, and that had to have meant something. I imagined he'd figure out where our lake house was and leave me some sort of message, maybe a rock or a feather. Of course I'd know it would be him.

We finally went back up for the annual End of Summer Festival and my stomach sank when I learned we weren't going to the diner for breakfast that Sunday. Instead, we packed two baskets of food and ourselves into the boat and headed over to the village.

I knew for sure I'd see Joe, and that when he saw me, he'd come over and say "hey" and introduce himself to my parents. I searched in vain for him everywhere I went.

"Looking for Mr. Dreamboat?" Loni asked.

"Oh, shut up." I said, trying desperately to hide my disappointment.

"Oh, look. There he is," Loni said, pointing off to our right. She was gloating so much I thought she was going to pop.

And there he was, walking towards us.

He was with a tall blond girl who laughed as she leaned into him. She looked up at him and he kissed her.

My entire body sank with heartbreak, and I felt as though I couldn't breathe. Of course, he would be in love with someone so blonde and pretty. I couldn't look at him, so I quickly turned and started collecting the empty plates and cups from our blanket.

"Why, that's thoughtful of you," my mother said. "It looks like the celebration is coming to a close already."

"She's just hiding from someone," Loni said.

"Shut up."

"Annie, you know I hate when people say that." Then she looked up and saw Joe and the girl walking past us. "That's that nice young man from the diner, isn't it?"

I kept my head down, pretending not to hear her.

"I knew he wasn't interested in you, you dork," Loni said dryly.

"Shut up," I said again. Sometimes I really hated her.

We spent Thanksgiving Week at the lake house. We waited to do our grocery shopping until we got up there so we didn't have to load the car with food. There was a large market near the house, and I was still young enough that I enjoyed the holidays, and looked forward to riding the cart up and down the aisles picking out everything we didn't need. Because it was a holiday, I stood a fifty-fifty chance of getting what I asked for, so I asked for everything from crazy cereals to cookies.

"Firewood," I called out as we were checking out.

"Good call," my mother said, pointing my father in the direction of the stacks of wood sitting at the store's entrance. "We'll take five," she told the cashier.

Although it was unusually cold, I was disappointed there was no forecast for snow, for I'd hoped to try catching snowflakes as they fell around me. It was a good thing we'd collected newspapers and brought bags of them up, for the ones in our wood storeroom off the kitchen were damp and we had to throw them away. We used almost all of them to keep the fireplace constantly lit, and we set the heater higher to keep us all warm as we slept. We wore mittens inside and wrapped ourselves in blankets while we watched T.V. or read.

News spread quickly in a small town like Lake Arrowhead, and a few days before Thanksgiving, a young girl went missing. My parents instantly went into high alert and we couldn't go anywhere or do anything without one of them there with us. It only made sense, but I was confident nothing would happen to either of us here. Even being so cold, all I wanted to do was walk through our woods or go down to the lake.

The morning of the little girl's disappearance, Loni and I brought out several games, decided on Monopoly and set it up on a table in the window. We made constant trips back into the kitchen to grab potato chips and sodas, and then finally made tuna sandwiches. We quickly tired of the game, and for most of the afternoon, we sat outside all covered up in our Adirondack chairs, first complaining, then reading, then napping.

Late that afternoon, Mother told us she'd heard on the radio they had found the girl; she'd just wandered into the forest behind the campground where her family was staying and eventually made her way back to their campsite.

Mother stretched her shoulders and rubbed the back of her neck like she did when she tried to relax, and I was hoping the good news would make her stop worrying about us so much.

Thanksgiving morning, we got up early to stuff the turkey and put it in the oven. We peeled the potatoes, cut carrots and celery for snacks, made a dip, and my mother tried a new recipe for green bean casserole.

"Everyone's making it these days," she said.

I'd had the grand idea of making a pumpkin pie, but I'd baked nothing before but cookies. No one wanted to risk a potential disaster, so we bought our pie at the grocery store, and it sat on the counter covered in saran wrap.

"There's a slice missing," my father said, frowning. He narrowed his eyes. "Who did it?" he asked.

We all looked at each other and shrugged our shoulders.

"I wanted to," I admitted.

"Aha!" he said. "If none of you did it, then it must have been me!" Haha, he laughed.

My father was in charge of keeping the fire going, and before we ate, he brought in the last bundle of wood and stacked it by the fireplace.

"We'll have to go to the store tomorrow and get more wood. I think next fall we should have someone deliver it," he said.

We all watched "It's a Wonderful Life" on the big black and white television in the living room. My mother loved it and cried every time she saw it, my father didn't quite understand it, I liked it somewhat, and Loni read a book.

After dinner, I swore I'd never eat again.

A large burp escaped my lips and my mother said, "I heard that."

"Just making room for more pie later," I said.

Loni and I cleared the table, and then I called "I'll wash."

Around nine, I sneaked into the kitchen and ate another piece of pie with whipping cream on it.

On Friday, we drove into Big Bear to see what the stores had on sale. We bought our first ornaments for a mountain Christmas tree. While Loni and my father waited outside, my mother and I went into a little store and bought ribbons and trims, and then when we got home, I started gathering pinecones so I could decorate them to add to the tree when we set it up.

I missed the warmer weather and wished we could go down to our dock and sit with our feet in the water. During the summer, we'd watched people in canoes and kayaks, and now and then water skiers passed by us at what then seemed like great speeds. But few people had been out in their boats Thanksgiving week. Still, we could hope.

CHAPTER TWO

It would have been fun exploring and investigating the forest surrounding the lake house with someone my own age, but no matter when we came up, I never saw children at our neighbor's house. I learned to be satisfied hunting and foraging for arrowheads and rarities on my own, and hiding from the neighbor was part of the adventure.

They had two houses, both built with logs. One was small, about the size of a double car garage, and the other was much larger. Once, when I was just happening by, I noticed her husband's workshop full of wood and tools. He must have been a carpenter or cabinet man to have table tops piled high with stacks of unfinished projects and sawdust on the floor.

"Come say hello," Mrs. Richmond called to me one afternoon, but like an idiot, I turned and ran like I'd been caught doing something I wasn't supposed to be doing. The moment I did it, I realized I'd have to see her sometime, so I called out, "I'm late getting home," and kept running.

The next time we came up, I was determined to go see her garden. In truth, it was more than a garden; almost the entire property was filled with flowers and plants I'd never seen before.

"You're back," she said when she saw me.

"Sorry, I had to rush the other week. But I couldn't help seeing your garden," I said.

"It's quite lovely, isn't it?" she said. "I'm Mrs. Richmond, but you can call me Gloria."

I wasn't good with determining ages, and I couldn't help thinking anyone older than my parents was ancient. Which is what I figured Gloria was.

"You can call me Annie. And I have a sister Loni, although she's older than I am, and she always kicks me when she thinks I've done something stupid." I wasn't quite sure why I'd just told her all that, but it just slipped out.

"I had an older sister too when I was your age, and she used to pull my hair and blame me for things she broke...When we grew up, we ended up being *very good* friends, which I'm sure you'll see with your sister. Do you want to come closer and look at my plants?"

The first thought that ran through my mind was my parents warning me never to talk to or take candy from a stranger, but Mrs. Richmond didn't look like she was going to kidnap me.

Her garden was like nothing I'd ever seen before; there were gravel paths that led all the way through it, and bursts of colors were mixed in with all the green. The only plants I could identify were the ferns, and they were in all the shady spots. There were wood carved animals everywhere; a bear climbing an old tree stump, an owl on a tree trunk, squirrels chasing each other on another stump. A multi color raccoon poked its head around another. And there were metal planters hanging from posts in amongst all of it, overflowing with flowers.

"Would you like to learn something about plants?" she asked, motioning me to follow her. She proudly looked out at her property, and then when she decided where to begin her lecture, she stopped and said, "Here we have bracken ferns, which are all over the mountains. People sometimes stop along the roads to pick them to eat. I've never tried one, and I hear they're poisonous. But they're beautiful. The first year I was here, I almost dug them all up because they were brown and wilted. But I learned they come back year after year.

"And these are lilies of the valley. They produce bell-shaped flowers that smell sweet." She then pointed to another area and said, "And all these in here are hostas. You see, they come in all shades of green. Did you know that green is green, whether it's solid, variegated, light or dark?

"And then I have my hydrangeas. When they bloom, the garden explodes with colors; these come in all colors of pink, blue, lavender and white. When I first planted them, I tried to mix them so it would always be a surprise to see what combination I'd have each time they bloom."

"What's that over there?" I asked, pointing to a green area surrounded by a makeshift wire fence.

"That's my vegetable garden; I have to keep it protected so that deer and other animals don't get in and eat everything. Come, can you figure out what's growing here?"

We stood in front of the gate and I looked at all the rows of green leaves. I'd only seen gardens in books, so I jogged my memory and pointed out what I was fairly sure of.

"Those look like tomatoes, and carrots, but what are those rows of tall round things?"

"Those are Brussels sprouts. Have you ever had them?"

I wanted to say 'no and I don't plan on it,' but I could tell she saw the look on my face for she said, "Well, when they're ready to pick, I'll make some for you and your family to taste. I think you'll like them."

I couldn't imagine it, but I did like vegetables and was game for trying anything once.

"And here are red and green peppers, beets for canning, cucumbers, and green beans. Yum."

"Who eats all this?"

"Well, we do, and of course we share it with our neighbors and friends. You know, in the old days, even before I was born," and she winked at me, "people grew their own fruits and vegetables so they could feed their families. Now, everything is grown for us, or put into cans. I guess that's progress." She let out a little sigh.

"The next time you come by, I'll make you some lemonade and we can sit out here. I'll teach you about the animals up here."

"Cool," I said. I then looked at my watch and said, "My mom will be worried about me if she doesn't see me right about now. Thanks for the gardening lesson."

"I saw Brussels sprouts," I called to my mother as I pulled the screen door open and rushed to find her.

"Don't let the door..."

I realized too late the door was going to slam behind me. "Sorry!"

I thought for sure I was going to be scolded, but instead, my mother sat me down at the kitchen table and asked all about my visit with Mrs. Richmond. I told her about the garden and the carved animals, and how I was going to try Brussels sprouts.

"And then she's going to teach me about the mountain animals," I said.

I'll never forget the way my mother would sit and listen to me when I had something to share. When I was younger, I sometimes tripped over my own words if I was excited about something, but she always made me feel that what I was saying was important. I didn't realize it at the time, but the time she spent with me was part of her love for me.

"You smell like you've been outdoors. Why don't you take a bath before dinner."

That was love, too.

CHAPTER THREE

For once, it worked out that my birthday fell on a weekend. To celebrate becoming a teenager, I invited three of my girlfriends, including my best friend Sarah, to have a sleepover weekend at the lake house. The four of us would take the bunk beds in the Bunkhouse room, and I had all kinds of games planned. Loni brought one of her girlfriends along and while I made her promise she wouldn't try to crash my party, I knew she'd find something to aggravate me; it had just become her way.

Once we'd loaded the car and everyone was ready, we all stood outside and waited for Sarah. I was getting worried her mother would change her mind and tell her she couldn't go with us. Finally, she rounded the corner and I could tell she was stomping mad.

"What's wrong?" I asked

"Everything's fine. I needed to let off some steam," she said, handing me her bag. "Here, carry this. My hand is numb."

"Keep these chips in the back in case you get hungry," my mother said, tossing me the bag.

Loni wanted shotgun up front, so she and her friend sat with my Mom. No one else really cared, so my friends and I climbed in and sat wherever there weren't bags and suitcases. You'd have thought we were going to be away for weeks.

Friday night traffic added over an hour to the trip, and of course Loni started complaining. My mother said nothing to embarrass her, just reached out and touched her shoulder, which did the trick.

"We're starving," I called from the back seat.

"Open the chips. We'll eat when we get there and then go to the grocery store."

When we finally got there, we went directly to the diner in town, and Loni and her girlfriend sat at a table as far away from us as possible.

"Will I be cramping your style if I sit with you ladies?" my mother asked.

"Not at all, Mrs. C."

"Hamburgers and malts?" I asked.

"Sounds good to me too," my mom said. "After dinner, we'll shop."

We roamed the aisles of the grocery store and because it was my birthday, I got to pick out every junk food I wanted while my mom was in charge of making sure we had the basics.

"For my birthday," I'd say as I dumped yet another thing into the cart, and my mother would just shake her head.

Loni and her friend stocked up on sweet drinks and cookies. I had an idea what the drinks were for, and I was hoping she wouldn't do anything stupid while we were up there.

Once we got to the lake house, Loni and her girlfriend took one of the guest bedrooms and I led my friends to the Bunkhouse room.

"Wow," they said.

"Since I'm the birthday girl, I call one of the bottom bunks. You guys can draw straws if you want," I said, and everyone just threw their bags on a bed and that was that.

We unpacked, hung our clothes, and got into our pajamas.

"These are cool," one of the girls said about my arrowheads.

We took our blankets off our beds and with only the glow of the nightlight, we could see our outlines as we lay bundled up on the floor. We were going to tell stories and see who could stay awake the longest. I started first, but soon my voice grew softer and when I stopped talking, I could tell everyone had drifted off to sleep.

The next morning, my mother let us sleep in. She made a huge breakfast of pancakes, bacon, and eggs.

"I'll leave Loni's breakfast in the oven," she said when we were finished.

"Can we go to the Village?" I finally asked.

My mom dropped us off, and we spent the day going through all the shops. We stopped in the pet store and stuck our fingers in the puppy and kitten cages before I bought a bag of duck food. We checked out the fossil store, and bought some postcards of the lake at the bookstore, had ice cream cones, and then bought a bag of chocolate-covered almonds at the candy store.

We walked from one end of the lakefront back to where we could sit and watch the water skiers circle around in front of us, and then we fed the ducks.

I could feel the warmth of the sun on my face and I could tell I was turning pink. I pushed my finger on to Sarah's cheek and it turned white before it went to pink as well.

"Sorry, guys. I forgot to bring suntan lotion. You ready to go back to the house?" I asked.

We found a pay phone, and I called my mom to come get us.

I was hoping Mrs. Richmond, *Gloria*, would be outside when we returned from the Village, and sure enough, there was a note on our door inviting us to come over for some lemonade. I wanted the girls to meet her and see her garden.

"I don't think I ever told you about some of the animals we have up here. Or if I did, I've forgotten," she said, laughing to herself.

It was a warm afternoon, so we stayed outside and after she showed us her garden, we sat at a table and drank what I remember being the best lemonade I ever had.

"Well, of course you all know we have bears and foxes up here. I have a fox that comes to my door and I feed it an egg; sometimes he runs off with it and I find shells in the yard, but if he's especially hungry, he'll break the egg right there and suck out the insides. Of course, feeding animals here isn't the best thing to do because then they feel comfortable getting close to humans and their foraging skills diminish. Not all people love animals the way I do.

"I also feed peanuts to my squirrels. They come to my door, tapping on it to remind me they're hungry. I love to watch the way they pack the peanuts in their mouths, then they run off and hide their treasure so they can come back here for more."

"Have you seen a bear?" one of my friends asked.

"Yup. We see them mostly at night though, and we can always tell they've visited us if we leave our trash cans out. They make a mess everywhere. We've seen a bobcat, and coyotes. And sometimes in the afternoons a few deer come through the property on their way to find something to eat. If I have extra apples, I leave them out on the ground for them to find."

She seemed comfortable just sitting and watching us eat her cookies before she went on to another thought.

"Now you've seen what's left of my daffodils. They come from bulbs that I planted years ago, but they also produce more on their own...did you make it to the Sequoia Trail?"

We shook our heads. "No."

"Well, if you don't have time *this* trip, you'll have to do that the next time you're here. There's plenty of hiking and plants to see there."

I felt like we were in a mini classroom, gathered around Gloria.

"What I didn't want to forget to tell you about today," she went on, "were the birds. We have more kinds here than even most mountain folk know. We have finches, chickadees, robins, pigeons, and some I can't remember. Our two most famous are the woodpecker, which is a handsome bird. It has a red cap, and it feeds off some of our pines, drilling holes with their beaks to get to the insects inside. But they've also damaged our houses, so many people have put up wire to deter them.

"I think the most popular, is our Steller's jay. They have beautiful blue feathers with a black-brown head and a crest on top. They love sunflower seeds, so of course I have a couple of feeders throughout the property. Now, any questions, class?" Gloria chuckled. "Take these cookies," she said, shooing at them in the air. "I don't want them around."

That night, we made a fire in our pit, and we roasted hot dogs and hamburgers for dinner. After we put the fire out and cleaned up our mess, we went inside to get ready to go to the movies. "Son of Flubber" and "Bye Bye Birdie" were playing at the theater, and when we couldn't decide which to see, we flipped a coin.

Bye Bye Birdie with Bobby Rydell and Ann-Margret won.

When my mother dropped us off at the movies, Loni and her girlfriend only pretended to go in. The minute she drove off, Loni turned around and said, "See ya. We'll be back here when Mom comes back."

The first thing we did was buy buttered popcorn, soda, Milk Duds and Jujubes. I was so caught up in the movie, I didn't realize I hadn't thought about Loni until the credits rolled onto the screen. Sure enough, she was outside waiting when we all came out, and she pushed me to the side when my mom pulled up.

"We'll get in the back," she said.

"What a bitch," my friend Sarah whispered.

When we got home, my mom helped us light a new fire in the pit so we could roast marshmallows, then we told spooky stories. Once the fire started burning out, the nighttime air chilled us, so I took the gallon of water we'd brought out and doused the fire, then covered the remnants with dirt.

When we made it upstairs, we heard music blaring in Loni's room.

"Let's play Monopoly," I said.

We opened bags of pretzels, Cheetos, and more soda. When we were about halfway through the game, I realized my mistake in not locking our door, for Loni opened it and stood in the doorway looking pale and unsteady.

"What're you dipshits doin'?"

She was shitfaced and had to lean against the door frame just to stand. She made it in a few steps before she said, "I think I'm going to

17

be sick," and we scrambled as she threw up all over our game and snacks. With all we'd eaten that day, I thought for sure I was going to be next.

Our shrieks brought my mother, who took one look at the mess and said, "My god Loni, you obviously ate too much junk. Good god."

I don't know how mothers do it, but after she quietly got Loni cleaned up and into her bed, she tackled cleaning the mess in our room. We didn't want to sleep in the Bunkhouse room that night, so we pulled out four sleeping bags, put new logs in the fire, and slept in the living room next to the fireplace.

"It'll be like a camp out," my mom said, trying to cheer me up.

"I'm really sorry," I said to my friends. "Loni can ruin a one car funeral."

After everyone else fell asleep, I added a few more logs to the fire then just lay there, unable to sleep. Loni had ruined my birthday. Being thirteen meant I was no longer a child, and becoming a woman. I didn't feel like one. I was angry and hurt. I tried to think of ways I could pay her back, to make her as miserable as she'd made me.

The only thing I could think of was to tell my mother about the drinking. Loni would definitely get in trouble, but it would also make my parents unhappy, and I didn't want to hurt them.

For now, I would stay silent.

Finally, I slept and was the first to wake when the sunlight filtered through the large living room window the next morning. After all the salt I'd consumed, my mouth was so dry it took two glasses of orange juice to make me feel normal again.

My mother left a note on the kitchen counter letting us know she'd gone to the store.

"Let's eat," I suggested.

I cooked the bacon, Sarah made the pancakes. Jilly scrambled the eggs, and Janice set the table. We made more than what we could eat, but the leftovers went down the garbage disposal.

"Loni and her girlfriend can feed themselves." I insisted.

My mom came back with a carpet shampooer and went upstairs to clean. Between vomit and spilled soda, it must have been quite a mess, but I wasn't about to go up and see. Instead, we cleaned up after ourselves downstairs and put everything away. I was hoping we could stay until the afternoon before heading home.

"Will you take us out on the boat today?" I asked.

"Let's get the laundry done, and the beds made first, and then we can see," my mother said. "I want to make sure Loni is okay."

"She just has a hangover," I muttered. Then to my mother, I said, "Can we go down to the dock? We're bored."

I waited for my friends outside, and the minute I closed my eyes and took a deep breath, I let the calmness of the morning relax me. I loved listening to the wind and watching it sway through the trees. I opened my eyes as a pinecone fell to the ground. Above me, a squirrel was sitting still on a branch, watching me, and I thought it might have been trying to reach it to eat the seeds. It scampered away, and I reached down to pick the pinecone up; I would keep it in my collection to mark my birthday. I closed my eyes again, listening to the silence.

When my friends finally joined me, we took our shoes and socks off and sat on our dock, dangling our feet in the water. I wanted to apologize for my sister's behavior, but no one seemed to even care, or at least there was no mention of it. My friend Sarah was the only one who affirmed her loyalty to me with a wry smile.

"We've had a great time, right, ladies?" Sarah asked.

"The best," the others added.

We never had time to go out on the boat, which gave us something to look forward to if we all came back again. We made sandwiches before we started packing the car for the ride down the hill. Loni looked terrible, and I was hoping the winding roads wouldn't make her sick again, but we were in luck. She slept in the very back of the car and we never heard a peep from her.

I wasn't sure how long a hangover lasted.

The next time we went up, Loni wanted to stay in her own bedroom.

"It's a great idea," I said to my mother, hoping to encourage her.

"No, it means more work for me when we leave," she said. "You guys can work it out."

Besides Loni, the problem with having the bunk beds in our room was there wasn't much wall space left over for furniture, so Loni and I shared the only dresser. In my forest explorations, I'd collected acorns, small bird's nests, and cracked egg shells I'd found on the ground, which I'd carefully placed on top of the dresser. At the end of the day when I returned to the Bunkhouse room, I'd find everything carelessly pushed over to one side. Once I found one of the shells on the floor and was just grateful Loni hadn't crushed it.

I knew Loni delighted in annoying me. One time when we were there, I found some acorns under my covers; she swore a squirrel must have come into the house and gotten in my bed. Or I'd randomly find a small branch or dried pine cone scale in one of my shoes, with no logical explanation of how they'd gotten there.

Eventually, our trips to the mountains grew less frequent. We both had school activities, eventually boyfriends, and Loni was nearing high school graduation. I could tell my mother only made the trip up for us, and it had also become obvious Loni had lost interest in going anywhere with me or my parents.

I, however, treasured my quiet time when I was there. If I didn't bring a friend with me, I'd read or wander down to the lake by myself. I was still amazed how I could see stars at night, and I still tried to capture the fragrances of the forest by bringing in pine cones and broken pine branches whenever I could.

At home, Loni spent most of her time locked up in her room and only came out for meals. I knew she was still drinking, but my parents suspected nothing.

I was grateful I had my friend Sarah. She'd tell me things about her whacky family that made my problems seem so small. And I could always count on her if I needed someone to talk to.

I was sixteen when we finally sold the Pinecone Lake House. Loni had gone away to college, and that left only my mother, me, and my friends making the trip. She made our meals, cleaned up and did laundry. She never complained, but I saw that I was being selfish. Without my father being able to join us, I understood she didn't have the companionship that had been part of the magic of the lake and the property.

On a weekend Loni came home from school, we made our last trip up so we could go through the house and decide what we wanted to keep once we sold it. My parents had listed the house, and there were realtor brochures on the kitchen counter showing photos of all the rooms. When I looked at them, I almost felt like I was looking at someone else's house. I realized then, I was going to be leaving an entire world behind me.

On our last night at the cabin, even though I was exhausted from packing, I had a hard time falling asleep. Obviously, I knew it was going to be the last time I'd stay in the bed I called mine. And I remembered how difficult it was for me to sleep the first few nights we'd stayed in the lake house in the beginning. I was grateful Loni slept in one of the other rooms, for I wanted to be by myself.

I waited until the last moment to carefully pack my mountain treasures; the feathers, bird shells, some pinecones, and the arrowheads I'd found. Since we wouldn't be returning to the mountains, we packed boxes of warm jackets, heavy socks, mittens, and boots, which we donated to the local thrift store. And as we drove away, I thought of movies I'd seen where the main character turns and looks through the rear window, waving. And that was me, tears in my eyes and everything.

"You're such a baby," Loni said.

"Shut up," I whispered.

Alyce Murphy

1934–1980

CHAPTER FOUR

Even before she went into the home, Mama used to talk about Daddy and she didn't always make sense. She'd start by saying things like "after Daddy's heart attack," then end with statements like "he never thought about us when he did it."

But let me start at the beginning.

My name is Alyce Murphy.

I was born and raised in Paramount, California, just north of Long Beach, back when it was hay and dairy land. If you weren't from here, you could always tell you were gettin' close cuz of the smell of the dung. Mama and Daddy said it reminded them of home. Once someone told me I smelled like shit, and I knew what they meant. That smell of horses and cows just stuck to our clothes, but we were used to it.

Paramount was heaven, as Mama told it; she and Daddy came out from Kansas right after they were married so my daddy could find work. My grandpa had already decided to move.

"The way I figure it, with Grandma gone, I don't have nothin' to keep me here anyway," he told them.

Homes were a lot more expensive in California than in Kansas, and they were still reeling from the Depression, but they figured if they put all their money together, they could find a house to share. They bought a small two-bedroom house which had enough land to build a garage one day. They had a goat, so'd they'd have milk and butter, and Grandpa built a large pen so it had its own place to stay and not eat the vegetables they'd planted.

When I was older, Mama tried to teach me how to sew and mend our clothing, but I hated doin' both. Grandpa loved to tease me by remindin' me how the women back home did their washin' by hand.

"That darned wind would come up and would blow dirt on them as soon as they were hung on the line."

"That's nice," I'd say, then run.

Mama saved any money she earned by selling her eggs, and when she had enough saved, the first thing she planned on buying was a clothes washer with a wringer. I was more interested in using that than sewin'.

We baked our bread and canned just about everyhin' and she taught me how to make soap from bacon fat, or goat's milk. We didn't have a double boiler yet, so when we had enough old soap scraps left over, we'd put them in a glass bowl which went in a saucepan filled with water. First the soap melted, then once it hardened, we grated and mixed it with 20 Mule Team Borax to use in the washer.

Old habits die hard, and even after she started using Tide powdered laundry soap, Mama saved soap scraps for years; kept them in a glass jar in the bathroom.

"They make it smell nice," she'd say, "Especially if someone does a poop."

On my seventh birthday, my daddy got his induction papers for World War II. We were getting ready to cut my cake, and I'd been scolded for sticking my fingers in the frosting to taste it. Daddy brought the letter in as everyone started singin' to me, but the look on his face made us freeze.

He left not long after that.

They had some savings, and she borrowed the rest from Grandpa so we could take a train ride back to where Daddy was in boot camp at Fort Benning, Georgia. She wanted to spend time with him before they sent him off into combat. I loved that train ride; it was full of soldiers (kids, Mama called them) who laughed and joked the whole trip.

They were a courteous bunch, holding open the corridor connection doors for us, and even offerin' to keep an eye on me if Mama needed to make a 'pit stop', as she called it.

"Unlike today," Mama would later say, "those were the days when there was no fear of handin' your child over to a stranger." There were very few small children on board, so every time one of the soldiers passed us, they made over me and of course, that made Mama feel the way parents always do; proud, like they'd created a big miracle.

"They were all so young," she'd tell me years later, "and I wondered how many of them were leavin' their own families behind so they could serve their country. I wondered if they didn't think there was a possibility they'd never return from their missions."

She ended up giving them the all the home-baked cookies she'd made for my daddy, figuring she'd replace them when she found a bakery when we got to our destination.

When we got back home to Grandpa, he was mighty glad to see us. He'd planted some apple and orange trees while we were gone, and he'd worked on the coops he'd made for the chickens and rabbits he was raising.

He told me I needed to help out more now that my daddy was away, and as long as I was with him, I didn't mind what I was doin'.

During the war, we all had ration books, and everyone always complained about not having enough fresh food to eat. To make extra money, Grandpa had the idea of starting a delivery route, and he filled his truck with apples and oranges when we had them, along with eggs and butter Mama made. He brought old coffee cans and had the women save bacon grease for its use in makin' bombs, and he took it to the little store across the street from us where someone else would come and pick it up.

He carried cages of live chickens and rabbits, and would kill them fresh for his customers. It was then I first saw him wring a chicken's neck, and the memory of it kept me from eatin' chicken for many years. I never did touch rabbit. I could never look at them as anything but a pet.

When he returned every afternoon, he unloaded his pickup and put the animals he didn't kill back into their cages. He'd take his shirt and pants off outside and dump them in a metal bucket so Mama could wash them. He'd scrub his hands with a brush, but no matter how hard he tried, he could never get all the dried blood out from under his nails and cuticles.

My job was to always make sure the rabbits and chickens had clean cages, fresh food, and water.

While he was away, Mama used to show me photos of her and Daddy, "to make sure you don't forget him," she'd say. Like that was going to happen.

For a while, the only man in my life was Grandpa, and I loved him dearly, animal smell and all.

Daddy was injured in France, so they sent him to a hospital so he could recover enough to be sent back home. When he finally came home, Mama cried a lot, but she never did it in front of him. Sometimes she'd stand at the kitchen sink, with tears silently running down her cheeks, or once when she was hangin' laundry, I heard her cryin'.

"Are you okay?" I asked.

"It's just dust got in my eyes," she said. "And I'm just so glad to have your daddy home."

But I could hear him sometimes crying out late at night, and then Mama would try to comfort him so he could go back to sleep. She'd cry then too, and once when I went to their bedroom door, I whispered into the silence, "Are you alright?"

When that happened, I had a hard time goin' back to sleep.

It took awhile for all of us to get used to living together again; I no longer had Mama to myself, and our routines had completely changed. Until Daddy got a job, we ate breakfast, lunch and dinner together. Sometimes I could hardly wait to get outside and play.

But I always loved seeing Grandpa comin' through the door after he took his boots off; and I loved the way he smelled after his bath.

For some reason, I was shy around Daddy when he first came home, so even though I could read myself, Mama'd have him read to me before I went to sleep, like Grandpa used to right after Daddy left. She later told me at first I was more curious about my father's face and whiskers, or the hair on his arms than I was in whatever it was he was reading. He was the same, but *he was different. With time, our lives blended back in together again, and we were one big, happy family.*

Since he liked working on cars, Daddy got a job in a body shop. My parents didn't have a lot of money, but after only a year, they were able to save up enough to put a small down payment on the large piece of property next door to Grandpa. It only had a small one-bedroom house on it, so even though I was almost ten by then, I slept in what was originally the laundry room where there was just enough room for a child's bed.

"You're still little, so you don't take up much space," Mama would say. Then she always tricked me into raising my arms so she could tickle me. I loved it when I made her laugh. The only place for my clothing was in the hall closet where we kept all the towels. Mama eventually bought that new washing machine, and Daddy built a covered lean-to for it outside.

I remember images of Mama with clothespins in her mouth and her apron with pockets tied around her waist while she sorted and hung our laundry. After pleading with her mercilessly, she'd let me hold the clothing as she ran it through the ringer to squeeze out most of the water. If Daddy came home in a good mood and saw the laundry hanging, he'd say, "Did you get your tit in the wringer today?" Mortified, Mama'd hit him with whatever was handy. Then she'd look over towards me to see if I'd heard him. I didn't understand what he meant, so I pretended not to hear him.

We planted our own vegetable garden, and I ended up with more chores. I helped hoe the dirt, and my favorite part was planting the seeds. Mama made markers and stuck them in the ground so we'd remember what we'd planted, and one of my chores was to water. I had to be careful to only water in rows, but every now and then I'd sprinkle the water on the top. I couldn't figure out how the plants would get enough water otherwise.

Sometimes when we grew more than we could eat, the neighbor ladies would come over and pay Mama for the left over harvest. She kept her money in an old coffee can in the cupboard just high enough, so'd I get no crazy ideas of takin' some of it. I knew Daddy would have straightened me out if I ever had.

"It's for a rainy day," she'd say.

Because our house back then only had a floor heater in the hall, most of the time the laundry room on the other side of the kitchen wouldn't stay as warm as the living room and bedroom, so if it was especially cold, Mama would bring me into their bed where I could snuggle close to her and Daddy to stay warm. But Daddy soon put his foot down.

"It's not proper to have a young girl sleep with a man in the bed," he said, and I was no longer allowed to do that. Of course I didn't understand, so I did what all little girls do; I cried. Instead, he let me get a dog, so not only did I have a new best friend, but I had a built-in bed warmer.

I named her Daisy, and after school, she and I spent most of our afternoons and weekends with Grandpa. I'd sit next to him in his truck, with an arm draped over Daisy, so she could look out the window. Grandpa's outstretched arm held us back if he came to a sudden stop. While he didn't have as many customers as he once had, we still made the rounds to see if he could sell his eggs along with the rabbits and chickens.

I was always told I was never to ask adults for anything, so when we'd drive by the diner I'd lean against the dashboard and point, "Grandpa, they sell ice cream in that store," and of course my grandpa would answer "They do?" and we'd stop. Daisy waited impatiently in the truck while we went in and had our ice cream at the counter. He always ordered a root beer float, and I had a scoop of vanilla with chocolate syrup, whipped cream, and a cherry.

Mama was one of the first of the neighborhood ladies to have Tupperware, and it was Grandpa's idea to sneak one of her bowls out so we could put a spoon of ice cream in it to bring back to Daisy as her reward for havin' to wait in the truck. Whenever Mama would complain she had an extra lid and no bowl, Grandpa would keep a straight face and shrug his shoulders. I, on the other hand, would have to go into another room to keep her from seeing me giggle.

In those days, few women worked outside the house, so Mama was home during the day. The house was always clean, and meals were made and promptly served at five. Until I got married and moved out, if I wasn't home at that time, I went without dinner. After finding out she meant business, there weren't too many times I was late! Of course, on the flip side, if I wasn't home for dinner, I'd get into trouble.

Daddy saved enough money to open his own body shop with his WWII bazooka buddy, Ralph Smith, known to us as Smitty. Business was good enough that my parents got a loan to build a two-bedroom house next to the small house we'd crammed into for the last few years. They also built a two-bedroom apartment over three garages in front. The way they figured, the rent from the apartment would cover the payments on the loan. And that's how it worked, but of course, at the time, I didn't know or care anythin' about that kind of thing. All I cared about was that I finally got my own bedroom.

Part Two

Marriage

CHAPTER FIVE

By the time I was eighteen, half of the girls I knew were enrolling in community college or planning weddings to their high school sweethearts. Sarah had executed her plan to leave; her bus out of town left the night of our graduation. She was now in Las Vegas.

Not that I didn't *want* a boyfriend, but the high school boys I knew were mindless, unstimulating, and exhausting. By nineteen, I was beginning to feel like I was going to be an old maid. And at twenty, I struggled with boredom.

Unlike my sister Loni, who *wanted* to go to college, I felt that attending my general education classes at our local community college was a waste of time. I could be a great student; I just didn't want to apply myself. I was a romantic, and I was looking to be swept off my feet. Not only in love, but in passion for whatever I chose to do with my life.

"What about a secretarial school?" my mother asked. Or, "You could become a teacher or a nurse."

Instead, I got a job in the cosmetics department at Walker's department store in downtown Long Beach.

I met David on a blind date in mid-May, at a dance place I'd been to before. Most blind dates I'd been on ended in disaster, so I drove my own car in case I needed to make a quick dash. The minute I saw him, though, I knew he was the man I was going to marry. I'm not sure what it was that made me think that, for he was not tall, dark and handsome like what most girls dream of, but of average height and looks. My heart didn't pitter patter, but I felt something different.

He had a distinguished look about him and even though he was casually dressed in tan slacks and a dark shirt, he looked sophisticated. He laughed with his friends and drank beer with a confidence that came with his years. He was sure of himself, and must have been equally interested in me, for only a few minutes after meeting me, he asked if I wanted to dance.

"I didn't think you were twenty-one," he said. He narrowed his eyes. "And you're different."

"I'm not, and I am. I've been here before with no problems, and I'm part Taiwanese."

"Well, you're quite extraordinary."

"Thanks." Despite myself, I felt myself flush.

"And what type of work do you do?" He asked.

I knew he was an attorney, and I immediately felt inadequate and embarrassed to say I worked in a department store. So I just said, "I work in cosmetics."

"Well," he said, "Sounds like you haven't figured it out yet. You will."

"I'm not looking to start a new family," he told me quite clearly about a week into our relationship. He wanted to nip any motherhood issues in the bud. I knew he'd had a vasectomy, and he wondered how important it was for me to have my own children.

The only experience I'd had with babies was watching a girl I knew who had a one-year-old walking around with poop falling out of his diaper. Her apartment was dirty, and I could smell the diaper pail the moment I went in.

She'd tucked her hair behind an ear and said, "Sorry," as she cleaned the floor.

What I *wanted* to say was "*Oh my god*," but what I said was, "It looks like you're keeping busy."

"Children aren't high on my list right now," I finally told him.

Sometimes we dined with his friends, but mostly it was just the two of us. And afterwards, we spent most evenings and weekends at David's small, sparsely furnished one-bedroom apartment. The first time I saw it, I was underwhelmed. Disappointed was more like it.

He apologized and said, "My divorce wiped me out and honestly, I just haven't felt like it was worth the effort to settle in."

It contradicted his maturity and character.

Of course, I never told my parents exactly where I was when we went out, and I was always home between one and two to avoid too many questions.

"I feel like I'm a teenager again," David said once, "having to get you home by curfew."

I loved watching him, whether it was his sureness when he ordered our meals, or how he acted so confident around his friends. He was obviously comfortable being in charge. He was so sophisticated to me; refined but complex, with what could be considered a bit of abruptness. Small wrinkles formed around his eyes, but he had no gray in his hair. His hands were soft, and I wondered if he had manicures to keep his nails and cuticles trim for professional appearances. I'd never seen him in a suit, but I imagined how striking he'd be.

It was thrilling to have an older man interested in me. People would sometimes glance up at us as we walked into a room; no doubt it was because of our age difference. He was almost the age of my father.

Sexually, I hadn't realized I was as inhibited as I was, for none of the young men I'd been with in the past ever wanted to truly make love. David was different. He liked to watch me undress, and then he would wait for my reactions as he touched me. He was easy to satisfy, while I had a hard time letting myself react naturally to him.

After about two weeks, I was trying to keep him aroused after an evening of heavy drinking on his part, and I murmured, "Love me. Love me."

And David said, "I do. You're my little China Doll."

I told him about growing up and feeling different from other children. How I was sometimes teased. How Loni started drinking. How I once went to a bar and drank so much I drove home in the fog and didn't know if I was ever going to make it home alive. And I'd wondered if I was going to have the same problem she had.

He told me his wife was pregnant when they got married and how he was never truly in love with her. After their third child, he had a vasectomy and admitted he wandered. When he found birth control pills in a dresser drawer, he knew the marriage was over.

Even though he could have had a lawyer friend fight for him, he let his wife have the house and paid alimony plus child support. In the end, all he walked away with was his car.

I wanted to know details about other women he'd been with; were they beautiful? What kind of work did they do? Was he ever in love with them? David never wanted to know about any relationships I'd had. Once, when I began to share one of my experiences with him, I noticed an abrupt clenching of his jaw and I quickly realized I'd touched a nerve. He wasn't interested in knowing about my past.

I didn't tell him that my parents were unhappy I was seeing him. They wondered what a man his age would see in such a young girl. They didn't understand he was like anyone else trying to start over.

He told me he hated the way he was living and thought I might be the person he could start a new life with.

I told him I too had been trying to find my way, and I thought he might be the best person to help me get wherever it was I needed to go.

On a warm Sunday afternoon, after we'd had brunch, I met David's parents. I was unprepared for how old they were and hoped the surprise didn't register on my face when his mother opened the door. They had a modest three bedroom, one bath home in Lakewood near the mall. It was filled with antiques and oil paintings Ruth had done. Her painted ceramics were on every tabletop, and they filled a china cabinet in the dining room.

"Is this to be our new daughter-in-law?" his mother asked as I came in to their family room. She was glowing!

"It is," David said.

"Well, come sit by me," Ruth said, taking my hand and leading me to a sofa. "I want to know everything about you." I could tell his mother loved me instantly.

"I was forty when I had David," she started. "We'd been trying for years..." as if to explain their age.

"And I'm sure you've met the children," she asked tentatively. "Robert is growing so tall and handsome, and Lucy needs a watchful eye; she's very smart and tries to get away with murder. Poor little William, he's still a Mama's boy, I'm afraid, but he's a loving child. I'm glad they'll have you to make sure David sees them regularly." She smiled at her son and patted my hand.

I was having my period, and I suddenly realized my cup had runneth over. I'd forgotten to change my pad! Hoping to avert an emergency, I stood to find the bathroom, and realized I'd bled through my pants, leaving a large red spot on their sofa. I thought I was going to die of embarrassment.

"Good god, Annie," David recoiled. *"That's disgusting."*

"Oh, stop it, David," his mother said. Then, as I rushed to the bathroom, she said to me. "Don't you worry about it, honey. It's happened to the best of us. Let me know if you need anything."

I wished I could have stayed in there forever, but eventually I came back out. I'd started to cry, and I knew my face and eyes were red.

"I'm so sorry. I just didn't think about it." All I wanted was to disappear.

"I've cleaned it up and put a towel over the spot. We'll just clean the couch tomorrow, won't we, Ed? It was way beyond that time already."

They wanted me to call them Mom and Dad, so I did. It was awkward at first, because I'd only called my own parents that, but I learned to feel comfortable over the years. They were called Mom and Dad, Grandpa and Grandma, your mom and dad, and my in-laws, depending on who I was talking with.

My parents were not the least bit happy about any of it. My father had adopted the American way of life when he came here and married my mother, who was born and raised Californian. I always knew he wanted to see at least some of his Chinese heritage passed down to any children my sister or I might have. And now there was no way it was going to happen with me. There would be no grandchildren. I knew my mother wished for the same, but there was nothing I could do.

"I hate it when he calls you his 'China doll'," my father said when I told them I'd agreed to marry David. I never should have told him David called me that. "And why so big a hurry? You just met him. You going to have baby?" When he was upset, he fell back on using broken sentences.

I thought my parents would be happy for me. I was planning a wedding and a new life. I finally had something I was interested in.

They'd only met David a few times, and I knew they weren't pleased with my choice of husband. I was annoyed with them. This was what I wanted, and I thought it should be good enough for them, too. I thought they should be happy for me. I'd found something I thought would help me become an adult. I was looking at the world through a twenty-year-olds' point of view, not through theirs.

Once it became clear I wasn't going to change my mind, they didn't try to dissuade me again. I still felt their disappointment, but they outwardly accepted my decision. It was what I wanted. They also accepted their fate as being overnight grandparents to David's children. I realized my sister Loni was their only hope now.

With resignation, my father said, "At least he has a profession. You have made your decision and now you will go forward and make a life of your own. You will be respectful of your husband, and you will become a mother to his children."

I didn't want to spend my first 'married' night at David's, so I started looking in the newspaper for apartments to rent.

"What I have is fine for now," he said when I mentioned it was something I wanted to do.

"I know it makes sense, but I want a place where you've never been with anyone before. And I'd like to find something I want to come home to. I've called a couple of places and we can see them on Saturday."

"You've done what?" his voice sounded edgy.

"I'd like to go on Saturday. We can decide on one and get it ready for when we return from our honeymoon. Mother said she'd take me shopping."

"That means we'll have to give them a deposit..."

"We have the money, don't we?"

"That isn't the point. I wasn't planning on spending more than what I already set aside for the honeymoon."

"Oh, c'mon David. Don't be such a fuddy-duddy. Plus, we'll need a room where the kids can sleep when they come to stay with us."

I went to tempt him with a kiss, but he stepped back.

"Oh." was all I could think to say.

I found a small chapel that had an opening, and a wedding dress that didn't need altering, and six weeks after I met David, I became his wife.

That night, when I took my shoes off, I remembered my father had put a Taiwanese coin in my shoe for good luck. He'd worn a smile on his face, but it couldn't hide how he felt. I knew I'd broken his heart. I'd wanted to tell him how much I loved him for letting me go. But because he wasn't raised to show or voice expressions of love, as a family we never said "I love you." I wasn't upset with him any longer, but I wasn't sure how to express that. So I hugged him and whispered, "Thank you, a-pah," which was father in Taiwanese. For a quick instant, I saw his eyes begin to fill; then he looked away.

I was in love with a new life. And I thought I was in love with David. Plus, I could still be exotic looking, but I now would be known as Annie Parker, instead of Annie Chang.

That was nine years and a lifetime ago.

CHAPTER SIX

I didn't want a wedding shower, so before the wedding, my mother took me to J. C. Penney's to shop for bed linens, pots and pans, towels, dishes and silverware. David's parents gave us two hundred dollars, so at the grocery store we bought dish soap, laundry soap, and hand soap. We bought all the grocery staples, like I was suddenly going to cook, and we stocked up on Kleenex, toilet paper and paper towels. I'd always hated ironing, but we ended up buying an ironing board and iron too.

"I'm sure David will need you to iron his dress shirts," my mother said cheerfully as I resisted.

"Ugh," I grimaced.

Our first morning in our new apartment was just as I'd envisioned it. We slept in and I brushed my teeth and took my shower first. When David finally woke, I told him I wanted to go to breakfast. He sat on his side of the bed, scratched his head, yawned, and then came to kiss me good morning. His morning breath stuck to my lips, and it was all I could do to not wince and turn away.

I quickly learned dating differed from marriage; we'd never spent the night together. Learning the personal side of being in a marriage was something that came as a surprise to me. My parents taught me the basics; get along with others, tell the truth, be a good person and do your chores without being asked. My mother never talked to me about what it was like to actually *live* with a man.

The first few months we lived together, I was always on guard. If David was home, I didn't want to use the bathroom other than to pee, but he didn't seem to care; he just did his thing and went about his business. I'd never bathed in front of anyone except for my mother and sister, and I was grateful the glass doors on the tub were obscured.

I didn't always feel comfortable falling asleep, or waking first and getting out of bed and having him see me without makeup. I'd also never experienced waking to find someone already aroused and wanting to make love. And I never wanted to have sex unless we both took a shower.

There was a lot I was going to have to get used to.

Before we were married, I'd only met two of David's friends. His law associate, John, and his wife Susan, had joined us for dinner several times, and although she was at least ten years older than me, we got along really well. While the men talked, Susan and I talked about how she got started in real estate and, assuming I was in college, she asked what I thought I wanted to do when I graduated. This caught David's attention, and he interrupted us, saying, "We're still working on that."

"Oh," was all Susan said.

His other friend, Bob, and his girlfriend, Debbie, met us for brunch one Sunday. She also was older than me, attractive and friendly. David suggested I use her as my role model.

"She always looks good, dresses well, and understands her role," he'd said.

"Honey," she said to me, "I can tell David adores you; you're quite exotic. Make him proud of you. Get your make-up done and whatever you do, when someone asks what you do, don't tell them you work in a department store. Tell them you're the assistant manager of the store. These guys like to impress their acquaintances; it's good for business, you understand? Stick with me. You'll catch on."

I later asked him if it embarrassed him that I worked in the store, and at least his answer was truthful.

"I'm not embarrassed; I just think you can do more with yourself. You need to figure it out, and I know you will. And as my wife, I want you to be the best you can be. In the meantime, I can see about getting you a job with John's wife, Susan. She might need someone to help her in the office. That sounds better, doesn't it?"

His words momentarily stung me, but as I thought about them, I knew he was right. I took what he said to heart and decided I would indeed do as he suggested.

With marriage came his children. Lucy was thirteen. She was a beautiful young girl, much prettier than I was at that age, and she wasn't afraid to tell me what she thought. When I first met her, she watched me from afar; I was certain she was curious about me, for her eyes bored into me.

"What *are* you?" she asked cautiously.

"What are *you*?" I asked back.

She looked amused.

"I'm part Chinese," I finally answered. "What is your heritage?"

She looked at David and asked, "Dad, what am I?"

Robert was eleven, and quite handsome, with his full head of dark hair and brown eyes. When we met, he just shrugged as if to say, 'whatever.'

And William was nine. He'd just had a fresh haircut and I could tell he was self-conscious about it, for he kept touching his hair as if he needed to brush it off his forehead.

"Aren't you a cutie?" I asked.

"No," he replied.

"Well, I think you are."

At first I'd tried too hard to win their acceptance; if we went out for dinner, as they were handed a menu, I'd say, "Get what you want," and David would give me a sideways glance. Or I'd tell his daughter how pretty she looked wherever we went. I'd ask them about school. What hobbies they had. I wanted to do fun things with them, like Disneyland or Knott's Berry Farm.

When I asked my mother what she thought about my new role, she reminded me that David and I couldn't always entertain them; we also needed to do everyday things with them, like go to the store, cook dinner, do laundry and watch movies.

"I think the less you try to impress them, the more you can help influence them."

I thought about that for a few minutes, and then said, "How did you get to be so smart?"

"Age," she answered.

Not long after that, David was on an out-of-town trip, and I had the children for the weekend. They asked if we could go to Disneyland, and I thought about my mother's comments. Did I want to take them to make them like me more, or did I want to do it because I could? Once I decided my motives were pure, the four of us piled in my car and we headed out for an exhausting day.

We had a great time. I went on most of the rides, which David would never have done, and we ate hot dogs, snow cones and Mickey shaped doughnuts. We were sugared out when we came out into the parking lot looking for my car. I'd forgotten to make a note of where I'd parked.

"I think it's over here," Robert said.

"I think it's over here," Lucy said, pointing in an entirely different direction.

"Here it is," I called out.

I unlocked the doors and started to get in when I noticed clothing in the back seat that definitely wasn't ours.

"Get out! This isn't my car!"

I turned to see if anyone had seen us. My heart was pounding. We stood there so I could regroup.

"Don't tell your dad!" I said. "All we'd need is for him to come home and find us in jail!"

We all started laughing.

"Okay, now we really need to find the right car," I said.

Over the years, I'd play little tricks on the kids. The best one was when David wasn't with us. I'd drive us somewhere, and I'd constantly push the brake pedal so we all lurched forward. And just when we stopped laughing, I'd do it again.

When they came over to see our restored player piano, I'd inserted a paper piano roll, then called the three of them in to hear me play. I moved my hands on the keys while I pumped my feet. Their eyes widened in surprise at my talent. Then I casually removed my hands to scratch my head. Obviously, the piano kept playing and when they realized I'd tricked them, they tackled me, almost knocking me off the piano bench.

I started working in the real estate office with John's wife Susan, and I found I enjoyed helping her prepare her listings and organizing paperwork. I was curious what the homes we listed looked like, and I talked her into taking me when she showed one of them. If she was busy, she began letting me sit at an open house, and I loved talking to prospective clients as they looked around. I began to feel comfortable pointing out the strong points, giving them ideas about what they could do with a room; how they could make changes to make it their own.

One day Susan called me into her office and I thought for sure I'd done something wrong.

"The clients that came to see the house when you sat for me last weekend are going to make an offer," she said.

"Great," I said, clearly relieved.

"And they loved your ideas about how they could decorate it. I've noticed you have a knack for it. Have you ever thought about going into decorating?"

I hadn't, but the idea intrigued me.

"I have a friend who is a decorator, and if you're interested, I'll give her a call."

My heart sank. How would I tell David I'd lost my job?

"Are you letting me go?" I asked suddenly.

"Of course not," Susan said, with the beginning of a smile. "I'm thinking we could start doing something together to do a better job of selling these houses. It could work for all of us. She'd hopefully get more work, and we'd sell more properties. And as a bonus, you'll learn to do both. Her name is Emma. You'll like her."

Once I saw the decorating studio, I fell in love. Books of fabrics and swatches of carpet were strewn about everywhere. There were what looked like several projects spread out on a long table, and I immediately went to them.

"These are wonderful," I said, absorbed in the colors. "I love the idea of learning," I said, then tentatively added, "but I'm almost overwhelmed."

Emma said, "It sometimes seems that way for me too, even though I've done this for years."

She pointed to one of her projects.

"You just have to have a starting point. Start with a color or a fabric that gets you excited. Then you work from there. That's the fun. Discovering different ways you can pull a room together. If you love it, you'll learn quickly."

I could hardly wait to tell David about my meeting with Emma.

"Good for you," he said. "I knew you'd figure something out. I'll take you to dinner."

With Emma's encouragement, I enrolled in several interior design classes at our community college. I had an eye for color but wanted more formal training. The three of us worked out a plan to list a property, make suggestions to the homeowner on how we could make the house look more appealing to prospective buyers, and to possibly bring in a few accent pieces to add color and interest. I continued to either sit at the open houses or go with Susan on showings so I could make suggestions to potential buyers in person.

The idea was to not only sell the property, but to gently remind the buyer we could also help them furnish it. We included the seller in our plan too, reminding them we could help them decorate their new home, which we hoped to find for them.

"Now what?" I asked Emma when some of our friends started asking if I could help them decorate. I realized I had another opportunity. I had never run a business by myself, so once I built up my nerve, I asked her if I could somehow become a partner with her.

"A junior partner, of course," I quickly added. "I wouldn't take on any projects that were out of my field of expertise; those I'd refer to you. But I'm interested in learning more and doing more."

Amazingly, she thought it was a good idea. And that's when I went to my first furniture show in San Francisco.

CHAPTER SEVEN

"We have a wedding to go to," my mother said one afternoon when I called to see how they were doing.

I didn't know why it surprised me to hear Loni was planning to get married. We'd been out of touch since she'd been away at school, and I'd been busy with my new life.

"When?" I asked.

"In a couple of months."

"Is she pregnant?" I asked.

"*Of course not*," my mother answered defensively.

"*Well*, you asked me that when I said I wanted to get married."

"That was different, Annie. You didn't even know your husband to be."

"Well, I guess *that's* good."

"Good, what?"

"Good, she's not pregnant and good she's getting married."

I had mixed feelings about the upcoming event. I hated the thought that she might ask me to be in the wedding. Not only did I not know any of her friends, but I'd put on a few pounds, and didn't really relish the thought of going out looking at dresses.

As it turned out, I didn't have to worry. I wasn't on her "A" list.

The wedding was going to be in Arizona, where she'd gone to college and where her fiancé was from. I was hoping it wouldn't be in the dead of summer when it was so blasted hot, and sure enough, that's exactly when it was. David had already told me he wasn't interested in going whenever it was going to be.

"I'll be busy," he said. "So you can go with your parents."

We flew in early Friday before the wedding, in time to meet the groom and his family before the rehearsal dinner. I immediately didn't like my new brother-in-law to be. His name was Jerome, and he was as dull as dishwater. He made sure we knew he was a nature history buff, like his father, and I was sure the two of them would have been happy to talk about themselves all evening if allowed to. His mother was heavyset and timid, deferring to her two men, "Jerome Jr. this," and "Jerome Sr. says..."

She'd brought what she was wearing for the wedding and when she unzipped her dress from a dress bag to show my mother, it was a drab chiffon and satin taupe number layered in sprinkles. I was no fashion expert, but even my mother's eyebrows rose when she saw it.

Jerome and Loni just didn't go together. I couldn't figure out what she could possibly see in him, and vice versa. He acted like a dorky intellectual, and she apparently hadn't stopped drinking, for she was sloshed before dinner. He was attentive to her needs, but I saw his parents silently watch her every move.

And my parents didn't miss a beat either.

The day of the wedding, I'd wanted to sleep in, but they included me with the mothers, bridesmaids and maid of honor for beauty and makeup appointments. When it was my turn, the stylist commented on how beautiful my hair was, and wondered if I minded if he trimmed it into a more *current* style. I thought, 'what the heck' and let him do this thing. I watched as he cut off what I felt were chunks of my hair, and when I looked at the final results, I loved my new look. Instead of straight dark brown hair, I now had a layered look, shorter in the back and longer in the front. I'd never seen anyone wear their hair that way, and I loved the thought of being different.

"You look wonderful," my mother said. "I can't believe you went ahead and did that."

"I can't believe I did it either." I said. "David may not like it, but I can always let it grow back."

"I have a headache," I heard Loni say to her maid of honor.

"I'll bet you do," I said, giving her a quick look. You know how they say all brides are beautiful? Well, she looked terrible. Her skin was splotchy, and her eyes were bloodshot.

"Fuck off," she said tersely. So I walked away.

I wasn't really sure why I said that to her. It was what I was thinking, but I could have kept my observations to myself. I almost felt angry with her. I looked at her and wondered how she was going to pull this off.

It surprised me that the ceremony brought tears to my eyes, but I've been that way at every wedding I'd gone to, even if I wasn't close to the bride and groom. I realized it's the part where the pastor talks about the future and how bright it can be. And the vows. And how eternal love is supposed to be.

Other than Loni tripping on her dress as she turned to walk back down the aisle, the wedding came off without a hitch.

The reception was a different story. The bride and groom sat at their table surrounded by the wedding party, and every time someone tapped a glass, they kissed, and then Loni took another drink. I could see her husband loved her, but I had no misgivings about how their future looked. Loni was drunk on her ass.

They made it through the first few dances, and then Loni somehow broke the heel off one shoe, and fell. The guests collectively drew in their breath and several people rushed to her, but the groom lifted her up and steadied her while she kicked off her other shoe and went barefoot. The evening dragged on, and I was ready to leave as soon as the bride and groom were whisked away in a waiting car. I could tell my parents were stressed and exhausted. My mother's face was pale, and she hadn't re-applied her lipstick after the meal, which made her look even more drawn.

We went back to the hotel in silence, and I didn't sleep right away, so I got up and went for a short walk so I could have a cigarette. At David's insistence, I'd quit after we were married, but every now and then I just couldn't resist the urge. I hadn't missed what words of wisdom David would have had about the whole evening, and after a long hot soak in the tub, I found I surprisingly relished having the bed to myself for a change.

The next morning, after breakfast, we flew back to Long Beach. My parents were visibly distressed, and periodically my mother would dab her eyes with her tissue. For once, I was proud of myself; I didn't say a word. There was nothing I *could* say to comfort them, and I felt to commiserate would only make matters worse.

The minute my parents dropped me off at my house, I saw that David's car wasn't there, and I instinctively touched my shortened hair. What would he say when he saw it?

It turned out I needn't have worried; when he came home, he left his golf clubs in the entry and went upstairs to take a shower.

"I see you cut your hair," he finally said.

CHAPTER EIGHT

Three years after we married, we started looking for our own house to buy. David suggested an area called Belmont Heights, close enough to the beach, so we'd enjoy cool breezes but not as crowded as Belmont Shore, the beach community originally built in the 1920s and 1930s.

At the real estate office, I looked through the multiple listings book and found a house I was dying to see. And when we drove up to it, I knew it was the one I wanted; it was the same feeling I had the day I met David when knew I was going to marry him.

There was a small metal engraved box nailed to the frame of the front door, and I asked what it was.

"It's a mezuzah," Susan said.

"It means Jewish people lived here," David added.

"I don't understand," I said.

"*Annie*," he said curtly, urging me aside so he could be the first to enter the house. I felt my face flush.

"Oh, that's okay, David," Susan said, gently putting her hand on his arm to stop him. To me she said, "It means doorpost. There's a parchment scroll inside, and it's a sign and a reminder to people of their faith. I'm surprised you haven't seen one before on any of the houses we've sold."

The moment she opened the front door, I took a deep breath, and although the house smelled musty from being vacant, I could envision us living there.

"They built this house in the late forties and is all original," she pointed out, but I didn't need her or anyone to point out all the charm.

"Look, David. The living room has a bay window and a fireplace with a wood mantle." I almost danced with giddiness, and although I realized David was still perturbed with me, I didn't care. There were seven steps leading up to the three bedrooms and an enormous bathroom with pink fixtures and pink and gray ceramic tile on the floor and about five feet up the walls. Downstairs was a narrow sunroom, dining room, the kitchen with a wall that would have to come down, another bathroom with a shower and a laundry room. I could hardly wait to put my touches on it.

I'd told my parents we were going to look at it and that we'd saved one-half of the down payment. I asked my father if he could loan us the other half, which was thirty-two hundred dollars. I was so excited; I didn't see how he could have refused me, and he didn't. I knew before we looked at it, it was a little out of our original price range, at thirty-two thousand dollars. Susan calculated our house payment would one hundred ninety-seven dollars a month. I was determined we could swing it.

David was livid when I told him I'd worked it all out beforehand.

"I can provide for us," he said. "We don't need your father." I could tell his pride was bruised.

Once I pointed out how his offer was going to benefit us financially, how we could afford to buy a nicer house now, his entire attitude changed.

"I'm still not happy you went to your father without asking me. And did you talk to Susan about this? Does she know we're borrowing money for the down payment?"

It seemed he cared more than I thought he did about what people thought of him.

I didn't care. I was turning twenty-three, and I felt the world was mine to conquer.

We had enough money left over to hire a painter and buy new carpet, and in a little over a week we were ready to move in. We enlisted the kids to help me move and in between getting boxes out of the hired truck, they ran from room to room calling out, "Wow."

In my excitement, it never dawned on me this was a much larger home than theirs was.

"Now they'll tell their mother we've bought an expensive home, and I'll have to pay more child support," David said, certain the children would hear.

I was sure they'd tell her about the house, and at first I'd felt a bit of pleasure that I had something better than his ex-wife did. But when I saw their faces, I suddenly felt ashamed of myself for taking such pleasure in having such a wonderful home. I'd seen their house in North Long Beach, and it was hard for me to picture five people crammed into a small three bedroom, one bath house. Unless David's ex-wife married someone with money, they'd never have a house as nice as ours.

When my father and mother first saw our new house my father said, "I knew you'd find something you loved, but I didn't think you'd buy something so extravagant."

Of course, unless you were wealthy, where my father came from, few people could afford a nice home. My parents lived very conservatively but comfortably in the house I grew up in.

"It's not extravagant. It's an excellent investment in a good area," I answered proudly.

I couldn't believe how much we'd accumulated in such a short time. David's parents wanted us to keep their old furniture from the apartment, but once it was all inside, the house looked like a disaster had struck.

I managed to get through a number of boxes and was mostly concerned about getting the kitchen in order. I hadn't mentioned it to David, but I already planned for it to be the first room we'd remodel once we saved enough money. In the meantime, we'd have to live with the old linoleum floor and tile counters for a while.

The kids brought their sleeping bags and split up into the two extra bedrooms that first night. Once I made our bed, I was tempted to just fall into it, but I knew I'd never have the energy to get back up and take a much needed shower if I did. Within twenty minutes, I was out of the bathroom, and I plopped down, exhausted. David took his shower next and came to bed, dropping his towel to the floor so I could take him in. He was a very appealing man, and wanted to celebrate our new house by making love, but I honestly was too tired to respond like I would have liked. Plus, I felt extremely uncomfortable having sex when the kids were in the next rooms. I knew if I turned him down, he'd be unhappy with me. If I had to look back, I'd have to say that was the first time I went through the motions and made him feel like he'd satisfied me.

Afterwards, when he asked me if I wanted him to touch me, I knew I'd feel too self-conscious and said, "I'm fine. That was just what I needed."

After David fell asleep, I got up to check on the kids. I figured they'd be conked out and Lucy was. Robert and William were talking, and I stood outside their door for a moment.

I heard Robert say, "Mom says she's young enough to be one of Dad's kids."

"I like her," William whispered.

"So do I."

I tried living with it for a few days, but I hated the way our hand-me-down furniture looked in our new house. I finally convinced David I'd rather have an empty room than have something I didn't love in it. I knew it sounded petty, but I felt strong enough about it for me to stand my ground.

"Then you're the one who needs to call my parents," he said. "I'm out of it."

"Would you be terribly offended if we donated the furniture to a needy family?" I asked Ruth the next time I spoke with her on the phone. "We have what we need for now, and we haven't decided what we'd like to buy. I can buy what we want through my decorator at wholesale." Like that was going to make her feel any better.

"Well, I suppose if that's what you want to do. We just thought it was something we could do to help you out." The line was silent, and then she said, "You know, why don't you go ahead and donate it; someone else can probably use it. And then when you're ready to buy something new, we can chip in and help that way."

"That's a great idea, Mom. I really appreciate it."

Once the house was set with what furniture and décor we had, I started working on the front yard. There was a family-run nursery close to the house, and they were very patient with me since I had no idea what would work best in our soil. Each time I went there, I'd fill the back of my car with plants and if the children were with us, I'd have them help me weed and plant another section of the flower bed. David never expressed any opinion about what I did, and that freedom to do as I wanted further boosted my self-confidence. If I was happy, he was generally happy, too.

The first of every month, David paid our bills, and I knew he resented writing his ex-wife a child-support check. I hated to admit it, but sometimes I shared that sentiment, too. I was working hard, but when our own budget was tight, I felt we were giving the money to her instead of the kids. In defiance, he'd always write 'Child Support' on the front of the check to make it clear he how he felt.

When I mentioned something to my mother, she was a bit surprised by my comments.

"Annie," she said carefully, for she was always kind in her feedback, "I understand how this makes you feel, but you have to remember that those children did not cause their parents to divorce. And now their mother has to bear most of the financial responsibility for raising them. I hear it all the time from mothers who say they don't have enough money to feed their children and that's why they're in the meal program at school."

What she said made sense, and I immediately wished I'd said nothing to her because I'd exposed my selfishness and lack of understanding.

"I'm sorry," I finally said. "I never thought about it that way."

"I know you didn't, dear, and that's okay. Now it makes more sense, doesn't it?"

I sighed deeply. "Of course you're always right, *Mother*," I said, teasing her.

"That's my job," she said. "And it's your job to talk to *your* children when they need you."

Summer was ending, and I reminded David we should probably take the kids shopping for school clothes. I felt his irritation, and I saw it in his eyes. He looked at me like I was intentionally aggravating him.

"Come on, they're your children," I said, disappointed in his reaction.

"Let their mother spend some of that money I give her for clothes."

When he turned to walk away from me, I said, "Stop it, David. She can't possibly have enough money to buy them everything they need. Shoes and socks aren't enough."

"*Fine*. You take them." And he left me standing there.

I held my hands out as if to say '*what was that all about?*'

That next weekend, we went shopping. Robert knew exactly what he wanted and went directly to the areas of the store where he found everything. Lucy had us going to three different stores to find everything she needed. And sweet William had a hard time deciding, wondering aloud, what his mother would have him choose.

Throughout our shopping trip, I noticed sales clerks not really being very helpful. They looked at the four of us and smiled, but only one finally said, "Cute kids. Is big sis taking you shopping?"

And then I realized what was so obvious to everyone else; David's children could have been my siblings.

"Nah," Robert answered with a big grin, "She's our stepmom."

I could have killed him.

When we got home, I left our purchases in my car and decided I would take the kids home myself after dinner. David's parents were coming over and I knew he wouldn't broach the subject of shopping while they were there. He'd figure out how much I'd spent once he got the credit card bill, but I didn't care. I was comfortable with what I'd accomplished.

In those days, I cooked a big dinner on Sundays, and we'd have David's parents over. Ruth was always emotional when we had the children, for it was really the only time she and Ed got to see their grandchildren. The children would come with us if we were having dinner at my parent's house, and I was amazed how once my parents met them, time lessened my father's disappointment in my decision to marry.

My mother graciously took on the role of doting grandmother, and she invited David's parents when we celebrated the children's birthdays with a dinner of their choice and lots of presents. For Christmas, the children spent the morning with their mother, and we'd have a potluck dinner with both sets of grandparents at my parents' house.

CHAPTER NINE

Alyce

Daddy never talked about the war; I'd hear his stories in bits and pieces, but only if he'd been drinkin' with his war buddy Smitty. Sometimes when they were sittin' outside, if we were havin' a barbeque or something, they'd have a couple a beers, and they'd start out talkin' about cars and eventually get around to the war.

They'd been on the front line during the war, and their job was to use the Bazooka, which was basically a two man portable rocket launcher. Because it was so heavy, they'd change up their routine. One day, my dad would carry it and Smitty would shoot it and the next day, they'd trade off. They shot at tanks, armored vehicles, and bunkers.

That's when they'd drift off and quit talkin'.

"I never thought we'd get back home...." one of them would say.

"Me neither," the other would agree.

"You were lucky," Daddy would say.

"Nah, you were the lucky one. You got to get out of there. Even getting shot up and in the hospital was better than what we were doin'."

They also had to go in and secure towns that had been liberated, often killing what turned out to be children who were left behind to stand guard and kill any soldiers who came into view.

When Daddy had a nightmare, Mama would say to me, "It was a miracle someone could survive as long as he did with that kind of hell."

I wasn't sure what Hell was, but I knew it must be bad.

In the end, Daddy got wounded in France, where it took three months for him to recover enough to come home. Mama once told me that the whole time he was away, he was sure he'd never make it out alive. He told her that it was only his thoughts about her and me, kept him goin'.

I was too young to know the difference between bouts of being in a bad mood and depression. The way Daddy struggled, the sounds that woke me in the night, Mama told me, made her decide they'd never have any more kids. It was Daddy's anxiety and lack of patience that scared her. Another child would have been too much for him.

He was always a good man, always helpin' other families out, and he never raised a hand to either of us, no matter how mad he got at something. But Daddy ruled with an iron hand and when he said 'no', he meant it. I could tell by the way he took a breath and held it, that he was on the brink and that was enough to make me step away. I never crossed him.

Within about a year after opening the body shop with Smitty, they went to work as civilians, doin' body and fender work at the Air Force base in Terminal Island.

"If we work during the week, then we can keep our shop open on the weekends," Daddy told us. "It'll be a lot of work, but worth it."

I could tell when Daddy was pushing it, though. Sometimes if he was home and working in the garage, I'd take him his lunch, and he'd be sittin' there, just starin'. Or he'd have a tool in his hand, and say something like, "Dang, if I can't remember what I was doin'," then give me a laugh.

"You should take a day off, John. Give yourself a break," Mama said.

Then he'd remind her how much easier life was with that extra pay comin' in.

It was too far away and would cost too much for us to go back to Kansas, where all of our family was from, so we spent most of our vacations and holidays with Smitty and his family in Compton. They had two boys, so when we went there, I looked forward to doing 'boy' things. They had other ideas, though, and they always tried to hide from me. I'd always find them, and once I did, they gave in and played with me.

Once I told them, "I'll tell my dad."

And they said, "If you do, you big whiner, then we'll never play with you again. So there."

Most of our neighbor kids were boys too, but I never had a problem fittin' in with them; I was a tomboy at heart. Two girls around my age lived across the street, so if I ever got tired of gettin' dirty and wanted to do girl things, I went over there. But that wouldn't last long. I was never into dolls and dressin' up.

Down the street there was a family who'd come from Oklahoma to work. They'd stay a couple of years, then they'd move back home. A couple of years after that, they'd move back into the neighborhood and everyone was glad to see them again. I think they did that twice again while I was growing up.

"Why do you suppose that is?" I asked.

"It's called being persistent," Mama would say. "And some people have big dreams of living here in California. I don't blame them."

My dad, who was never really friendly with the neighbors, would say something like, "Well, you'd think it'd cost them more to keep moving back and forth than it would if they would just stay here and get second jobs. Or have the kids deliver papers or somethin'."

Across the street there was a one room grocery store called Ma & Pa, and I used to love it when Mama would send me out to buy something she needed. If she wanted more than a couple of things, I'd have her write it all down and I'd check to see if her female stuff was on the list. I hated bringin' her personal 'necessities' as she called them up to the counter, especially if there were other people in the store. My worst fear was that she wouldn't give me enough money, and I'd have to stand at the cash register tryin' to figure out what to put back because I couldn't pay for it. I'd seen it happen to one of our neighbors, and while they didn't seem to mind, I was embarrassed for them. Thankfully, Mama was a good counter, and it never happened to me, but even to this day I think about that when I'm in the supermarket. I wonder if I brought enough cash.

The meat counter was my favorite. I got to watch my order being wrapped and secured with a piece of string. There was an order to it; place the meat at an angle on the paper, fold the center in, then fold the left side and right side, and roll it all up. I wished I could have gone behind the counter and done it myself. Mama wrapped our leftovers that way in tinfoil or saran, and I still do.

Some of the families had accounts at the store. They could buy what they needed and Pa, as we called him, would write it all down in a long book with lots of columns. I saw it once. The customer's name was at the top of the page, and there were totals of what they owed. When payday came around, they came into the store and paid their bill. When that happened, there was a date, and a zero written underneath it. Pa kept it under the cash register counter.

A couple of my friends could go in and charge either a drink or candy, and I was always jealous, because I was never allowed to do that. One time I told Mama how I felt about that, and she gave me a look that made me ashamed. But the minute she left the room, my grandpa winked at me and handed me two quarters.

"Don't tell anyone," he whispered, as I gave him a hug.

It wasn't quite the same as keeping a tab, but I never refused his quarters!

We played fort in the dirt, building hills and roads, and I had my own set of toy soldiers. We were young, and it was so easy to let our imaginations take over. Every adventure seemed so real. No one ever wanted to be the bad guys, and most of us didn't even know who the bad guys from the war were. It didn't matter. We just built more forts and advanced our soldiers.

We took full advantage of every day, and even in the scorching summer sun, we'd play badminton and baseball. Sometimes Mama would come out and bring her homemade lemonade.

"Come on," she'd call, and we'd run to a shaded area she'd found and sit on the ground. "Thanks, Mrs. Murphy," one of the kids would say, and then we'd all chime in.

I'd say it too. "Thanks, Mrs. Murphy." And my mother would smile at me.

One time when we were playing baseball, I was up and I hit the ball so hard it broke a neighbor's windshield. I knew Daddy would kill me when he found out, but Mama and I went over there and after I apologized, she offered to pay for the damages.

Of course, I had to pay her back by doin' extra chores, but I thought that was only fair.

"It'll be our little secret," she said to the neighbor, and he just nodded his head.

We never mentioned it to Daddy. A couple of times I caught myself referring back to it in conversation, and yet when I looked over at him, he never seemed to catch on to what I'd been saying. Years later, when that neighbor died, I remembered how he'd never yelled at me for doin', and he kept his promise; he'd never told Daddy.

We'd ride our bikes down to the school and race around on the playground. If there were enough of us, we'd set up teams and race against each other. Or, if we didn't feel like doin' that, we'd pick one person to lead us on an imaginary journey across the blacktop.

One of the neighbor kids built a pushcart, and since we had the longest driveway of all the houses in the neighborhood, it became our runway. We'd use it to compete to see who could go down the driveway the fastest. We'd see who could spin out without flipping it over, and then we were the champ. A couple of times we ended up with pretty badly skinned knees, but there was my mom again, playing Florence Nightingale with antiseptic and Band-Aids.

And on special occasions Mama and I would take the bus to Compton where there was a Sears Roebuck & Company, a Woolworth's dime store with a soda fountain, and a shoe store where you'd step onto a new contraption that took an X-ray of your foot. This was a time when furniture stores sold the first televisions. We'd stand with a group of people in front of the store window and watch a program. The furniture store would set a speaker box outside so we could hear the sound. The television sets were large, and the screens were small, and eventually we got one.

I remember Grandpa and Daddy bringin' it into the house, both makin' groanin' noises because it was so heavy.

"Get all the stuff off that wall," Daddy called from the doorway.

There was only one wall it would fit on—the one opposite the couch, and that's where it went. Sometimes, if nothing was showing, we'd just sit and look at test patterns. During the summer, Mama would make cookies and lemonade and all the neighbor kids would come over. We'd sit and watch Mighty Mouse, Tom and Jerry, Bugs Bunny and Woody Woodpecker until she had enough of us and scooted us back outside.

That was the year Frankie Miller got a paper route, and we were all green with envy. No one wanted to wake up at four-thirty in the morning to fold papers, but he made almost fifty dollars a week. Because I was a girl, I wasn't allowed to have a route, plus our neighborhood was already taken; so I had a better idea. Frankie and I went into business together. He got a second route, and I'd work with him to fold the papers while he delivered them.

One time, when he noticed one of his old lady customers hadn't picked up her paper in about three days, he told his mom, and she called the police. They found her unconscious, and that call saved her life. Another time, Frankie saw smoke comin' out of a neighbor's house and pounded on their door to wake them up.

Frankie got all the glory, but I earned thirty-five dollars a month. And at Christmas, Frankie shared his holiday tips with me.

We had party lines on the phone, with phone numbers beginning with words. Ours was Metcalf, then numbers; ME-43479. When you picked the phone up, you never knew who might be on the other end of the line. Sometimes we could listen in and hear the latest gossip. Once I heard two women talking about their husbands.

"I know he's cheating on me."

"How do you know that?"

It sounded like Mama's friend Ruth, and I immediately hung up.

"So how's Ruth?" I asked her later.

"She's fine," Mama said. "Why?"

"Just curious. Haven't seen her around lately."

On the other side, we learned to listen for the sound of the click that told us someone was doin' the same and listenin' to us. When we heard the click, sometimes we'd start talkin' in gibberish, like a foreign language, or we'd make up a silly story.

My father was never one to sit idle, so if he wasn't too tired from workin', after dinner he'd go out into the garage and work on his boat. He built it from scratch; he started with the wood, then added fiberglass, and when he'd finished paintin' a name on it, he'd start workin' on an engine. During the summer, he'd take a day off here and there, and take Mama and me down to Marine Stadium in Long Beach, where the 1932 Summer Olympics had been held. Although he was tough on me, he taught me to water ski and he eventually let me drive the boat so he could ski himself. He was much better than me, able to use just one ski, and those were the times I saw the tension actually lift from him; he stood taller and would look up at the sky and breathe in the salt air.

He made me a single ski, telling me I could learn to get up with it, but we never did get to go out once it was done. There was always something else to do, then winter came, and it was too cold.

That was also when he gave me one of his pocket knives. He always kept one in his front pocket, and he taught me how to open and close it without cutting my fingers.

"I know you're a girl, but girls need knives too," he'd said as he put it in my hand.

I go back to these memories when I look back on being thirteen again. Because in 1947, my world changed forever.

That was the year my father left and never came home again...

CHAPTER TEN

David joined me the first time I wanted to go to the furniture market on my own. There was so much to take in, and I was excited to show him all I'd seen on my first trip with Emma a year earlier. Initially, he showed a little interest in the business of decorating, and he tried to maintain his attentiveness, but it soon waned. I knew he wanted me to succeed, but he tired of the showrooms and décor, choosing to sit in the hallways and 'people watch' as I looked at everything I wanted to.

I'd never been to a Chinatown, for my father thought of them as commercialized and belittling. So when David suggested we go there to eat at one of his favorite restaurants, I instantly recalled my father's feelings, and my first thoughts were to say "no." From my father, I'd learned a little about the mainland Chinese immigrating to San Francisco during the California Gold Rush, but no one from his family had come to the United States back then. In some ways, he'd always felt distanced from that period of history.

We peeked into shops filled with souvenirs and "authentic treasures" and I bought tea for my mother, chopsticks for the kids, and a jade necklace for David's mother. At an amazing Chinese restaurant, David had several glasses of Baijiu, a white wine, and we had an excellent meal of chow mein and Peking roasted duck; afterwards, we gorged on a bag of almond biscuits.

I believe this was the first time I realized that for David, a trip away from home included drinking, a delicious meal, and sex. I was so tired and my feet were killing me from so much walking. The last thing I wanted to do was make love, but I didn't want to come out and say so. I felt I owed him this, and after cringing at myself in the unflattering bathroom light, quickly took a shower and made myself ready.

These were the years I went with David most places; business trips, car shows, or outings in his Porsche. Mostly I found pleasure in being introduced as his wife; one time a fellow car enthusiast clapped him on the back, and if David had been a peacock, he'd have spread his feathers high and wide. Expressions on their faces spoke volumes; some were bemused, some were surprised, and some were welcoming.

Eventually, the repetitiveness of it all grew mundane, and I found I would be thinking of things I'd rather be doing. I grew more confident and comfortable when I didn't have the added pressures of 'always being on' as David's wife. It became obvious he didn't need me by his side. Most of the time, if I went with him on a business trip, he suggested I go find something to do that would be of interest to me.

Eventually, I wasn't included in his plans, and he wasn't always tactful about letting me know.

"Just John and I are going," he'd say. "Wives aren't coming this time."

"I have projects I can work on," I'd say.

I was working on albums filled with magazine pages of ideas I could show my clients. I'd found most women knew what they liked when they saw it, but couldn't articulate what styles they were drawn to. Once they could identify with a particular style, the project went so much easier.

While I grew to look forward to them, I knew David only tolerated my trips to Market, and eventually, he opted out completely. So, I started going by myself, and realized I had a much more relaxed time without him; meeting vendors for dinners and talking about what the newest design trends were, what new fabrics were being shown, and what the trends were for artwork and home décor. I found myself content in my world, able to unwind from the day after a long soak in the tub. I'd sit in bed with a book, exhausted, relishing my time away from home, and it was then, in total silence, that I began wondering what was missing from my life.

On weekends, even if we had the children, I became a golf widow. I'd never been interested in the sport myself, but I encouraged David to play, as it was a great way for him to relax and entertain clients. Several times a year, there were legal conferences around the country and he attended those too. And then the "guy trips" started.

David seemed to have no problem finding extra-curricular activities to keep him occupied. And if I ended up going out with him to meetings or entertaining his clients, I found myself more and more turned off when he drank too much and acted like he knew everything.

Most of the time, his friends would go along with his behavior, but once one of the guys gave him a bad time, and David took him seriously.

"Well, you're an asshole," he said.

The group fell silent. His friend, John, looked at me.

"Hey, just kidding," David said, and laughed. "I still love ya."

Then everyone loosened up and laughed with him.

I didn't like the David I'd seen that night. It was as though he'd been changing, but I hadn't noticed it.

The problem was, I was changing as well.

It was on one of my trips to market that I ran into one of the designers who'd worked with me and Emma several years before. While she greeted me warmly, she looked anxious. She turned, as if looking for someone.

"It's Annie Parker," I reminded her.

"Yes. Yes. Of course," she said. "I know who you are."

I could sense this wasn't the time for getting reacquainted, so I told her I hoped to run into her again and quickly went on my way. At the end of the hall, I turned back, and I saw her greeting one of the sales reps I knew with a kiss. I knew *he* was married, and unless anything had changed with her, so was *she*!

Throughout the rest of that day, I couldn't help but let my mind wander back to the "secret lovers" and I hated to admit that I envied them the excitement and lust. They probably made wild, passionate love in their room at night, and then were forced to carry on with business as usual during the day.

I certainly wasn't looking for clandestine love, and yet, I was still a true romantic at heart. My thoughts kept rushing back to imagining them together, while I ate alone in one of the hotel restaurants that night. I sat in one of the lounges and had a glass of wine while people watching.

A young couple caught my eye, and I observed them starry-eyed and amorous. I tried to think back to when David and I first met, and I didn't remember him ever being so engrossed in me. Of course, he was more mature and because of his profession, I wouldn't have expected him to act like this couple did.

I recalled, though, how he'd show affection by proudly putting my arm through his before we entered a room of his friends and acquaintances. Now I wondered, was that affection, or showing me off as his trophy?

That night, even after my soak in the tub, romance filled my mind, and I had a hard time concentrating on the book I'd brought. The next day, I wondered if somehow I was sending out some type of signal, for a rep I knew came up to me as I entered his showroom. His face brightened.

"Hey there," he called out.

A few heads turned to watch me walk in, and I felt flattered at the attention.

"Hey, yourself," I said back.

"I haven't seen you the last few times I've stopped into the studio," he said.

"I've been really busy lately," I said, not refusing his light hug. I couldn't bear to tell him his name escaped my mind, but I remembered his eyes and how they were a stunning blue.

"It wasn't the same without you. Without all the questions." He laughed.

Sales representatives were the best way to learn about products, so I usually had a lot of questions for them. Plus, it was their job to teach and to create interest, just like we did with our clients.

"You're looking splendid," he said. "Business must be good indeed. If you have a minute, I'd love to show you some new pieces. I'd like to see Emma put something on the floor."

He took my arm and led me to some new displays.

"Sit."

I did.

I remembered now his name was Ray. He sat next to me on a sofa and said, "What do you think? It's very well made and well priced. What price points do you think you'd look for?"

"Well, honestly, I go by what suits my clients, but I'd like to offer good, better, and best. I believe everyone deserves a beautiful home."

"That's a great tagline. Do you have room to squeeze in a couple of pieces?"

"I'd need to run it by Emma."

"What about *your* living room?"

"That's a really good idea." I said. "I've been thinking of doing something, and I can photograph it and put it in my album. I can pull that off."

Ray tilted his head slightly and studied me, then nodded his head as though he'd just decided.

"What?"

"Nothing. I always thought you were not only attractive but smart too."

"Well, thanks Ray, for the vote of confidence. I'm loving what I'm doing."

"Excuse me, I need to see someone," he said, catching his sales manager's eye. "Why don't you look through some of our fabrics and see if something works for you. Then we can get an order placed. I'll be right back."

With a plan in place, I started pulling fabrics I could live with on a day-to-day basis and by the time Ray came back, I had them laid out, along with some of the new introductions.

"Wow, you've done an outstanding job. Hey, we're having our market cocktail party tonight, why don't you stay and join us? There'll be plenty to eat and we've even got a band coming in."

While I didn't normally enjoy parties, I was feeling recharged, and said, "Why not?"

I still had time to go to a few more showrooms. "I'll be back," I said with a bounce in my step.

The party had started by the time I got back, and the showroom was packed. Somehow, Ray found me and took my sample bags.

"Are you hungry?" he asked, taking me by the hand and leading me to the buffet tables. "I waited for you."

"I'm starving," I said, taking in all the appetizers and main entrees.

"Let's fill our plates and find a place to sit. Then I'll get us some wine." It surprised me we found a sofa away from where the band was setting up, and we set our plates on a cocktail table. "So, how was the afternoon? Successful?" Ray asked after we'd settled in.

"It was great. I love market. I can hardly stand it," I said, bringing my glass to his. "Here's to a great beginning," I said, then realized I hadn't meant that as it sounded. "To a great market."

"Here's to you." He seemed amused.

"What?" I asked, taking another sip of my wine.

"Nothing. Just thinking of when I first met you and you so openly showed your interest in everything. How sometimes you apologized for asking so many questions."

"You remember that? That's frightening." I grimaced.

"No, it was refreshing. I've been around designers for so long, they've somehow learned to hold back any excitement. Any genuine interest. Never get that way, Annie."

I didn't know what to say, so I said, "I hope I won't."

After we ate, I fought the crowd to the dessert table and loaded a plate with a variety of tempting diet busters, and came back to see Ray talking with another designer. For a moment, I was surprised and slightly disappointed; I chastised myself for such a silly response, which was foolish and reckless. I didn't own him, and I certainly wasn't interested in him romantically.

"Hey there," Ray said as I approached. "This is one of my favorite clients, Elaine Smith-Hudson. Elaine, Annie."

"Annie Parker," I filled in. "Nice to meet you. Where are you from?"

"Leave it to Ray to snag the young pretty ones," she said slyly. "I'm from South Orange County, and you?"

"Long Beach."

"Well, Ray, call me in about a week and I can order some new pieces for the showroom." She turned to me and shook my hand. "Nice to meet you, Annie Parker."

"Let's dance," Ray said, pulling me to the temporary dance floor. The band was just starting a slow tune. "Elaine's a great gal, isn't she?"

It took a minute to get into rhythm, but once we did, dancing with Ray was smooth. He didn't do any crazy moves, which was perfect for me. I could feel the heat of his hand on my back, and he clasped my right hand in his. Even though we were just dancing, I hadn't been in anyone's arms since I'd met David, and it felt strange but a little exciting. We danced for a few minutes, and I let my mind wander.

Ray took my left hand in his as he led me off the floor, and he fingered my wedding rings.

"So, Annie Parker, how long have you been married?"

We locked eyes, and I tried to deny the interest I sensed.

"Oh gosh," I said. "Almost seven years." I felt a panic rise in me, and it wasn't all bad. "What about you?"

"Not married. Was once, but I still haven't found the perfect woman."

"Ah," I said, shaking my head and smiling. "I don't think you'll ever find her."

"Maybe not. I'll get us more wine," he said, touching my arm.

When he returned, we toasted again, and as he watched me, I realized where this could all be leading, and I tried to quell the spark in me. I knew I wasn't truly interested in betraying David, but having a fling could be, well, very exciting. However, I remembered how uncomfortable I'd be with another man, and quickly decided against it. I knew without a doubt I could be headed for trouble.

"Thanks for working with me, Ray," I finally said. "But I really should go. I promised David I'd call him once I got back to my room. Plus, I'm dying to sit in the Jacuzzi and soak my feet."

I could tell I took the wind out of his sail and the smile disappeared from his eyes. He was visibly disappointed. I could see he'd turned red, as had I, but he hugged me and said, "Sounds good. The Jacuzzi, I mean. I'll get your order in and as much as I hate to see you go, you've made some excellent decisions today...Annie Parker."

"I think I have too," I said, and I turned to leave.

As I soaked in the tub, vivid images of being with someone other than David kept running through my mind. There was no harm in fantasizing. But what I thought was strange, was that I couldn't remember when the butterflies I now had, had stopped for me.

In the beginning, David couldn't get enough of me.

"You're skin is so beautiful," he'd say. "You're my China doll. You're like no one I've been with before."

I wasn't so naïve to think there would constantly be romance, but it felt wonderful to know that someone was attracted to me. Thinking back, even the first time David and I made love, he hadn't tried to seduce me or capture my heart.

Although I had done nothing wrong, I went to bed feeling a little guilty about it all. The next morning I grabbed a quick breakfast in the hotel restaurant and while I was waiting for the shuttle, I saw Ray talking with a woman and my heart skipped. I sensed his familiar flirtation, and my stomach rolled. I didn't call out to him; in fact, I didn't want him to see me. I was embarrassed by feelings he probably didn't even know I had. How foolish I could have been.

I checked my sample bags and luggage in the lobby and spent the rest of the day trying to focus on projects I was working on, and how I'd lay out my living room as an extended showroom. When I got home late that afternoon, David wasn't there, and it looked like he hadn't been there all weekend. I tried to remember if he'd said he had plans as I focused on unpacking and doing laundry. Depending on when he got home, we'd go have something for dinner; I wasn't cooking.

CHAPTER ELEVEN

I can't say it surprised me a year later when my sister Loni told my parents she was getting a divorce.

"She gave me no details," my mother said when I asked what had happened.

I wondered if her husband had gotten fed up with her drinking. I'd only seen her once since her wedding, and that was when we celebrated my parents' anniversary. Loni drank the entire weekend, and I wondered how she never got sick. Her husband was fidgety and acted like he could hardly wait to leave.

Loni and I had grown further apart, which made sense; we never spoke. My mother was the one who shared the news; she'd tell me what Loni was doing, and vice versa. We never even exchanged birthday cards. Apparently, I wasn't the only one who thought we had nothing in common.

"Hey, lil' sister," she said when we arrived at my parents' house. "Hugs."

Her words were thick and when I drew nearer, I smelled alcohol. It had permeated her pores. I tried not to flinch, and I quickly pulled back from a brief embrace.

Out of the corner of my eye, I saw David, and he said a quick "hi" and went into the kitchen to make himself a drink.

When I saw her, I remembered how I'd always thought she was prettier than I was. In the short time since I'd seen her, she'd started smoking again and had aged drastically. There was blankness in her eyes, and her coloring wasn't good. I wondered how much her drinking had damaged her brain and liver.

David made it clear he would be absent for everything except the actual anniversary dinner, and even throughout that, I could tell he was just barely tolerating everyone. He was cordial towards my parents, but he didn't engage in any conversation. It was obvious to me, at least, that he felt my family was somehow beneath him, especially my sister. And it made me uncomfortable. It was ironic; when we were with *his* parents, he expected me to wait on them, and wasn't shy about reminding me. The difference was I loved his parents.

I looked at him with the same level of disapproval that I felt for my sister. When the evening was finally over, I was angrier with him than I'd ever been. My instinct was to lash out at him, which, of course, would have started an argument I would never win.

"It's so like you to think your family's better than mine," I said when we got in the car.

He said nothing, which of course angered me more. He climbed into bed, gave me a perfunctory kiss, and then rolled over. He then promptly fell asleep. His snoring infuriated me even more, making it harder for me to drift off.

That summer, I learned the cause of David's most recent disagreeable and somewhat confrontational behavior.

I was just walking in the door from a much needed nail appointment when the phone rang. I rushed to the kitchen counter where the phone was.

Our friend Susan asked, "Do you have a minute?"

Instinctively, my stomach went cold, and I was certain she was going to tell me something had happened to David.

"Yes," I finally answered.

"I've been wrestling with myself for a week now and it's making me a nervous wreck."

I was silent.

"Annie, I saw David, and I think you need to know."

As if it could, my stomach sank even further.

"He was with someone."

"When?" I almost whispered.

"When I was in Vegas for my birthday. A couple of my girlfriends came with me and I saw him in the casino. Oh, Annie," she said. "I'm so sorry. I had to tell you. I'd want to know if it happened to me."

I didn't say a word.

"*Are you okay?*" she asked.

"I don't know," I said. I stood there for a minute. I couldn't even think. I needed time to digest what I'd just heard. I literally felt the blood rush from my head.

"Yes," I finally answered.

I sat at our counter. Of all the things I'd been thinking about that morning, mailing a package, making a deposit, picking up David's dry cleaning, I'd definitely not thought about the state of my marriage.

I realized my purse and my keys were sitting on the kitchen floor. I hadn't heard them drop. I hung up the phone, not even thinking Susan was still on the line. I went upstairs to our bedroom and stood in the doorway. The room didn't look any different from when I'd left that morning, but I felt a chill pass through me. I looked at the bed we'd shared for over eight years and wondered where we'd gone wrong. Then, I couldn't help but wonder if David had ever made love to anyone else in here. The thought turned my stomach.

I knew he wouldn't be home for a few more days, so I went through his things to see if there was anything he'd hidden...anything that would give me some idea what he was doing. I carefully started going through his dresser, then thought *what the hell,* and dumped everything out on to the floor. What difference did it make now anyway if he knew I'd gone through his things? After a few minutes, I hated to admit I was disappointed; there wasn't anything incriminating anywhere. Of course not.

I went through his sport coats and jackets, and there I found a few credit card receipts, but nothing unusual stood out. I closed his closet doors and then opened them again. Rage burned through me and, like a madwoman, I ripped everything off their hangers and let them fall to the floor. I hoped that would make me feel better, and as I looked at the heap before me I instantly felt a quick stab of remorse for behaving so childishly, but my bitterness pushed it away.

I pulled our wedding album out of one of my drawers and I looked around at the carnage I'd created. By now I was numb. I brought the album into the living room and found my way to my favorite chair. The only sound in the house was the tick tock, tick tock of our antique grandfather clock. Gradually, my breathing returned to normal and, as it did, I sighed.

I opened the album and there on the first page was a close-up of me looking away from the camera. The rest were of me and David, of our parents and the kids. I proceeded to rip each page out, dropping them all on the floor in front of me.

About an hour later, I still sat there. I'd been lost in a daze, and the incessant ticking of the clock reminded me that thinking about my problems was just wasting time.

Even though the weather outside was warm, I was chilled, so I pulled a throw over me and tucked it around my neck. Eventually I dozed, and when I awoke, it was dark in the house.

I knew I'd never be able to go back to sleep, and there was no way I was going to climb into our bed, so I made my way into the kitchen and found a bag of chips and a soda. "Just what the doctor ordered," I said aloud.

As I mindlessly ate my way through the bag, I remembered my emergency cigarettes in the kitchen. David hated it when I smoked, and I'd never done it in the house. Now I didn't care. I lit one up in defiance and when I finished it, I dropped the butt into my soda can.

I thought about calling David at his hotel, but I wasn't sure what I'd say to him. Had he taken this woman on his business trip?

I tried to remember just how long it'd been since David and I shared intimacy or any tenderness towards each other, and it left me with a feeling of emptiness and loneliness. I thought of all this now, and it shocked me to realize I wasn't so much devastated that David had sought out a sexual relationship elsewhere, but that he humiliated me by doing it behind my back. And what was worse, other people must have known about it.

I dropped another cigarette in the empty soda can and decided I was going to show *him* what it felt like to be betrayed. I took a quick shower and re-did my makeup; as I searched in my closet for something sexy to wear, I wished I'd taken the time to lose those few extra pounds. But what the hell, I still looked good.

It was almost ten by the time I drove into the parking lot of a night-spot I'd seen that had dancing and a band, and the place was hopping. I got the lay of the land as I walked in and went to the bar and asked for a glass of red wine.

"Hey there," someone said, coming towards me.

"Hey yourself," I said, thinking he wasn't so bad looking. I hadn't bothered to take my wedding rings off, and he didn't even notice. I could tell he was younger than me, which was okay. I concluded I either didn't look that bad, or he was desperate. I almost smiled at that last thought. But my mission tonight was to drink and find someone to go to bed with.

Sometimes people say that when they drink, they don't mean to do what they do, but that wasn't the case with me. I knew clearly what I was doing. We danced a little, had another drink, talked a little, and then he kissed me. I knew he was the one.

"Can we go to your place?" he asked. "The way you look, you must live somewhere nice."

We went to his car first, and that's where I saw the car seat in the back.

"What's that?" I asked, stupidly.

"Oh...my sister borrowed my car," he answered calmly. "It's her kid."

When we pulled into my driveway, I wondered if any of our neighbors would notice.

"Wow, this really is a nice place," he said when I opened the front door.

"Don't mind the mess," I said as he stood in our bedroom doorway.

"Whoa. What happened here?"

"Just doing some spring cleaning," I said.

I had him take a shower, and then plain and simple, we had sex in the bed I would never sleep in again.

"At least let me try again to satisfy you," he said when I got out of bed.

"I'm good," I said as I went into the bathroom. When I came out I said, "My husband will be home any time so you should probably get on your way."

"Husband?" he asked, surprised. "But I didn't think..."

"Yes. Like your sister's car seat in your car," I said.

"Shit."

I watched him dress then said, "Thanks for a good time."

"Can I give you my number in case you want to do this again?"

"No, I'm good."

I took a couple of aspirin and another long, hot shower. I purposely left the bed unmade and added a pair of sexy underpants to the mix; it was obvious what had transpired there. My time frame was all turned around; it was three AM, and still dark enough out that I could try to get some sleep. I sat back in my living room and everything but me was the same as I'd left it; the sofa, the chairs, everything I loved so much. They hadn't changed, but I had.

I ran through multiple versions of my future, trying to consider the consequences of any rational decision;

One, I could divorce David. Assuming I got the house, how would I afford it on my own? And did I even want to stay here?

Two, I could confront him. Of course, he'd notice the mess I'd made of his closet and bed, but I'd still have to make the decision as to what I'd do in the long run.

Three, I could live with the fact that David had been unfaithful and would continue to be so. But why would I want to just accept my life as it was? Just to be married?

Four, I could stay married and get a boyfriend myself and have my own secret life.

But the bottom line was always the same—how could I continue to live here with him?

For now, I just needed to leave.

Part Three

A Cabin in the Woods

CHAPTER TWELVE

I passed a small market and a gas station before I turned one last curve to read the sign that said "Dogwood Cabins." Once I got out of the car and stretched, I took a deep breath and relaxed my shoulders from the drive. I'd found the B&B with little trouble; I followed the directions the innkeeper had given me once I turned off State Highway 18. It took an hour and a half from Long Beach, which was just far enough away that I could be by myself, but close enough in case I had to go back down to check on the house.

On the way up, my ears popped with the changes in elevation, but now they seemed to settle. I didn't know it at the time, but parts of Lake Arrowhead are a mile high. Everywhere I looked, tall trees were green and abundant, and the air was crisp and clear. If a sky could ever be perfect, it was now, with not a cloud in sight. It surprised me that the trip, with all the winding roads, didn't bother me, but thinking back, it never had. In fact, it made me focus on something other than my situation.

The B&B was all cabins. The main office was the quintessential cabin, probably from the early thirties, and the minute I opened the front door, I smelled the remnants of fireplace and evergreen. The walls were knotty pine, the floors were old oak, and pine trees were visible from every window.

It was just what I'd envisioned.

"Annie Parker," I said to the older man behind the counter. I guessed him to be in his mid-seventies. His face was lined and weathered, and thinning gray hair covered his ears a little, but it didn't diminish his still handsome face.

"We were looking forward to your stay with us," he said, pushing the worn and yellowed guest register towards me. He had a sadness about him that was hard to place. "We have you down for one week, but you said you might want to stay longer. That's okay too. Just let us know."

"It's so beautiful here! Do you call them cottages or cabins?"

"We call them cabins and we can give you a one bedroom or a single for the same price. It hasn't been that busy this week." As an after-thought he added, "They all have a fireplace."

"They all seem so charming, and I think the single would be perfect. Thanks," I said as I looked around. There were old photos of the lake, and several of winters where it looked like there was so much snow piled up against the buildings you wouldn't even be able to get out to the stores and businesses. The photos were from the forties by the look of the cars that parked outside one local business.

An old red paisley patterned sofa and two worn leather chairs were centered in front of the old stone fireplace, and a large painting of the cabins and the surrounding trees hung above the mantle. On the dark oak coffee table were magazines with homes for sale in the area, a tat-tered guide to the activities at the lake, and a stack of maps.

"It didn't seem real busy on the road up," I said.

"Well, Mondays are a bit slow. Everyone's gone back home from the weekend or if you live here, by this time, everyone's already gone to work."

"How long have you been up here?" I asked.

"Oh...about twenty years running the cabins."

When he was satisfied with the registration, he said, "My wife used to do this part, so I'm a little slow. I'll take you to your cabin if you'll follow me."

I got my suitcase and travel bag out of my car and followed him down a gravel pathway lined with tree trunks. Each cabin had its own turn off path, a front porch and a garden area. The trees surrounding the cabins were majestic. The sound the wind made as it whistled through them was just what I needed.

"I'm Sam, by the way," he said. I'd seen the yellowed name tag he wore. "Sam Jackson."

"Glad to meet you, Sam. Obviously, I'm Annie. Do you have a lot of guests staying with you?" I asked, although I'd not seen any other cars on the property.

"We'll be busier on the weekend. During the week we don't get as many visitors. But that's okay, I'm not getting around as quick as I used to, anyway."

The moment Sam opened the door to the cabin it was just like a picture in an old magazine advertising cabins for rent. Like the office, the walls were all knotty pine, each with a window that not only let in light but looked out into the forest. Dark plaid curtains added the right amount of color, and they coordinated with the faded comforter on a bed that almost filled the room. Old mountain photos hung on the walls, and a wonderful bear painting hung over the fireplace. It was exactly what I would have selected if I were working with a client. The older worn carpet was brown, but it fit the room.

"Hope this will suit you," he said.

Sam turned slightly when he heard a truck pull into the parking space outside the office. But he turned back to me. "The fireplace works, although it's kind of warm out right now. It does get cooler at night. Paper's there to help start the fire," he said, pointing to a basket filled with old newspapers and cut wood. There's even a T.V."

"It's perfect, Sam, thanks."

As I set my suitcase on the bed, I saw the doorway darken. A man stood blocking the sunlight, and I wasn't able to get a clear image of his face. By his physique, I could tell he was young and fit, and tight jeans accentuated his long legs. His work boots were scuffed and dusty.

"Hey, Sam," he said.

Sam turned again. "Well, hey there, Noah."

Noah left his baseball cap on, but nodded to me. "I had to pick up some supplies at the lumberyard, so I thought I'd stop in."

We were all quiet for a moment.

"Oh, Annie, this is Noah Chambers. He's a local, and since my wife died, he seems to think he has to check in on me." Sam shook his head and opened a cabinet. He pulled some towels out and set them on my bed. "But I do appreciate it," he whispered conspirationally.

"I heard that," Noah said, and turned around. "It looks like you're in good hands for now, so I'll get back to work. Nice to meet you, Annie," he said, and then he left.

I could hear his shoes crunching on the gravel, then his truck driving out. I was curious who Noah was, but not curious enough to ask Sam.

"Well, you're all set," Sam said, handing me the keys. "If you need me for anything, call the front desk. But give me a few minutes to get back there before you do," he said, smiling.

"I think I'm good for now. Once I put a few things away, I'm really looking forward to a quick nap. I may come down and look at your maps after that if that's okay."

"Got nowhere to go. I'll be there," and Sam closed the door behind him.

I could hear him walk back down the gravel path, and his obvious loneliness saddened me. I wondered when he'd lost his wife.

I unpacked and put my things away, then pulled the comforter off the bed so I could sleep directly on the sheets. I hated to sleep on hotel bed coverings that someone else had possibly used. I closed my eyes, and it seemed within minutes I was out.

It surprised me I'd slept an hour! I had no timetable, and no one to account to, but it still felt strange to take a nap during the day. I ran a brush through my hair, touched up my lipstick and decided the clothing I had on was good enough for the rest of the day. I finished unpacking my toiletries and brushed my teeth.

I was hungry.

I made my way back to the office. Sam was there but napping in one of the chairs facing the unlit fireplace. I tried to tiptoe in, but he heard me and sat upright.

"You're back," he said.

"I tried not to wake you but I'm starving and I was hoping one the maps here showed places to eat."

I picked one up and started looking.

"The Sports Grill in town is always good. The locals go there, and then there's Ginny's Coffee Shop. Sometimes I have them make me a sandwich if I don't have anything around here to eat, and sometimes I even get delivery," Sam said with a wink, then showed me on the map where they both were.

"Great. I'll try the Sports Grill. And I'll keep this so I can figure out where I'm going. Again, sorry to wake you," I said and headed out.

The Sports Grill was easy enough to find. It, of course, had a bar area with three televisions, and most of the dining tables were in another area off to the right. Sports memorabilia and a hand painted map of Lake Arrowhead took up about ten feet on one wall. The place was half full but noisy, and a server with an imprinted t-shirt motioned me to a table. I ordered a chicken club and iced tea, then pretended to watch one of the TVs on the wall while I waited for my meal. When it came, it looked great and tasted delicious too. I hoped I didn't look like I was as starved as I was.

"Hey, there." I heard a man's voice and looked up. I hated it when men just walked up to a woman to check them out. I gave him a look.

He noticed and put his hands up in mock surrender. "Hey, I'm Noah," he said. "I met you at the cabins. With Sam," he added. "While you were checking in."

I'd not been able to see his face, but when I looked down at his work boots, I recognized them as the ones I'd seen when I was checking in. Because the sun hadn't been in *his* eyes, he'd obviously had a better glimpse of me than I'd had of him. He was cute. Handsome, even. A little dirty from working, but still cute. I could tell he worked out in the sun a lot, for his arms were tan, and while a baseball cap covered most of his brown hair, several longer strands had escaped. His beard was neatly trimmed and short, and his eyes were a gorgeous blue.

Noah apparently didn't notice the ring on my finger when he asked, "Mind if I join you?"

"Sure."

"Are you by yourself?" he finally asked.

"Yes, I am."

"Where're you from?"

"Long Beach."

"I'm originally from up here. Never did like it down the hill."

He was full of questions, and I liked his openness. And his smile. He was very friendly and comfortable to be around.

"How long are you up here?" he asked.

I sighed. "A week, or maybe two. Depending how I feel. I'd forgotten how beautiful it is here, and I need a break."

"So you're not new to the mountain. What break, if you don't mind me asking?"

I thought about my answer for a moment, which made him say, "I didn't mean to be so blunt. It's just not usual to see a single woman come up here," Noah said. Then I could tell he didn't quite say that the way he'd intended. "I mean, there are single women here, but not many come up by themselves." His face colored a little.

"Well, I'm not really single. My husband's on one of his business trips, and I'm tired of sitting at home. So I decided to break out and do something for myself for a change."

Noah nodded slightly, "I admire that."

He was studying me, so I asked, "What about you? What do you do up here?"

Leaning back in his chair, he said, "I'm a carpenter by trade. I also build homes now and then. So I stay pretty busy."

"Have you lived up here your entire life?" I was interested to see how someone made a living here, especially in an area where there didn't appear to be much commerce or many business opportunities.

"Yup. I tried moving down once. While I was seeing someone, but neither worked out very well for me. I wanted to be up here and she wanted to be down there. And my work was up here." He shrugged his shoulders slightly, as though that explained it all.

"I'm sorry," I said genuinely. I momentarily thought about my own situation.

"Well, I've interrupted your lunch, so I'll let you go," Noah said, rising from the table. "If you find you need something to do at night, there's a local cowboy bar just across the street. It's very casual, and you don't need to wear boots," he said with a smile that made me smile back.

"Thanks. I'll keep that in mind. I'm sure I'll be looking for things to do," I said.

He then looked down at my heeled shoes and said, "I *do* suggest that if you're going to be here for a while, you get out of those *city* shoes and put on tennis shoes. Or mountain boots," Noah said, still smiling. Was he flirting with me, or was he just a charmer?

"I'll keep that in mind."

He turned to leave, and I rearranged my unfinished sandwich and started to eat. He seemed nice enough, and I felt a little flush.

Once back at the cabin, I pulled one of the Adirondack chairs into a sunny spot outside in my garden area. The air was cool and crisp, and the best part was there were no sounds other than those from the mountain...the wind whispering through the trees and the pleasant chatter of birds. I closed my eyes for a few moments and just breathed.

I found the book I'd brought and started to read. But after a few minutes, I realized I was restless and wasn't able to focus. Instead, I decided to walk around the property instead. Pinecones of every size were scattered everywhere, and I could smell the earth as pine needles and branches broke beneath my feet as I walked. A squirrel scampered up a tree so quickly, I only saw him out of the corner of my eye.

I wanted to peer inside windows to see what the other cabins looked like, but even though I knew I was the only guest for the moment, I felt like I'd be intruding if I did. I walked further out onto the grounds, and there was plenty of land behind the cabins, so no other neighbors were visible. I closed my eyes again and just listened. I'd done as Noah suggested and changed into my tennis shoes, and one lace had become loose. I bent down to tie it and I felt a little light-headed when I stood.

In a moment, the spinning feeling disappeared, and I was back to my old self.

After about a half hour, I went back to the chair and picked up the book, starting from the beginning; this time my mind was clearer, and I could get engrossed in the story.

"Hey Annie," Sam said.

"Oh," I said, surprised to hear anyone.

"Sorry if I scared you," he said. "Mind if I sit?"

Sam didn't wait for an answer, but pulled the other chair near me.

"It's awfully quiet up here, isn't it?" he said. "That's what I love."

I nodded in complete agreement.

"I forgot to give you a bottle of water when you checked in. You need to drink a lot of it when you're up here. Altitude can do funny things to you if you're not used to it. We're not that high up, but I've had guests get sick and think they were having a heart attack when it was just dehydration."

"Ah, would that be a reason I just felt funny when I bent down to tie my shoe?"

"That would most likely be it. Just be careful when you bend over, or get up too fast. Walking will wind you too. It'll get you every time. You can feel like you're out of breath when you just went a few feet."

"I think I got the picture," I said.

"So keep a bottle of water with you."

"I definitely will."

We sat comfortably in silence for a few moments.

"So where's this cowboy bar Noah was talking about?" I asked.

Sam gave me a quick look, but answered, "If you have the map, I'll show you. It's not too rowdy, but it is noisy. But then again, it could just be my age!" he grinned.

I went to my cabin and got the map off the dresser, and brought it to him.

"It's just across the street and a few buildings down from the Sports Grill."

"Thanks," I said.

I thought I might check it out tonight.

"Well...I got my fix of fresh air. It isn't like I have customers waiting, but I guess I'll get back to the office," Sam said, heaving himself out of his chair. "I swear these things get lower all the time," he muttered as he walked away.

In the short time I'd been up here, I couldn't say I'd come to any conclusions about life. I felt I was just thinking blank thoughts, so at nine that night I pulled into a full parking lot at The Cowboy Bar and it surprised me there was a place for me to sit at the bar. I ordered a glass of Cabernet and almost wished I had brought my cigarettes so I'd have something to do with my hands. A young woman came in a few minutes later and took the last seat next to mine.

"Hey Joe, I'll have a beer," she said to the bartender. Then she looked at me and asked, "Are you new in town?" It sounded like a line from a western.

"Yes, I am," I replied congenially.

"Well, I'm Laura. I'm kind of regular here, along with half the others in the place," she said. "You up for the week?"

"I think so. I just needed to get away, and this seems like a great place to do some thinking. Not the bar," I laughed, "but the mountains."

Laura glanced at my ring.

"We get a lot of part-timers up here. Personally, I couldn't live down the hill again... too crazy." It reminded me of what Noah had said earlier at the Sports Grill.

"I think I'm just used to the hustle and bustle. But I also think I could get used to living in a place like this."

"What do you do?" she asked.

"I'm an interior designer. What about you?"

"A hairdresser."

I took another sip of wine and looked around the room. Some people were dancing, and it looked complicated.

Laura caught my focus and asked, "Ever dance the Two Step?"

I laughed again, "No, I haven't. It looks fun, but I don't know if I'm coordinated enough."

"You should try. Come with me," Laura said kindly.

"Maybe the next one," I said, feeling a little self-conscious.

Within minutes, a nice looking older man asked me to dance, and I felt a little funny telling him no, thanks.

"That was awkward," I said. "I didn't come prepared to meet anyone."

"You're fine. A lot of guys come in hoping to find someone to dance with. No big deal."

Other than my recent big night out, it had been years since I'd been out on my own; I wasn't ready to deal with the singles crowd.

When another man asked me to dance to a slow song, I also politely declined, then said to Laura, "I'm not really looking to dance with anyone. I feel terrible telling these men 'No'."

"Aw, they'll get over it. They're in here all the time, and you're new. Don't worry about it."

After about an hour and a half, I'd nursed my glass of wine as much as I could, then left a nice tip for the bartender. "I'm heading for home," I said to Laura. "Not that I have to get up in the morning"

"Nice meetin' you, Annie. Hope to see you again."

"Same here."

Even for summer, the evening had cooled down. Once in the cabin, and snug under the covers in my bed, I lay there unable to sleep. The wine should have relaxed me, but instead, I started a fire in the fireplace. I lost time as I sat in one of the room's chairs, staring at it, mesmerized by the dancing flames. I suddenly couldn't help the burst of satisfaction I felt, picturing David coming home and finding our bedroom in chaos. At first, he'd think we'd been robbed, but then as he looked around, he'd see that none of my things were out of order; my drawers were still in place, my clothing was still hanging in the closet. He'd figure out it was me. Would he wonder where I was?

"Ha," I thought.

But when that moment of satisfaction left me, I plummeted into anger.

"How dare you," I said aloud. "You righteous bastard."

At some point, I was going to have to decide what I wanted to do.

I stared into the fire again, and then I thought about my evening at the Cowboy Bar tonight, and I wondered if secretly I'd hoped Noah would have shown up.

Just for a familiar face, I thought.

CHAPTER THIRTEEN

Eventually I slept until sunlight glared through the window and shone right into my eyes. When I saw the clock on the nightstand saying seven AM, I rolled over to face the other direction. There was no need to get out of bed this early, so I went back to sleep.

It actually felt great to sleep in. A little mischievous, perhaps, but I had no one to account to; no clients calling, no projects with problems, and no David. I'd call my current clients to let them know I was out of town for a couple of weeks. Even if I didn't stay up here that long, I'd have time at home if I went back down early.

I thought of David and wondered if he'd come home yet. If so, would he be curious where I was? I suddenly felt a small void being by myself. And while he'd no doubt been having a good time, I felt slightly guilty that I was on my own trip...but one that differed greatly from his. He was cheating, and *I* was trying to figure out what to do with my life.

Once I showered, I wondered what exactly I was going to do for a week. Or two. Now that I'd taken the time off, I wasn't sure what to do with myself.

I was hungry and decided to try Ginny's Coffee Shop for breakfast. French toast and bacon sounded decadent, so that's what I ordered, and while I waited for my food to arrive, I started looking through one of the magazines that listed houses for sale in the area. No matter where I went, I always liked to check on real estate and market prices. Not that

I thought I was going to buy something up here, but it also gave me something to do while waiting for my breakfast.

I was about to ask the waitress who'd come up to my table for a refill of iced tea, but when I looked up, I was surprised. It was Noah.

"You need to quit following me," he said, and smiled down at me.

"*Me following you*? You're following me." I was actually happy to see him, and again he made me smile back.

"Mind if I join you?"

At least everyone up here was polite enough to ask, although it seemed they all just went ahead and sat, anyway.

"I guess you already did," I said as he slid in across from me.

Noah looked like he'd just gotten out of the shower; his hair was still slightly wet and combed back, and for the first time I noticed it was in a short ponytail. His beard was neat and combed. His shirt sleeves were rolled up, revealing muscular forearms, and I couldn't help but notice he had a lot of hair on them. To me, body hair on a man could be sexy. I thought of David then; he had hairy arms but no hair on his chest.

"Hey, Molly," Noah called to the waitress. "I'll have the hungry man breakfast and a strong cup of coffee."

"What else is new," Molly said, cracking a wry smile.

"I guess you're a regular here too?" I asked.

"Yup. If you live up here, you're bound to be a regular just about everywhere you go."

"I have that at home, at some restaurants I go to a lot."

"You go by yourself?" Noah asked, adding sugar and creamer to his coffee.

I thought for a minute then answered, "I guess I do... my husband is always working, and my schedule is all over the place, so yes, I guess I do."

"What does he do? Your husband."

"He's an attorney. He refers to himself as 'a slip and fall' guy."

Noah just looked at me, and I could read his mind.

I said, "He's kind of jerk," and I could see the surprised look on his face. "He's a jerk, but if you need something done, he's the one to go to."

97

"How long have you been married?"

"Almost nine years." I finally set the magazine aside.

"Wow. You must have married young. Any kids?"

"No. They weren't on the menu. But I knew that when I signed up. He came with a family. And you?" I asked, catching him looking straight into my eyes.

"Nah. Almost, but it wasn't meant to be. We never got officially engaged, but we talked about marriage. She wasn't ready to settle down, and looking back on it, neither was I." Noah paused, then said, "However, she wasted no time marrying someone else not long after that."

A flash of sadness crossed Noah's face, but it quickly dissolved. "So that's two for two. But that was a long time ago, and I guess I wasn't meant to be with either lady," he said.

I wasn't sure what he meant, and then I remembered him telling me about the girl who wanted to stay down below when he wanted to be in the mountains. So he didn't seem to be very lucky in love.

Breakfast came, and we ate mostly in silence until he said, "You have powdered sugar on your upper lip."

"I do? Where?"

He mirrored his own face, and said, "Here," pointing above his lip. I tried to lick the spot with my tongue, but missed it. He took a clean napkin and started to reach across the table, but I could tell he thought the better of it. Instead, he used it to show me wiping his own mouth.

"Did I get it?" I asked.

"Not yet. One more try."

"Now?"

"Yup."

I grinned.

"What?"

"Just déjà vu all over again."

"What?"

"We used to come here for breakfast when we had our cabin, and I was in love with the young man who cleared the tables. He pointed out I had syrup on my chin and I knew when he winked at me, he liked me too."

He seemed to study my lips, and then he looked up at me. I felt an instant jolt of electricity pass through me, and it took me by surprise. Was I the only one who felt it?

"I was all of ten at the time. And my sister called me a dork."

"What's on your schedule for today?" he asked, changing the subject and wiping his own mouth again.

It took a moment for me to compose myself. "I thought I wanted some time to do nothing up here but think, but I really can't picture myself sitting outside my cabin all day and reading; I believe that's also called procrastinating," I answered, being honest. "What do you have in mind?"

"I have a light day today if you want to check out some job sites and take a trip around the lake." There was that smile again. It was infectious.

I pretended to think, but only for a moment before I agreed. I could tell it was going to be a beautiful day, and I wanted to get out and do something besides sulking. Plus, seeing Noah's work was a good enough reason as any.

"You're on," I said.

We left my car at the coffee shop and took Noah's Jeep. Because it was four-wheel drive and raised, I needed a few tries to get in.

"I can see you'll need the step stool," Noah said, giving me a mock shake of his head.

"Don't pick on me," I said, teasing back.

The first stop was at a small home, probably built in the twenties, with a ton of steps leading from the driveway up to the front door. By the time I made it into the house, I was out of breath, but I did my best to not show it.

"We're doing a kitchen remodel here, and as you could tell from the steps up, it's a challenge getting all the materials inside." My breathing was still labored, and Noah took one look at me and gently took my upper arm. "You okay?"

"Whew. I'll be alright. I'll just have to pace myself the next time I climb this many steps."

"That's what happens to city folk," Noah teased. "It's the elevation. Can you imagine those stairs when it snows? Driving up and entering on the same level, with no stairs, is the best. It's called entry level. But it's not always an option since most everything here was built on the hilly mountain."

I went immediately to the bay window, and the view was incredible. I could see the shoreline and boats on the lake.

"This is beautiful. I guess I can see why the steps didn't keep them from buying this place."

"The style and age of this home make it a Charmer," Noah explained. "It's one of the original homes on the lake. They're usually on the smaller side since they were vacation homes, but they have a lot of personality. The trick is to remodel them while trying to keep that charm and character from the past. To do it right, everything needs to be custom made. I have a couple of buddies who help me out on these."

He went to the table and looked at some paperwork lying there, and once he made some notes and looked satisfied, he said, "Ready to go to the next job?"

I tore myself away from the beautiful view.

"Sure...can I look around a little first?"

"Go for it. We're not doing anything in the bedrooms or bathrooms yet."

From down the hall, I asked, "Do they live here?"

"No. They come up on the weekends, mostly. They can still stay here while the remodeling is going on, but I haven't seen them as much since we started."

He locked the front door behind us and then grinned. "Going down won't be so hard."

"I'm grateful for that."

Noah drove the long way around the lake so I could see all the homes along the road, and I only periodically got a glimpse of the lake itself. "It's too bad you can't see much from the road," I said.

"That's because the houses sometimes are two to three levels above the lake and the trees take up a lot of the views. But maybe we can go out in the boat and get on the lake itself so you can check it out," he said.

Our second stop was a much larger home, on more land. It also looked like a Charmer, but more like a cottage, painted a blue green with dark red accents. It definitely had character. The circular driveway was gravel, and in the center was a tall red lifeguard chair and an old wooden boat. Painted red strips of wood were laid in the dirt to look like a dock. Two large round logs were sunk into each end to resemble pilings. What looked like a guest house or apartment was to the right above the garages. It was really cute. In fact, if I was looking for a home up here, it would be just what I would want.

Branches tied together in a split rail fashion, created fencing, and medium-sized rounded rocks lined the flower beds. To the left was the main house, and from the front deck I could see that the windows looked straight ahead to trees and a gravel walk way lined in more medium-sized branches. I wondered if this was where they got the idea of lining the walkway at the B&B, or vice versa. Either way, it was a great way to enter into the private forest that lay straight ahead.

Inside, the mudroom and sunroom had original brick floors, and packed cardboard boxes were covered in sheets of plastic. There was a step up into the living room and the rest of the house. It was more like a large cottage. It looked like the hardwood floors went throughout the entire first floor, and they were covered in protective paper to avoid damage during remodeling. Someone had installed skylights, adding much needed light throughout. The kitchen had new white cabinets with a black granite top, and an old O'Keefe and Merritt stove with red knobs sat in the middle of the floor.

"What a great blend of old and new," I said. The wide pine plank floor in the kitchen was taped off in squares. "What are you doing here?"

"Truthfully, I wasn't sure which way to go. I'd like to paint the floor but I'm stuck."

Immediately I said, "Why not paint black and white on a diagonal like diamonds?"

Noah rubbed his chin and nodded.

"I am a designer after all, and I love coming up with unique ideas."

"I had no idea what you did," Noah said. "That's a great idea."

I loved the surprised and pleased look on his face. I gave my shoulders a modest shrug. "You never asked."

He took me on a tour of the rest of the house; three bedrooms and three newly remodeled ensuite bathrooms. The dining area had French doors that opened out to a side deck that overlooked more of the property.

"This is so charming, Noah. I'll take it."

"Whoa there, this place isn't for sale.....it's mine."

"What? You're kidding. It's wonderful!"

"Thanks."

It was true. I could have lived there. I turned to go back out the front door, and in my mind, I *saw* the wide step down, but I missed it and fell into the sunroom. In seconds, Noah was right there, and although my heart was pounding fiercely, I knew I hadn't broken anything.

"Annie, are you okay?" he asked, helping me to my feet.

Of course, I would never admit my elbow hurt like hell.

"I guess that's a step I should do something about," he said sheepishly.

"I guess that's a step I should have remembered!" I straightened myself out and stood there, looking at him for a minute. He really was cute. I could tell he felt bad about my fall, so I dragged out his agony by wrinkling my face and saying, "Ow."

Once Noah saw my smile, he relaxed and figured out I'd been giving him a hard time.

"You sure you're okay?" he asked again.

"I'm fine. Just embarrassed."

After a moment, Noah said, "I need to go to one more job site. Do you want to come with me or have me drop you off at Ginny's?"

I tilted my head in thought. "Let's continue. It's actually nice to have company."

"Wait," he called before I tried getting into the Jeep. He went into the garage and found a plastic milk crate for me to step on to make getting in easier. "Here you go, shorty." I could tell he was pleased with himself, and he gave me a silly grin.

"Thanks."

"I'll have to get you that step stool."

As we continued to drive to Noah's next job site, I basked in the sun that radiated through the passenger side window and while I took in everything along the way, I had no particular thoughts going through my head; it was almost as though I'd pushed them all from my mind.

"You're awfully quiet," Noah said, glancing towards me.

"Just daydreaming."

I looked at all the different styles of homes we passed along the highway. Some looked unoccupied, and some had several cars parked outside, no doubt with visitors. I wondered what it would be like living in a small community like this.

At Noah's next job site, there was a new deck under construction, so I was eager to see a view and I followed him to the back of the house. There were tons of trees, but no view of the lake. I was disappointed, and I also didn't care for how close the houses in this neighborhood were to each other.

"What are the trees out here?" I asked.

"Mostly we have pine and cedar. They're some of the most beautiful in the world. The forest is magnificent, isn't it?"

"It is."

Noah checked with the men who were working, and in no time, we were ready to leave. For a contractor, his organizational skills impressed me. He seemed to be very detail oriented.

"Hungry?" he asked once we were back in his Jeep.

"I can't believe I am."

We stopped and had lunch.

"All I've done so far up here is eat and sleep. I'm blaming it on the altitude."

I wondered if I was using any excuse I could think of just to avoid thinking.

CHAPTER FOURTEEN

That night, I had dinner at the Cowboy Bar. I felt comfortable there, and maybe Laura would show up and teach me to dance. I got there around eight, and there were only a few cars in the lot.

I found a table out of the main traffic and started looking at the menu. I was famished. My nose felt a little sunburned from the day's outing, but by morning I'd be fine.

Dinner was delicious but filling; a real country meal...rib eye steak and baked potato. I ordered another glass of wine and felt relaxed.

The room started filling up, but after about an hour, I began feeling conspicuous and I hadn't seen Laura. If I was honest with myself, I also wished Noah would have come walking through the door. But neither happened, so I left a tip on the table and headed back to the cabins.

Once inside, I lit the fireplace and put my PJs on. I sat in one of the chairs and got my book out. Before I knew it, I had a crick in my neck from falling asleep, so I resigned myself to go to bed. It was midnight.

The next morning, I slept in again, and after a quick shower, I decided to forgo makeup and pulled my hair back in a ponytail. Today I would buy some boots!

I had breakfast at the same little coffee shop. Ginny greeted me when I came in and introduced herself. She was about five foot six, pleasantly plump, and wore her gray curly hair in a ponytail herself. Throughout my meal, I could hear Ginny's contagious laughter, and it made me want to laugh, too. Noah never came in, so when I checked out the shops in the village I remembered there being a shoe store there years ago, and indeed it was still there. I found a nice pair of boots and bought several pairs of socks. I'd wear them tonight. The candy shop was also still there, so I stopped in and bought some dark chocolate-covered almonds to snack on later.

There was a small refrigerator in my kitchenette, so on the way back I stopped at the store to buy some apples, bottled water and chocolate.

When I got back to the room, I put my groceries away, then grabbed my book and went outside. As soon as I sat, an obviously pregnant calico cat made her way to me, rubbing against my leg.

"Well, hello there. You look like you're about ready to pop," I said, scratching the cat's head. "Who do you belong to?" I asked, as if the cat could tell me.

"There you are, Jezebel," Sam said, his feet crunching on the gravel walkway. "We have us a pregnant cat, as I'm sure you can see," he said, reaching down to pet her. "I'm trying to keep an eye on her so she doesn't have those kittens outside. Never know what's out here at night, and I don't want her losing them to wildlife."

"I'll look after her. Can she come in if she wants to?" I asked, petting her again.

"Sure. If you leave, will you see if she'll follow you up to the office so she'll stay in tonight?"

"Absolutely."

Jezebel and I spent the afternoon reading and napping.

Around seven-thirty, I started getting ready for another dinner at the Cowboy Bar. I donned my jeans and new boots and did my makeup and hair. I even sprayed on cologne.

By nine, I'd finished a much lighter dinner than the night before. I'd ordered my second glass of wine when Laura came in and she walked over to where I was sitting.

"Hey there, stranger," she said, pulling out a chair. "Wow, look at those boots! Planning on doing some shit kickin' tonight?"

Laura then went to the bar, and I could hear her ask the bartender for her usual.

"What have you been up to?" she asked, sitting down.

"Just a little of everything, I think. Reading, buying boots, grocery shopping, napping. What about you?"

"Just working. I rent a station from a salon about fifteen minutes away. I have a pretty good clientele going, so it works for me."

"Are you involved with anyone?"

"Not really. I'd love to find 'Mr. Right' but they always turn out to be 'Mr. Wrong.' What about you? I see you're married, but if you're up here for a break, it doesn't sound like life is perfect for you either," Laura said kindly.

I sighed. "We've been passing like ships in the night. And as much as I'd like to *be* married, I feel like there's so much more that I'm missing. Like, where'd the romance go?"

"I hear you. I was married once, but he kept cheatin' on me, and I finally decided I was tired of puttin' up with that. I'd rather be heartbroken and by myself than heartbroken in a dead end marriage." Laura drank from her beer. "So I told him to leave. And he did. Without a fight. And that hurt too." Laura was silent for a moment. Then the music turned louder, and it snapped both of us out of commiserating.

We stayed for another hour or so before we both headed back home. Laura had an early client, and I...well, I didn't feel like staying there by myself. Besides, my new boots were making my feet sore.

When I returned to the cabin, Jezebel was waiting outside. As soon as I opened the front door, she ran in, her tight belly swaying a little, and she tried to open the closet door. Sensing what she wanted to do, I opened the door and let her in.

"I think you need a place to have your babies," I said, looking around for an older blanket. I found one in the closet and laid it on the floor. Jezebel kneaded it for a moment, then lay down on her side. I petted her, then found a bowl and put water in it and set it down near her. By morning, there might be kittens.

I awoke the next morning to mewing, and indeed there were three kittens being cleaned by their mother and wanting to be fed. They looked more like rats than cats, but it wouldn't take long for them to start getting cute. I quickly dressed, then went to the office to see if Sam had any food and an extra cat box. He had something for Jezebel to eat, so I brought it and a cardboard box back to the cabin.

As soon as I showered, I grabbed my things to head for the store to get some cat essentials. I bent down for my purse and felt the same light-headedness I had before, and thought it would stop by the time I got outside. I stopped to get my balance on one of the Adirondack chairs outside my door. Out of nowhere, I was seeing stars. Since I had a bad habit of tensing my shoulders, I thought if I stretched my neck, they would go away. But they didn't.

Suddenly, I pictured David with someone else, and my stomach sank with dread. I had that cold sensation that comes with nauseating anticipation, and then I felt nothing. I was totally devoid of any emotion at all. It had to be adrenaline, and it took my breath away.

I sat down and tried to slow my breathing. I tried to focus on breathing deeply as I felt a panic race through me. *Breathe.* But the panic wouldn't leave me, and I felt cold rushing through my veins. I thought if I closed my eyes, I'd be able to relax, but that didn't work, so I opened them, and tried to find something to focus on.

The only thing I could see was a Steller's blue jay as it made its way to a bird feeder and water dish in my little garden. It pecked, swallowed, and pecked again at the seed, and it somehow relaxed me. Thankfully, the bird stayed until I could finally take a deep breath and resume a normal breathing pattern.

I'd never felt that way before, and it frightened me. By continuing to breathe slowly, I felt better, but my brain was still foggy, so I sat quietly until I knew I was going to be all right.

When the panic left, nausea and exhaustion replaced it. I could hardly keep my eyes open and I could barely stay awake.

I needed a few minutes to think, but suddenly tears welled up in my eyes and I wiped them away as quickly as they fell.

'How could I be so stupid?' And what was I going to do about it?

He must have been lying to me for months, and yet I saw nothing that made me question the status of our lives together. How does something like this happen? How do people become so blind?

I called the house, planning on leaving a message, and it surprised me when David answered.

"What the hell happened? My stuff's everywhere! Did someone break in?"

"No. How was your trip?"

"Annie, I came home to this mess. What's happened?"

Everything I'd been thinking fought to get out, but I chose to take baby steps.

"Where were you?"

"We stayed an extra day in Vegas."

"Were the guys there?"

"Yes, but I need to know…"

"I know you weren't with the guys. Where were you?"

The line was silent, and for a moment I thought I lost him. My heart was pounding in my ears.

"We need to talk." It was all I could think of to say. "I'll be home tomorrow."

"Where are you," David finally asked, uneasiness in his voice.

"I'm in Arrowhead. I came up to get away and to figure out what to do about *us* if the truth be known…and now you've just made up my mind."

I hung up.

I hated him.

My body went limp. I wanted to melt into the chair and disappear. I heard Jezebel meow and then felt her rub against my leg. I must not have closed the door to the cabin.

"Hi Momma Girl," I said, hanging my hand over the arm of the chair. I was so drained I didn't want to move. Jezebel found my hand and made me pet her. Something about her company made me relax a little.

Somehow I'd been able to keep my thoughts random these last few days; never thinking in complete sentences, rarely letting them fill me with complete despair, but suddenly it all came crashing down on me and I couldn't stop it.

How could David have done this to me?

And how long had he been seeing someone?

How many other 'road trips' had there been with another woman? Was it the same woman? Did she make him happy where I had failed?

Was this new? This cheating?

How could I have been so stupid?

I thought back to the times David had kissed my cheek when we went to bed, but had, thankfully, not been interested in having sex. And to pay him back, how I used to tease him, telling him I'd wait up for him when he said he was going to be late, then pretend to be asleep when he finally came home. It seemed we'd both been playing games.

I kept coming back to the same point. It wasn't the failing marriage itself, or the complacency we'd settled into that was bothering me the most.

The mocking voice inside me kept repeating, "He made a fool of you." The betrayal was the worst!

I sat outside most of the day, letting my mind wander, alternating between anger and self-pity, and I tried letting the crisp mountain air cleanse my mind. I walked around the compound again and absolutely loved the tranquility the area brought me. I could picture myself living here. I could easily run away. I had to figure out what to do; there was no way we could continue after this.

I found the street of our original Pinecone Lake House on my map and decided to pay a visit. My breath caught for a quick moment as I saw it. I sat in my car for a few minutes and finally built up the nerve to get out and walk the property. I wondered if Mrs. Richmond, our old neighbor, was still alive, and the moment I saw her wonderful garden, I knew she was. I didn't see cars on either her land or on the Lake House property, so I continued.

Our house looked smaller. The paint was peeling around a few of the windows, but the weather always took its toll on wood from one season to the next. The grounds had recently been raked, and they were well maintained; the rocks we laid still circled the many trees, making dams to collect and save water. A new hammock hung between two of the large trees, and I wanted to climb into it and curl up, but I didn't. I walked to the end of the property and looked out at the lake, and I think I was secretly hoping someone from our lake house would come out and ask what I was doing there so I could tell them it used to be ours. I would accept their invitation to go inside. Had they kept any of the artwork we'd left behind? Was our Bunkhouse bedroom still decorated with the cabin bedding and curtains?

A boat towing two skiers passed me, and then I saw two men in their canoes, laughing loudly as one tipped to the side from the waves.

The air was cool in the shade and I felt like I was a million miles away from everything, which was exactly what I wanted. I closed my eyes and envisioned myself living up here. The thought wasn't altogether impossible.

I wanted to sit on the dock and dangle my feet in the water, but I was technically trespassing, so I enjoyed the air for a few more minutes, and then drove back to my cabin.

By eight that night, I was at my "usual" table at the Cowboy Bar, and was ordering wine and dinner.

Laura came in around eight-thirty and brought her beer to my table. "What's cookin'?" she asked, pulling out the chair.

I wasn't sure how to start, so I just blurted it out. "My husband has been seeing someone." And I told her what had happened. And then I told her how stupid I felt.

"Wait a minute, Annie. I don't think you're stupid. Maybe you didn't see the signs of him cheating on you, but you're not stupid," Laura defended me.

"I didn't see it." I tried to fight it, but tears welled up in my eyes. "And I can't believe it makes me want to cry. I knew in my heart we weren't working out. I just didn't expect this." I used the cocktail napkin to blot new tears from my eyes.

Laura put her hand on mine. "Men are pigs!"

We both laughed.

"Yes, they can be," I agreed.

"I'll buy you another glass of wine," Laura said, standing and going to the bar. She came back with another beer for herself, too. "Why not drink to your misery," she said, trying to coax a smile out of me.

"I agree."

Suddenly Noah was there. "What are we drinking to?" he asked, not having a clue what was going on.

"Nothing. Just girl stuff." I said. I tried to look away.

He pulled out the other chair.

"Make yourself at home," Laura said, giving him a punch in the shoulder.

I had suddenly lost my appetite and when Noah asked if he could have some of my French fries, I pushed the plate towards him.

Someone asked Laura to dance, and she accepted the offer. It left Noah and me alone at the table. I wiped at my eyes.

"Hey, what's going on Annie?" I could see the concern in his eyes.

"A lot," I said. "I don't know where to start."

"Start with the beginning?" Noah said, reaching for my hand.

I didn't pull it away. "I'm going back down tomorrow, and I think I'm divorcing my husband."

CHAPTER FIFTEEN

"Dance with me," Noah said, pulling me up and almost dragging me to the dance floor. He drew me close to him, moving with a grace I hadn't expected. When he put his cheek next to mine, I felt the softness of his beard and then the warmth of being in his arms. His hands were a little rough as he held mine, but their strength gave me a sense of protection and calm. I could hear his breathing in my ear.

There was definitely a spark between us. I could tell he felt it too, and it was almost impossible to move away from him. But I sensed others would recognize what was happening between us. I had, after all, made sure everyone knew I was married.

"I need to talk to you alone," Noah whispered in my ear. "I need to know what's going on. Let's leave here."

"We can go to my cabin," I said, leading the way to our table so I could gather my things.

Laura was still on the dance floor, and I caught her eye as we left the bar.

The gravel beneath our tires seemed to echo in the silent night, and I hoped Sam wasn't able to hear us as we each pulled in and parked. For some reason, I felt guilty; like I was doing something I shouldn't. When I opened the door to the cabin, a hungry Jezebel instantly greeted me.

I was glad I'd picked up after myself before I left for the Cowboy Bar, so I motioned for Noah to sit on the sofa while I opened a can of cat food.

"Who's your friend?" Noah asked, taking his jacket off.

"That's Jezebel and three new kittens. I feel honored she chose to have her babies here. But now I have more mouths to feed." I smiled as I gently scratched under her chin. "I don't mind. I love animals."

"I've always had dogs," Noah said, "but for some reason, I haven't had one for a couple of years. When I finally settle into the new house, I'll have a place for one. Or two."

I took my boots off and then sat in the chair opposite Noah.

"So, what's goin' on?" Noah asked, fidgeting with his beard.

"Well, the short version is that before I came up here, I found out my husband was having an affair." I waited for that to settle in, and I could see a muscle tense in his jaw as he sat forward.

"*Are you kidding?*" He sat back against the sofa again and once more stroked his beard, deep in thought. "Wow." He studied me for a few moments before he asked, "What happened?"

"I've had a few days to sort it through, and when I'm not angry, I think about us and how we really hadn't had a relationship for a while. I think we just grew apart." I looked at him, and there were the beginnings of tears in my eyes.

"Do you love him?" Noah's voice was soft, but his mouth was tight. He wanted to know.

The tears stopped. "I don't think so. I believe I still care about him, but I'm not in love with him." I smiled, a little uncertainly. "And it looks like he feels the same about me."

Saying that last part aloud was what did me in. Saying I wasn't in love with David was one thing, but realizing he was no longer in love with me was shattering.

"God, Annie, I'm not sure what to say. Or do." I could see the pain in his face. All he did was look at me.

I went to sit by him on the sofa and said, "There's not really anything you *can* say, or do, except to continue to be my friend."

"Whew," Noah said again.

I snuggled next to him, and he put his arm around me.

"I'm kind of overwhelmed right now. Can we just sit like this?" I shivered.

"It's getting chilly in here. Should we light the fire?" Noah asked.

"That would be great," I said, tucking my feet under me.

I watched as Noah got the wood on the grate, then he started the fire with some of the rolled-up newspapers in the basket. He looked back at me once, a gentle smile on his face. Just checking on me, I thought. He was truly a handsome man. I remembered the softness of his beard and the smell of musk on him as we danced. I must have smiled at him, as he turned again and smiled back at me.

Noah sat back down on the sofa, and we both watched the flames build.

"We bought a house after we were married, and I loved it. I was happy. I had everything I wanted, and I thought we'd live happily ever after."

I laid my head on the back of the sofa and closed my eyes for a few minutes.

Noah gently touched my cheek, and the electricity was back.

"I think I never realized what I didn't have until about a year or so ago. I started looking at other couples who looked like they were in love, and they didn't look like us. I saw romance everywhere I went and wondered why I didn't feel that way about our relationship. "I even thought about having an affair."

I'd never said it aloud, and I waited for his response. It was as if he froze into blankness.

"That sounds awful, I know, but it seems I've been thinking about all this subconsciously for some time. I would never have had one, but I thought about it, and I could tell when men were interested in me. I was determined to make a success of my business and my marriage. They were the two things that changed my life for the positive."

My body turned icy, and I was hoping I wasn't having another dreadful episode. "Apparently David had been thinking the same thoughts, but he, on the other hand, did something about it. We never really had what I'd call a passionate relationship or even courtship, if the truth was known. No lust, just pretty basic. I guess I started comparing us to what I read in books or saw in movies, and I never saw us as those couples. It was always a quick peck on the cheek goodbye, or 'I'll be late so don't hold dinner' 'I have a client to see, or a meeting' and I just accepted that as our way of life."

I'd poured it all out. I turned to Noah and touched his arm. "Am I making you disappointed in me?" I asked. "I don't know why I felt comfortable telling you all this. And you haven't answered me."

He pulled at his beard.

"I'd like some wine," I said. "I think I have beer if you'd like one."

I got up. Even if he wanted nothing, I needed a drink.

"What will you do now?" he finally asked.

"Well?" I asked when I sat back down.

"You're certainly a complex little lady."

We sat in silence and Jezebel jumped up and made herself comfortable on my lap.

"What do you want to do now?" he finally asked.

"Right now?"

"Yes."

I knew I was being bold, but I said, "Right now, I want you to kiss me."

I set my wineglass down and moved close enough to whisper in Noah's ear. "I want you to kiss me." Just saying it made me ache inside. Jezebel jumped down.

I'll never forget that first kiss. I felt limp. I'd secretly wanted this all night. I wanted to know how it would feel to kiss this man who had taken me under his wing since I met him. I hadn't wanted to admit I'd been attracted to him while I was still trying to figure out what to do with my life.

However, today, talking with David had changed the game. And I was now going to be free to do as I wanted.

Noah's kisses were powerful. I leaned back to see the effect I had on him, and it was exactly what I'd hoped. His eyes slowly opened and

I could see tenderness and caring in them. Those beautiful crystal blue eyes. Right now, they were only for me.

"I've wanted to do this since I first saw you," Noah said hoarsely. "I knew kissing you would rock my world."

A secret part of me reveled in his confession.

"I've wanted it too. I just didn't know how much," I whispered. This time, *I* kissed *him,* and I realized I'd never felt so much passion in a kiss. I had no idea it would feel like this. But Noah's gentle kisses on my neck and face made me realize I wanted more.

"Annie, we need to stop." Noah's plea was genuine, but his fingers kept touching my face and my lips. "It's not the right time."

I desperately wanted Noah to keep kissing me, to hold on to that feeling of being wanted. And when he stopped, I tried to keep the tears from coming. Maybe it was the wine. I knew I wanted more from Noah, but he wasn't ready to give me more. I felt humiliated and angry with myself.

"Please, Annie, don't cry," Noah said.

But I felt utterly miserable.

Jezebel came and rubbed my leg. "I think you need to go." I was embarrassed. "I need to let her out and go to bed."

CHAPTER SIXTEEN

Alyce

When Daddy hadn't come home that next morning, Mama was frantic. He would never have just taken off without tellin' her. She repeatedly called the auto shop and Smitty's house, but there was no answer at either place. She then called the police to report him missing. She paced the floor as they asked her questions, and several times, I heard the panic in her voice.

"He'd never run off. He'd never not come home unless somethin' was terribly wrong." She was trembling.

"What kind of issues?" she cried. "We don't have no issues. No."

She pinched her head in frustration and closed her eyes in thought.

"I don't know...he was wearin' jeans, work boots..."

"A red shirt," I added.

"Oh, and a red shirt, my daughter says."

"He's never left us before. But he was upset about something. I could tell, but I don't know about what. He left that morning just like he always does. And he hasn't come back."

It was three days of hell for Mama. She wouldn't leave the house, afraid she'd miss a call. Because it was the weekend, I didn't know what I could do to help except to keep her company. She slept on the divan and she found one of her hidden pack of cigarettes and smoked like a chimney.

I wasn't much of a cook, but I made us some cereal for breakfast, and peanut butter and jelly sandwiches for lunch. Mama made hamburger patties and macaroni and cheese for dinner, but she said she didn't have an appetite. I didn't eat much either and I gave most of mine to Daisy. I kept the kitchen clean, the way she liked it, washing dishes and leavin them to dry in the strainer...

When she ran out of cigarettes, she sent me across the street to the Ma and Pa and I bought her a new pack. She smoked Kents then, and I hated being in the house with all that smoke. Daddy still smoked Lucky Strike from when he was in the service, but he told my mom he'd quit. I caught him sneaking a couple of times, but I never told Mama his secret. He'd always give me a little wink and say, "I'm just having one."

My grandpa came over and spent the days with us, falling asleep in a chair in the front room so he could keep Mama company.

"Now don't you worry," he kept saying. "He'll be okay. We'll find out what's happened soon."

But it didn't seem to give Mama much comfort.

I didn't go play with the neighborhood kids during those three days, but a few times I went outside and threw a ball to Daisy or picked up loose gravel and threw it back onto the driveway. When I did that, she'd think I'd thrown the ball and would run to find there was nothin' there.

"There's no ball, silly," I'd say, and she'd keep lookin'.

I didn't have a sense of what was happening; I just wanted them to find Daddy.

Grandpa took Daisy and me to have ice cream on Saturday, and I was so engrossed in worry, I almost forgot to put some in the Tupperware bowl for Daisy, but Lois, the waitress, reminded me. Daisy whined and waggled her tail the minute she saw us, and I had to say "Scoot," so she'd let us in the truck.

"There you go, girl," I said as she lapped it up.

Sunday night, Grandpa cooked fried chicken and corn, and I sneaked Daisy some as I ate. Mama didn't look well; underneath her eyes her skin was dark, and she only had a few bites to eat before she got up and said, "I just can't eat."

She went outside and had a cigarette.

It was Monday, while I was at school, when she got a call from the San Bernardino County Sheriff's Department. They'd found a man in a rented Lake Arrowhead cabin, with my father's wallet lying on the dresser; he'd apparently hung himself.

She didn't come get me from school, but waited until I got home. I knew somethin' was wrong when I came in the front door and Mama and Grandpa stood to greet me. I thought if I took my time putting my homework down on the dining table and getting a cookie out of my grandma's old glass cookie jar, they'd sit down, and it would be good news.

Mama told me he'd had a heart attack. I didn't ask many questions; I just accepted what she told me.

Mama and I went to the local funeral parlor to make arrangements for Daddy's burial, and we selected the most reasonable casket we could find that didn't make Mama feel guilty.

"Daddy always told me if he went before me, he didn't want me to waste any money on such nonsense. 'Just send me off,' he'd said."

I wasn't exactly sure how I was of any help. I cried the whole time. All the details were a blur to me, but I know Mama was grateful to have me there with her, for she was always huggin' me close. She told me she didn't want to be by herself.

Daddy's family came from Kansas; his daddy had already died, so it was just his own mama with her new husband and his brother. I was Mama's shadow, at her side constantly since I'd never met any of them. Most of our neighbors came too. But Smitty and his family weren't there.

I remember asking my mother why, and all she said was, "I'm not sure."

We didn't normally go to church, so the funeral director recommended a minister to do the service at the mortuary. He didn't know Daddy, but he talked about him like he did; about how he served our country, how he was wounded saving lives, and how he was a fine man. He said some prayers, and I looked around the small chapel to see if everybody's head was bowed.

They printed up a pamphlet with Daddy's war picture on it, and I did my best not to wrinkle it as I put it in my pocket. After the service, we all stood at the gravesite and listened to the minister read things from the Bible, but the passages weren't familiar to us. We bowed our heads in prayer again and there was talk about the valley of death.

The first thing I did when we got back to the house was smooth out Daddy's pamphlet the best I could. I watched myself in my dresser mirror as I put it in my pink ballerina jewelry box and saw the same old me. Somehow, I thought I should have looked different than I had a week or so ago when Daddy was still alive. But I looked the same. I wrinkled my eyebrows and made a big frown. When I straightened out my face and looked in the mirror again, I looked like me, but I'd changed. I was not the same person. I now no longer had a father.

People started showin' up for the buffet the neighbor ladies set up, and everyone talked about my dad. When they finally started to leave, they all told Mama and me how sorry they were. At that time, no one knew the truth.

Almost thirty years later, Mama told me she wished she'd told them all it was just a family affair. That way, she wouldn't have had to face them later. She also told me that the parents of my friends eventually knew what really happened, but she'd told them I didn't know. They kept this secret, even from their children, my friends. I know that now because, looking back at it, none of my friends ever brought the subject up or teased me.

We found out less than a week later why Smitty and his family hadn't attended Daddy's funeral. In a town just over from Lake Arrowhead, Smitty, his wife, two sons and their dog were found murdered in their newly remodeled cabin. At the time, there was no connection between the two events.

CHAPTER SEVENTEEN

After Noah left, I should have slept well because of the wine, but instead, I awoke several times during the night, first with too many covers, then not enough...restless regardless of whether I was on my side or on my back.

Morning finally came and when I pulled back my curtains, even though the sun peeked through the trees, I felt no nudge of motivation to make the trip down the hill. I fed Jezebel, took some Tylenol, and then showered. Despite a slight headache, I was going home.

Sam was up when I stopped by the office.

"Hey there," I said, bringing my key. "I'm heading back down, maybe for a couple of days, but leave my cabin as it is. I fed Jezebel and the kittens are doing fine. Will you check in on them?"

"You okay?" Sam asked, checking my face closely.

I knew I looked awful because I felt it, and I could see the concern on his face. I could tell Sam didn't want to pry, as he'd no doubt heard our vehicles last night.

"I'm good. Just didn't sleep well last night. I'll be back."

And I left. I needed something in my stomach before taking off, so I hoped Noah wouldn't show up at Ginny's while I ate. Thankfully, he didn't. I was tired, and I really wasn't sure what I'd say to him. I regretted my behavior, and I didn't want to face him.

An hour and a half later, I was unlocking my front door, and traces of my cologne filled the air. Feelings of "it's always good to get home" fought with "this will not be my home for long" and I felt empty inside.

I sat at the kitchen island and checked the mail. There was a note in David's handwriting, reminding him to call Beverly; my blood froze. Was this the woman he'd been seeing? I was so angry, tears stung my eyes. It was like salt on a wound. Was this proof he'd moved on and probably wasn't even giving me or our marriage the time of day? What an arrogant prick!

The opening of the front door startled me. Had I set the alarm? But keys dropping on the entry table told me it was David.

"Annie, are you home?" David called from the entry.

"Of course I am," I said under my breath, then headed to the living room.

My heart skipped when I saw him; he looked confident yet exhausted, and suddenly my anger dissipated. He didn't have that annoying, arrogant swagger. Was he possibly wondering about the outcome of our meeting?

David stood there, his Polo shirt and jeans accentuating a physique that belied his age; some gray had made its way into his beard and his temples, and he was still quite striking.

"We should talk," he said. "Let me get a bottle of water."

I waited for him in the living room. I loved this room. The walls were a gray green, the floors were hardwood, and the original wide crown molding matched the off white color of the trim. Very classic traditional. When I made it into an extended showroom, instead of having the traditional sofa and two accent chairs, I decided on six swivel chairs that faced each other so that guests could each have their own comfortable place to sit. I used that floor plan again for several of my clients, and it worked well.

How odd that I would think of this unimportant detail now when our lives, as we knew them, were about to change forever.

I sank into one of the chairs and closed my eyes. I was suddenly overwhelmed, and I was so angry with David again I could...could what? Yell and scream?

When David came back into the room, I looked at him, and realized that when he sat in a chair opposite me, his shoulders slumped and he wasn't nearly as confident as he had been when he came home.

"I'm really sorry, Annie," David started. He looked down at his hands, then up at me.

His smile was pensive, and just a sliver of emotion emanated from him. It surprised me. But it wasn't enough that he could come to me, to at least attempt to console me. For a split second, I wished he would take me in his arms, but he didn't. Then I realized I wouldn't have let him touch me, anyway.

"We've obviously been complacent for a while now; I could see it not only in me, but in you."

I just watched him.

"I've been seeing someone," he continued, then stopped. His gaze never left me.

"So I gather," I said dryly. "I don't think I'm so much disappointed that we've both changed, but that you felt you needed to be with someone else. I would never have done that to you." It was true. No matter how I'd thought about us as a couple, or even with my fantasies, I never would have had an affair.

"And I am humiliated that your friends knew what you were doing. I can live with the fact that we'll no longer have a life together, but you made a fool out of me in front of other people. And that's betrayal, David. How many others know?"

David didn't answer.

"And how long have you been seeing her?" Now I wanted to scream, but instead I bit the inside of my mouth. "And have there been others? Have you made love to them in this house? *My house?*"

His expression was grim. I had all the answers I needed.

"I want a divorce," I stated, with emptiness in my voice. "I'll make a list of what I want, and you can have the rest. I don't want the house, but I do want enough money to start my life over somewhere else. I'm not staying here around people who know what you've done to me!"

Now I was truly exhausted.

"You're the attorney," I continued. "Take care of it. I'll let you know the name of an attorney in the mountains, and you can communicate with him."

"Are you sure this is what you want to do, Annie?" David didn't plead with me, but instead seemed resolved.

"How could it end any differently? Yes. I've given it a lot of thought. I'll start packing some things now, and I'll make my list. If you want to be here when I pack the rest of what I want, I'll make arrangements with you for that."

It caught me off guard when David said, "I am truly sorry, Annie. I should have come to you and I didn't. We might have been able to fix this. But I see I've let my pride get in the way again..."

We looked at each other for a long moment. I thought of the first time we'd met; how he thought I was exotic...how I'd loved him, but now wondered if I was ever in love. I turned and then left the room. But before I did, I said, "I'd truly prefer it if you weren't here right now. I'll go back up this afternoon."

I would never let my own anger and hurt show in David's presence. As I made my way to our bedroom, I heard David leave. He'd put everything back into his dresser and his clothes were hanging in the closet again. It was like I'd never been there. Everything but my life had been put back where it belonged.

I knew there'd never be enough room in the cabin for all my clothing, so I found some tubs with lids in the garage, and took what I could; I packed my computer and office supplies, my current customer files, my printer and notebooks. Next I packed underwear, socks and shoes that would work in the mountains, and the rest of my makeup, toiletries and my wash cloths. I took mostly jeans and casual tops out of the closet, and a few work outfits in case I had to come back down; I didn't want to come back to the house until I was ready to pack everything else up.

Since I didn't have my own place, I'd either have to store everything in Long Beach, or rent storage in the mountains.

Thinking about starting the list of what I'd want, I walked into every room and put my interior designer hat on. I found some post-it notes and put some on some things I really treasured. I felt empty and mixed. I thought back to the day I met David, and how I knew I would marry him; his maturity had given me the opportunity to decide what to do with my life, and I'd be forever grateful for that. He'd also shown me another side of life, one of having almost everything I wanted.

But what I realized I'd really wanted was love.

Suddenly I was overwhelmed just thinking about what I would tell people. My parents, my clients, and my friends.

Right now, I didn't want to deal with any more issues.

I quickly jotted a note.

"We'll have to sit down and work this out. I'll come back down next weekend, unless you're planning on going away with your girlfriend..." I crumpled the note and started again.

"We have to sit down and work this out. I'll come back down next weekend. Let me know when you'll be home.

I took the crumpled up note and left. I'd decided there was no reason for me to stay in the house.

CHAPTER EIGHTEEN

By the time I got back up the mountain, it was dusk. I'd never driven the winding mountain roads coming up at night, so I was glad there weren't a lot of oncoming lights from cars speeding down the hill. I hadn't thought about it until I got near the cabins that I was famished. I avoided the Cowboy Bar and instead stopped at the Sports Grill. I was hoping I wouldn't recognize anyone while I ate.

After dinner, I checked in with Sam, who was surprised to see me back so soon. I wanted to let him know I was back and to see if he'd looked in on Jezebel, which of course I knew he would have. I was exhausted and decided to wait until morning to bring all my things in. I'd talk with Sam in the morning to see if I could get a larger cabin until I knew what I was going to do.

Jezebel and her kittens were sleeping soundly in the closet, so I started a fire in the fireplace, and with a full glass of wine, spent the evening trying to unscramble all the thoughts running through my mind.

Thankfully, Noah wasn't around that next morning when I grabbed a bite to eat, so I didn't have to face him yet. But my stomach lurched every time someone came in to the diner, and I finally admitted I was secretly disappointed I wasn't able to share my trip with him. Once I was resettled, I'd call him.

The door to the office was unlocked when I returned, and Sam was sitting behind the counter petting Jezebel.

"She needed a break," he said, chuckling.

"I see that." I said, and leaned on the counter. "I have two things to talk to you about. First is, I need a larger cabin, after all. I've decided to stay awhile if that's ok with you." Sam looked at me. "And second, I've decided I'm going to move up here."

Sam pursed his lips and slowly nodded.

"So, I'd like the largest you have."

"Okay. Can do."

Then a totally random thought entered my mind—what if the cabins were for sale? I'd love to get my hands on a restoration project like this. I had nothing keeping me down the hill, so why not? David and I had enough equity in our home to split it so I could figure out a way to make it happen.

"Sam, I have a crazy idea," I blurted. "Would you be interested in selling the cabins?"

"*What?*"

"Would you sell me the cabins? You could stay here, but I'd love a project, and I think these would be perfect for me."

"Whoa, there. Aren't you a married lady?" Sam asked, puzzlement showing on his face.

"That has nothing to do with it, for now. We'd need to work out the details, but I'd love you to think about it." I said, feeling a lot brighter than I had earlier.

Spontaneous and impulsive were two words that could describe me, and those personality traits had, mostly, helped me grow and mature. They'd helped me decide to marry David and become a designer, and they could certainly help me change the life I now had.

"Well," Sam said, "let me think on it for a bit."

"That's good. Think about it. I'll talk to you tomorrow." I looked at him pleadingly. "Just think about it." I headed for the door. "And Sam, thanks."

"For what? I haven't done nothing."

"But you have."

I made it halfway out the door, then turned. "I'll have Jezebel spayed when she's ready. We don't need more kittens!" I said, this time truly leaving.

The new morning air was cool, and a slight breeze had blown some pine needles into the birdbath, but it didn't stop a Steller's jay from coming to drink. I sat in one of my Adirondack chairs, thinking this was going to be a perfect day. I was trying to think of anything to do other than unload the car, and even though I'd never been one to hike, I could still appreciate the outdoors up here. I was certain I could survive and decided to go to out on one of the trails we'd always talked about when we came here years ago.

I headed for Heaps Peak Arboretum not too far away. One of Sam's maps showed me where to go, and the Sequoia Trail was only about a mile long. It surprised me how many people were there; lots of young couples and families with children and dogs.

I spent the time reading the signs posted throughout and was surprised I was interested in learning about the area. 'Acorns from the Black Oak trees are, and were, a staple food for wildlife', and I wasn't aware that Native American Serrano spent summers here, harvesting and eating acorns, preparing them to eat by pounding them into meal.

'Horseshoe Springs was a natural watering hole, which has always been a lifesaver for mule deer and black bears.'

I learned it would take centuries, but the forest that bark beetles had infected would gradually come back to oak and pine trees. And I learned that while we all dread the wildfires that spread quickly through the mountains, they in fact, helped thin out smaller trees and keep the forest healthy.

Now if I only had someone to share this new knowledge with.

The new cabin had a large bedroom, with an old claw-foot tub and a small separate shower. It had the requisite fireplace with an old painting hung over it, a larger living room, the same brown carpet, and some area rugs. It also had a larger kitchenette, which would be great for keeping a little more food on hand. I showered off all the dust from the trails, then for a change, soaked in the tub. I'd found space in the closet for Jezebel and her kittens and moved them into their new home, which seemed to suit them just fine.

I unloaded my car and found I had plenty of room to store what I'd brought. I'd have to look into storage for the rest of the things I wanted to bring up. I went back to the first cabin and stripped the bed, then cleaned the bathroom. Sam had a vacuum in the office and a laundry room, so I started washing the sheets.

"I'll be back for these when they're done," I said as I left the office. "I've cleaned everything else up."

For the rest of the day, I had such mixed feelings it was hard to focus on any one thing. I tried to sort my feelings of anger and resentment at David for being himself on one hand, and then on the other, I tried not to get too excited about the possibility of buying the cabins and opening a bed & breakfast.

Adrenaline had gotten me here, but now I wondered if this was a crazy idea. Where would I end up living? And how could I live by myself? My heart skipped a beat. If I went ahead with this, I was truly going to be alone.

Then I realized there was no reason I *couldn't* do it. The place needed my expertise and love. And what a perfect place to live. Just far enough away from the rat race down below, but only forty-five minutes away from major shopping. If my existing design clients needed me, I could work on projects down the hill, too. It was funny how I'd so quickly picked up the terminology "down the hill". It felt a little pretentious, but comfortable, too. In the end, this was going to be my new home.

Laura and Noah were both at the Cowboy Bar when I came in and joined them at our usual table. I was bursting to tell them everything, but I waited until I had my glass of wine.

"I asked Sam if he'd sell me the cabins," I announced.

Clearly caught off guard, both Laura and Noah just looked at me.

"*What?*" they both said at the same time.

"Yup. I did it. I asked him before I came here if he'd sell me the cabins. They need my love and it would be a lot of fun to restore them, and run the place."

Noah and Laura looked at each other, no doubt thinking I'd lost my mind.

"What did Sam say?" Noah asked.

"He said he'd think about it. I kind of sprung it on him, and I think he thinks I'm a little crazy."

"I do too, Annie," Laura said. "You've obviously made some decisions about what's going on?"

"Yes. In fact, I have. I'm moving up here no matter what."

Noah's eyes widened, but he only looked at me; Laura said, "I don't know what to say. Congratulations?"

"Yeah," Noah finally said.

"I'll have another glass of wine. Anyone else?" I asked, as went to the bar.

"I'm good," Laura said.

"I'll have another beer," Noah said.

I was dying to know what they were saying about me while I was gone, but I felt so liberated I wanted to shout to the world I'd taken the first step. In fact, when I got back to the table, I dragged Noah onto the dance floor. I didn't care that I didn't know the steps, I just let myself move to the music.

I thought about us as we danced and could visualize a future here. I knew I had no way of knowing what was going to happen with my marriage when I drove up here, just that everything was falling apart. Now, I knew all those pieces would fit back together again, even if it happened just a little at a time.

Noah didn't come to my cabin that night, which was fine. I wasn't ready to be with him. I didn't have it all figured out yet, but I felt certain I was on the right path. The hardest part right now was going to be waiting for Sam to make a decision.

The next day, I was so stir-crazy I couldn't think of anything to do with my time. I was dying to go talk to Sam, but I knew I hadn't given him enough time to decide what he wanted to do, so I got in my car and drove to Big Bear. I hadn't been there in years, and I remembered a lot of shops were downtown, so I'd have something to do while I was there.

There's only one way in and out of Big Bear, and the road was packed with people who had the same idea I did. It took me over an hour to get there. As I crossed over the bridge into town, it surprised me how beautiful the lake was. Big Bear is not a private lake, like Arrowhead, so anyone could take their boats out. The water level looked good, which, like in Lake Arrowhead, was always a concern.

Downtown had grown so much since I'd been there, and I finally found a place to park.

"Excuse me. Excuse me," I said, trying to weave through the tourists that packed the sidewalks. I found a place with outside seating and treated myself to a hamburger and fries before I went into the stores. Along the way, I stopped for ice cream and sat on one of the street benches where I could people watch.

I found an antique mall at the end of town and bought some treasures; a couple of old leather books to set on my dresser and a pinecone decorated box that reminded me of the one I'd made when we had our lake house.

There were some open house signs and I couldn't resist stopping and looking at a few houses. One was on the busy road leading uphill from the main boulevard. And one was on the lake. I was taken aback when I saw how far the water had receded down at this end of the lake. There was probably twenty feet of sandy soil before a small amount of actual lake started.

"It gets like this when we don't have a good winter," the realtor said. "But it always comes back."

Wouldn't that be awful if you bought a lake front home and there was no lake?

I eventually headed back to the cabins, where I was dying to take a nap. There was still just as much traffic leaving as there was coming into town, and I inched my way back over the bridge. There definitely was a lot more going on here than in Arrowhead, but with that, came congestion.

When I got back, I left my door slightly open so Jezebel could come and go, but she ended up sleeping with me for about an hour before her kittens cried to be nursed. I would not push Sam for his decision, but the anticipation was killing me.

I didn't have to wait much longer for him. I'd gone outside to read, and after a few minutes, I saw him walking up to the cabins. It was impossible for me to read anything from his expression—his face didn't give me any clues.

"Well now," he said, sitting next to me. I recognized a bit of concern in his voice. "Mind if I ask what you're thinking?"

"It's a long story," I started. "I came up here to think about what I wanted to do...my marriage was at an impasse." I spared him the details and gave him the short version. "My husband and I have decided to get a divorce. And I'll be starting over here. It's peaceful, and I know it won't be perfect, but I feel like it's a positive change for me."

Sam sighed, and then he drew in his lips in thought. "I was kind of hoping something like that wasn't happening, but then it's none of my business. My wife and I never had a lot of problems. We were lucky. Or, I should say, I was lucky." Sam was silent for a moment. "What are you thinking?" he asked again.

"Well, I suppose I could be happy with a cabin of my own, but I'd love to have a project to keep me occupied. I'm not sure how much cash I'll have to start, but we have the money, so financing shouldn't be a problem. I'm an interior designer, and since I won't have clients up here until I can get established, it would be a perfect time for me to tackle this. I'd stay here, work on the cabins, and run the bed-and-breakfast. I know it'd be a lot of work, but I'm willing to take it on and I'd hope you'd stay here and help me run it."

Sam raised his eyebrows and looked at me like I'd gone crazy. I wasn't sure which part he was most surprised about. He rubbed his face with one hand, and then said, "Let me think about it seriously. It just might be good for both of us. However, I haven't had a boss since my wife died."

I felt rejuvenated, like I had a new purpose. I felt everything would work out with purchasing the property. It was funny how when I pictured myself doing something, it generally came true. It was almost impossible to keep from thinking of all the things I'd like to do: redecorating, some landscaping, signage, marketing and advertising. It was just what I needed to make a fresh start.

The next day, I stopped in the office and Sam was sitting in front of a small fire in the fireplace. The room was warm.

"Well, here's what I came up with," Sam started. "I talked with my lawyer, and I can sell the property on a contract, where you make payments to me every month. Since you'll be spending a lot of money doin' what you want to around here, I figure that's down payment or investment enough for me. I don't have kids, so there's no one around to argue with me."

I could hardly contain myself! I should have tried to keep a poker face, but it was impossible. "Oh, my gosh, Sam, I can't believe it! It will not upset you that I want to re-decorate?"

"Not at all. I know you'll do a great job, and it'll do wonders for the place. Plus, we could use some fresh blood up here."

I gave him a big hug. "I can hardly wait to get started."

"I'll have my lawyer draw up the papers tomorrow."

I knew I might be overstepping, but I couldn't help but ask, "Can I have keys to see the other cabins? I'm dying to start making my lists of things to do."

He reached under the counter for the master set. "Here you go, kiddo. I have to warn you that cabin number five is a disaster. It's been a catch all since *we've* been here."

I knew I was going to have to tell my parents about David, and I'd put it off long enough, hoping I wouldn't be so angry about everything. I also knew how they still felt about him, and while they accepted my marriage, they wouldn't be broken-hearted to see it come to an end. But they would worry if I was unhappy.

I set aside thoughts of the cabins and called them. It surprised me how supportive they were until my father said, "I'm amazed you stayed with him as long as you did."

I knew he didn't mean to hurt my feelings, and I felt I was being overly sensitive. When I told them I was up in the mountains, they said they thought I should come and stay with them. I didn't need to go anywhere, and I wasn't in the mood for more conversation, so I cut our call short. I told them I'd let them know what I was doing, and where I was eventually staying.

"You know we're always here for you, honey," my mother said as we all hung up.

"*Well, I'm glad that's done,*" I said aloud. "Tomorrow I'll get my post office box."

To get back on track, I went into full design mode. I brought my notebook, tape measure and pencil and opened the first cabin. But my curiosity got the better of me; and I changed my mind and opened cabin number five instead. When I opened the door, a pungent odor assailed me and I heard a flapping noise from the back of the room. I definitely didn't intend to go inside; what I saw gave me a good idea of what I was in store for. Smelly carpet, stacked furniture and mattresses leaned up against a wall, and full plastic bags stacked five and six feet high. I got a chill and quickly closed the door.

I then went into the other six cabins and took measurements, both for flooring and windows. The vanities and kitchenettes needed updating, and I was hoping Noah could work on those. I made a list of what I'd need; mattresses, bedding, dressers, area rugs and art. I could order all the furniture at one time and place everything as I completed the updates. When I finished looking at all the cabins, I was even more invigorated.

The furniture market was coming up in about three weeks, and I could hardly wait to shop. I'd go prepared with each unit's information. The minute I got back to my cabin, I unpacked my Market Planner book and searched the exhibitors that were going to be there. I made a checklist of which showrooms I'd want to visit. Since there were two buildings, it was impossible to hit every showroom, so planning ahead was critical.

It would be great if I could take someone with me. Shopping as a team was always more fun, and it would give me the opportunity to bounce ideas off a partner in crime.

Who could I invite? Laura? I didn't know if she'd even be interested, plus it might be too expensive for her to fly. Anyone from down the hill? Then I wondered about Noah. I'd have him do some of the work in the cabins so he'd be able to see a complete picture of what I had in mind. Men weren't usually good shoppers though, unless, of course, it was car parts or sports equipment. Maybe I could ask. We could get separate rooms. And if neither were interested, I'd go by myself. I'd done it before.

When I brought the keys back to Sam, I told him I'd heard a flapping noise in number five, and he said, "It's probably bats got in there. I'll have to check it out."

Bats?

I sat outside and started drawing each of the cabins. All the carpeting would have to be replaced, so I'd stop at the flooring and decorating center in town to get some ideas, and possibly get some samples to take with me.

And then I'd have to find out what Sam was doing for marketing. It didn't look like he had a lot of reservations, but that would change once I redid the cabins. I'd work on brochures, business cards and a marketing plan with the local paper. I'd join the Chamber of Commerce and have a ribbon cutting ceremony...

On one hand, it was exhilarating, and on the other, a bit overwhelming. But I knew this was the perfect project to keep my mind busy, doing something constructive.

That night, I had dinner at the Cowboy Bar, and anxiously waited for either Laura or Noah to show up so I could share my great news. About the time I was ready to leave, Noah came in. Although I didn't have any claim on him, I felt he took his time talking to everyone before he came over to see me.

He studied my face, and I took in his neatly trimmed beard, and remembered how soft it felt when he kissed me. My stomach did a little flip, which it was doing a lot of lately.

He brought his beer to the table and sat. Maybe this was going to be a big mistake, but I said it anyway.

"Sam and I have come to an agreement."

Noah's eyes widened slightly.

"We sign the papers tomorrow."

Noah had been leaning back in his chair and choked as he swallowed his drink.

"I didn't think you'd be that shocked." I said.

"Holy cow. You *do* work fast!" Noah coughed again.

"Am I freaking you out? Do you think I've gone crazy?"

The corners of his mouth turned up. "A little. Just surprised at how quickly you move."

"Well, I can't think of a better way to get my life back together than to jump in. It's what I do." I thought for a moment. "Sometimes I *do* move pretty fast."

I then said, "So Noah, I wanted to ask you something...I'm going to San Francisco for the furniture market in a couple of weeks, and I could use some company. I need to buy furnishings for the cabins, and I'd love to have you do some of the restoration work. It'll give you an opportunity to see what goes on behind the scenes, not that you're interested in the details, but you have a good eye for things."

Noah's easy smile told me he was interested.

"I also thought about asking Laura if she wanted to go for a day. I don't know if she can get away."

I sensed a twinge of disappointment.

"Are you thinking of flying?" he asked.

"It'd be the fastest way to get there and back. "

"Would I have to look at girlie things all day?"

"No. I'm sure there are other things you can do while you're there. But I'd love to have you see it all."

He said, "Find out if Laura can go, then let me know what you two decide. A buddy of mine has a small bush plane and he might be headed that direction for hunting season in Idaho, anyway. I can always come out for a day and then we take a commercial flight back together."

I nodded my head in agreement. "That sounds good, too. Let me talk to her."

"Annie, are you sure you're ready to make this change? You haven't been through winter up here, and you've never run a bed-and-breakfast... or as Sam likes to call it, a bed and *no* breakfast." Noah grinned.

"I feel *really* good about this, Noah. I feel like a big void has just been filled. I know it's not going to change everything in my life, but it's a great start. I'm up for the challenge."

"Then I'm behind you too. I'm up for a challenge myself." He raised his beer bottle to my wine glass.

"One thing is for sure, Annie, you're going to need to get a four-wheel drive if you live up here. You'll need to be able to drive when it snows."

"Oh." I hadn't thought about that. I pursed my lips in thought. "I'm sure I could do it, but I've never bought a car on my own. Since you know what I need, would you go down with me to find something?"

"Sure," Noah answered wryly. "I love dealing with car salesmen."

We left the bar early and walked out into the parking lot. Noah walked me to my car, and before I got in, he took me in his arms and hugged me firmly. He pulled away from me, leaving just enough space to kiss me gently on the forehead.

"You're something else, Annie."

Apparently, I hadn't scared him away yet. I liked Noah.

CHAPTER NINETEEN

That next weekend, I was ready to meet with David. We had a lot of details to discuss; how we would separate everything, how I would get the money I needed to get the B&B up and running, and what the time frame was for processing the divorce. David had asked his friend John to handle everything for us, and I was fine with that. Even though he'd been David's friend before we met, I liked and trusted him.

The closer I got to our house, the tighter my stomach knotted. When I pulled up in front of the house, I braced myself for the worst; was I suddenly going to be broken-hearted? I was leaving the home I'd loved. I momentarily felt beaten, but then I remembered leaving was *my* choice, *my* decision. And like the roller coaster I'd been on lately, I unexpectedly felt bitterness. Almost like the betrayal came from the house itself. I knew I'd never be able to live there again.

When I opened the door and stepped in, I didn't know what I expected. I had butterflies in my stomach as I walked through the rooms; nothing had changed, but the rooms now seemed empty. I felt a little detached, knowing David would keep most of the furnishings; I'd wondered if he would have started sorting things without me, but he hadn't.

I'd brought more boxes to pack my remaining personal items, and I'd take back whatever I could and store it in the mountains. Noah had offered to bring his truck down, but we decided to wait another week or so to make sure I worked everything out with David.

I was emptying drawers and packing when David came in. He stood in the doorway to our bedroom and only said, "Hi there."

"HI there," I said, glancing in his direction.

There was a hint of arrogance and self-confidence about him.

There were those butterflies again. Looking at him now, I could honestly say I wasn't interested in trying to make things work with him, but I was sorry to see that our relationship had come to this. I still found David attractive, and my mind raced with images of us in various stages of matrimonial intimacies. I felt myself flush. I didn't hate him..... I just wasn't in love with him anymore.

"I have a tentative agreement written up if you want to check it out," David said. His voice sounded tired, and I sensed a hint of uncertainty. He held up a manila folder.

"Sure," I said, putting the last of a drawer into a box.

He watched me silently as I tucked the box tops closed.

"If you agree to this, we can both sign it and I can give it to John to formalize. I thought we could go through the house together and each write down what we were interested in keeping. That's the most amicable thing I can think of..." David said, "and I *do* think this can stay amicable?"

"Yes, I do too."

His confidence returned.

I was certain this was the only time in divorce history that both parties wanted to work with each other as cordially as possible. We each took a pad of paper and started in the living room. I looked at everything from a mountain decorating point of view. Anything else belonged in the house. I spoke first and said, "The only thing I really want in here is the mirror over the fireplace. It can work wherever I end up." And when David nodded, I wrote it down.

"Value? Two hundred dollars?"

"Sure," he said.

Next, we went to the dining room. "I'd like the sideboard, the painting, the lamps, the obelisks and the samovar. I like it just the way it is now," I said. "Value, a thousand?"

And so it went throughout the house. I agreed to leave him the essentials, including the pots and pans. I'd buy new when I finally had a home.

"I'll make a suggestion as to a value on all the contents," David said diplomatically and business like.

"If you trust me, I'll pay my own credit cards so we don't have to close everything down and start over," I said.

I startled him when I said that. "Of course I trust you, Annie. You've never made me feel otherwise."

I realized I'd offended him, but his last divorce hadn't gone so well, and he had never lost that wariness.

"I'm sorry, David. It's just you know how people can unnecessarily hurt someone they used to love..." The words stung him and hung in the air.

"I'll transfer all my obligations into my name, and you can do the same," David said with a twinge of defiance.

"Do we need to sell the house to split our assets?" I asked. I hadn't wanted him to have to sell if he truly wanted to keep it.

Now back to more businesslike. "We can split our cash, which will give you enough money to start over, since that's what you originally said you wanted. I haven't decided if I want the house now. I'd like a little time to think about it. We can state in our paperwork what we're agreed to so far."

I could tell his emotions, like mine, were subject to change as well. I went to him and put my hand on his arm. He'd cheated on me! And now I felt bad for him! His recent indifference to me had gone, and in its place was resignation.

"That's fine, David."

I smiled slightly, to show him I understood what he was going through, and then I went back into the bedroom to finish packing my things.

I heard David leave through the front door, and then I sat for a moment on our bed. Was he sorry he'd hurt and humiliated me? I'd never seen him so downtrodden and bruised. It didn't change how I felt about everything, but we were at an unfamiliar point in our relationship.

Once I loaded everything into my car, I started my trip back up. Instead of the Cowboy Bar, I stopped at the Ginny's to have something to eat before returning to my cabin. I was exhausted and wanted a glass of wine, a soak in the tub, and to sit in front of the fireplace.

Tomorrow I'd rent a storage space.

CHAPTER TWENTY

Laura met me for dinner that night, and I brought her up to date on my latest meeting with David.

"He was up and down, but I could tell he was truly defeated," I said.

"But he brought it on himself, don't forget."

"I know. I don't think he really thought about the consequences of getting caught. I know I'm doing the right thing, but when I'm not angry with him, I feel sorry for him. It's crazy. I sometimes have a complex way of looking at things. I can be unhappy about some aspect, yet sympathetic about something else."

"Well, at least you know where you stand now. And you can move on. It's for the best. I understand. You keep telling yourself that, but it still hurts."

I asked her about joining me in San Francisco, knowing we'd have a great time, but it just wasn't in her budget, even if I paid for the hotel.

"Let's plan something afterwards," she suggested. "I want to see everything you pick out. But what I really want to know, is how you're going to work this out with Noah joining you?"

"Don't be silly. We're just friends. He can sleep on the sofa," I said, raising my eyebrows a couple of times. "He *is* awfully cute though."

"Annie, *he likes* you."

"I like him too, but it's way too soon for anything serious."

"I just want you to be careful." In the short time we'd known each other, we'd developed a comfortable friendship.

"I will."

A few weeks later, I flew out of Ontario International Airport. I went directly to the furniture market and checked my bags there; I'd check into the hotel later. I had each cabin's details in separate folders and the list of vendors I wanted to visit, so I was ready to go. Each cabin had knotty pine walls, so the coloring was the same. This would make getting started easier than having to create complete color schemes.

The first showroom on the list was for bedding. I was in my element, laying out the bedding samples and options; I needed seven unique patterns or combinations, as I wanted each cabin to have its own look. Once I had that decided, I got samples so I could look for area rugs, which was going to be a lot harder. There were hundreds of rugs to look through, and yet it was so inspiring.

By the end of the day I had bedding samples and tear sheets of rugs I liked, and I was worn out. Shopping was great fun, but it took a lot of concentration, and it killed my feet.

"I need Advil and dinner," I said to one of my sales reps.

"A group of us are going over to Scoma's later if you want to join us," he said.

David and I had eaten there once when he'd come up with me. It was the first time I'd thought of him in over a week, and I could honestly say thinking about him now didn't dampen my mood or curb my appetite.

"Sounds great," I said.

I picked up my luggage and joined the rest of our group in the line for a taxi.

Scoma's was a well know seafood restaurant literally off the beaten path; it was between two buildings on the wharf and down an alley. I wasn't much of a fish eater, so I had their wonderful garlic bread and a San Francisco original shrimp Louie salad. I had two glasses of wine, and by the time we called a cab, I was ready to collapse.

Before leaving for breakfast the next morning, I sorted my samples and eliminated some I didn't need, and then I took the shuttle to the furniture market. I needed to look for furniture today. I'd had a great idea over breakfast; instead of buying mattresses at market and having them shipped, I'd talk to the local furniture store about providing everything I needed, hoping, of course, for a discount. They could deliver and help me set up, and I'd suggest they put their cards or a note in the room in case guests were interested in purchasing for their homes. I'd seen that done in a couple of boutique hotels we'd stayed in.

Everything was coming together for the cabins. I found a couple of sources for lodge furniture and would decide over lunch at the mart. At Ray's showroom, I found sofas and chairs and made tentative fabric choices, collecting even more samples to co-ordinate. I hadn't taken my wedding rings off and it was obvious his eyes went to them.

"Still married, eh?"

"For a while at least," I said.

Noah was flying in and would be in town around two-thirty. I was eager to see him and to show him everything I'd selected. Since we were spending the night, I'd have him come with me in the morning to decide on artwork. Then we could fly back and head up the mountain.

I called the hotel at three-thirty and Noah had just gotten into the room. It was too late in the day for him to meet me, so I mentioned the Wells Fargo Museum near the hotel and thought he'd enjoy visiting it. I told him to take his time, and as soon as I got back, we could have a big steak dinner at Alfred's Steakhouse, another of my favorite restaurants.

I felt myself getting a little intrigued by our time together tonight. I could not stop thinking about what it would be like to be with someone like Noah, although I kept bringing myself back to the reality of our situation; now that I had my head screwed on right, we were just friends, and I didn't need any new relationship complications.

Plus, he'd promised to sleep on the pull-out sofa, so that settled that. He was there for company and for help in deciding on the finishing touches for the cabins.

But once I got back to the room and saw him lying on the bed in our room with his shirt open, I couldn't help but smile. There went that old stomach flip as I realized it would not be as easy as I thought to be in the same room and not think about all the possibilities!

Noah immediately jumped up and fumbled with his shirt, but not before I took in his muscular upper body with a hairline that traveled from his belly button to below where his jeans started.

My breath caught. When I looked up, Noah was eying me mischievously and I could feel myself blush.

Noah finished buttoning his shirt and said, "Hungry?"

"Yes," I said, setting my samples and brochures down. "I have a great place for dinner, so I hope you don't mind that I made reservations. They said we didn't need them because it was early, but I wanted to make sure we could sit in a booth. It's one of the oldest restaurants in town."

"Sounds great. I'm starving,"

"I'll be just a second," I said, going into the bathroom. I closed the door and then looked at myself in the mirror. I was still a little flush. "What's wrong with you?" I said to myself harshly.

"What?"

"Nothing!" I called out. I finished with a touch up of powder and lipstick. "Ready to go," I said as I led the way out of our room.

Alfred's Steakhouse opened in the late twenties. With its dark red walls, ambient lighting, red leather tufted booths lined the walls, and large scale patterned wool carpeting, it was the epitome of old, fine dining. Chairs with red velvet upholstery flanked the dining tables in the center of the room.

Dinner was fabulous with New York steaks charred to perfection, Caesar Salad tossed table side, baked potatoes with butter and sour cream, lots of Cabernet wine, and cheesecake for dessert. We were both stuffed.

I shared my excitement about all that I'd accomplished the last two days, and Noah seemed genuinely interested. Tomorrow we would work on artwork, then leave for home.

I lifted my wineglass, and Noah did the same. "To a very exciting project and to someone whose friendship I really appreciate."

And Noah added, "To more than friendship, I hope," he said with a glint of hopefulness in his eyes.

I felt myself blush again, but gazed back into his eyes. The light in the restaurant didn't dim how beautiful they were, and I saw both eagerness and gentleness in them.

Noah set his wineglass down and reached to run his finger down my cheek, ending at my lips. His touch was like magic. I wanted to close my eyes and kiss him right now. I knew he cared about me, and that in itself was arousing; no one had touched me like that in a long time, and I'd forgotten how electric it felt. Then playfulness got the better of me, and with his finger still on my bottom lip, I made a growling sound and opened my mouth like I was going to bite him.

We both jumped in surprise and then laughed.

It was the perfect ending to a perfect dinner.

The question now was, had it really been a good idea for me to ask him to stay in the hotel with me? I could sense he was thinking the same thing, too. If my life was settled, it could be different.

Once we were back in the hotel room, I started taking my shoes off and groaned.

"I'll shower tonight since I'm assuming it'll take me longer to get ready than you in the morning." I then grabbed some things and closed the door to the bathroom.

I came out with my hair in a towel and I had a one piece nightgown on under a matching robe. I saw that Noah had pulled pillows off the sofa and was getting his bed ready.

I climbed into my bed and said, "Are you up for a movie? I don't think I can sleep yet."

"Sure," Noah said. He'd changed into his sweatpants and a t-shirt.

"If you promise to behave, you can sit here with me." I patted the spot next to me on the bed and looked for a movie.

About ten minutes into the movie, I fell asleep. I didn't realize he'd dozed off until I stirred about an hour later. Noah had moved me and put his arm around me so I could comfortably lean on him. "So much for the movie," I said, sitting up.

"Stay where you are," Noah whispered.

He raised my chin to meet him and he kissed me; first nibbling on my lower lip, then my top lip, then brushing my lips with his, teasing us both. Then he covered my lips with his; I'd never felt that sensation before, of being so enveloped in a kiss.

Slowly and seductively, he continued to kiss me and I felt a surge of excitement inside me. He very gently discovered my body and knew instinctively where to find that part of me that ached for him. He opened his eyes to look at me, and I couldn't believe how he turned me on.

I knew this wasn't a good idea, but I also knew this was what I wanted. I wanted him completely, and he knew it.

"Noah, I don't have protection," I whispered.

"There's more than one way to skin a cat," he said.

I could feel his heart pound against me as he slowly lay down on top of me. It was the first time I'd ever made love with my clothes on, and I couldn't believe how content he'd made me feel. He leaned on his elbows and kissed me, his breath slowing.

"You're beautiful, Annie," he said, and then touched a tear that had filled my eyes. "Are you crying?" he asked gently.

"No," I said as he rolled over. I whispered, "Will you hold me tonight? Even though we promised Laura you'd sleep on the sofa?"

And I smiled, knowing we'd have a hard time convincing Laura we hadn't been together.

We both took quick showers, and by the time I was back in bed, Noah was sleeping soundly. "Just like a man," I said to myself. It took me awhile to go to sleep, my mind continually playing back how amazed I was at the passion Noah had drawn from me.

That next morning, in the hotel restaurant, I couldn't help looking at him, remembering how he touched me the night before, and I felt my face growing warm. I didn't remember ever feeling that electricity, much less being touched that way. Seeing me watching him, Noah reached across the table and took my hand. He played with my fingers while he looked at the menu. His hair was still wet from another shower, and he smelled so fresh.

I called valet service to help us bring everything down; I'd take our luggage and my sample bags to the mart and check them in again until we were ready to leave.

There were two showrooms I wanted to go to and between them, I made a list of everything I'd need. Noah was a great help, expressing his opinions, especially if he really didn't like something. Several times, we touched hands and caught each other's eyes.

He watched me as I looked at everything, and I could tell it mesmerized him as I flipped through the wings of framed prints, making notes of images I wanted copies of. I felt comfortable talking with the sales representatives, not hesitant to let them know if something didn't fit with my overall plan. I felt on top of the world.

By around one, we were ready to leave for the airport.

It was hard not to look at his profile as we drove back up the hill. I loved watching him, and when he suspected I was looking at him, he'd look my way and give me a crooked smile, sometimes touching my thigh and leaving his hand there. Sometimes I'd touch *his* thigh, wanting to be evil and moving my fingers up and down his leg, watching as he got aroused.

"Hey, do you want us to get into an accident?" he'd say, but he'd hold my hand there for a moment longer. We could have pulled over five times to make love on that trip home.

Being with Noah made the time fly as we finished the drive back and I wanted this time together to last as long as it could.

"Tell me what you'd like me to know about yourself," I said.

"Well, I came to the mountains with my parents when I was three, and graduated from the local high school. Instead of college, I opted for learning to become a carpenter and eventually took over the construction company when my boss retired."

"Tell me about your parents."

He sighed and rubbed his beard. "My mother was a nurse at the mountain hospital, and my father was a Sheriff. When I was twenty, they were coming back up the mountain, and a driver coming down was going too fast. He lost control of his car, and they all died in a head-on collision."

His face had gone red.

"I used to wish the guy hadn't died, so I could have killed him myself."

I didn't say anything for a few minutes.

"I'm glad you didn't." I touched his arm with my hand. "And that's when you met Sam?"

"I knew Sam before, when I'd do odd jobs for him around the cabins, and he kind of took me in."

Once we got back up the hill, we had an early dinner and then headed over to my cabin.

"I had a great time," he said, leaning in and kissing my cheek.

"I'll bet you did," I laughed. Then I grew serious. "So did I. I'd love to just go to bed, but I'd like to lay everything out so I can get it ordered Monday."

"If I promise to behave," he said, raising an eyebrow, "I'd love to see how you decide what goes with what."

I wanted to get into my PJs but I also wanted his company, so I said, "If you really want to, and promise to stay on your side of the bed this time, then fine. I could use some final thoughts on what I've chosen."

Noah set my bags of samples next to the sofa. I fed the cats, then I changed into a sweatshirt and flannel sleep pants. I emptied all my samples onto the bed. I laid everything out by cabin; first bedding, then rugs, then artwork. Noah sat relaxed in one of the chairs and watched as I sorted, then mixed my choices again until I had everything coordinated the way I liked it. I had a bad habit of chewing the inside of my cheek when I worked like this, and my jaw was getting tired.

"What do you think?" I asked, chewing my cheek again.

"You're amazing," he said. "Would you help me with some of my projects too?"

"Really?" I turned to face him. "You seem to do a pretty good job by yourself."

"Yes, but you'd add the finishing touches. When you finish the B&B, we can talk about it."

"That'd be great, Noah. I need to start developing my client base here. I'll focus on it later." I turned back around and picked up one of my finished layouts, taking it to the small table.

"What do you know about bats?" I asked out of the blue.

"Bats?"

"Yes, bats." I spread more samples out. "I think when I went into cabin five, there were bats. At least that's what Sam thought."

"Well," Noah started, "I know they're supposed to be removed, not killed."

I looked at him, wondering if that was true.

"Why is that?"

"They eat mosquitoes and that reminds me, I heard a terrible story about a woman waking up to something warm on her face in the middle of the night, and it was a bat lying there..."

"Oh my God, Noah! That's awful!" I cried out, covering my face. I shuddered. *"Why did you tell me that? I'll never be able to sleep!"*

Noah's face instantly colored. "I'm sorry! I just heard that," he stammered, and I could tell he immediately regretted having said it. "I'm sure it's an old wife's tale." He tried to calm me.

"I don't think I'll ever get that image out of my mind!"

"I'm really sorry. I'm sure it never happened."

"That's really terrible." I grimaced. "Yuck. Anyway, apparently cabin number five has been a store all for forever. Even before Sam and his wife bought the place. I looked inside and it smelled like it hadn't been opened up in years. And there is a ton of stuff in there. Once we get a couple of cabins under our belt, I'd love your help in clearing it out."

"If you're not still mad at me?"

"Sam's going to have someone take care of the bats, so I don't have to worry about that, thank goodness." I couldn't help it, and made a terrible face.

I tried to turn my focus back to what I was working on. I started numbering each sample to match the cabin number, then listed what I wanted to order by vendor. There was a method to my process, and I was totally in my element.

The sun had gone down, and it was dark outside.

"I need to get back to my place so I can get ready for work tomorrow," he said. "I'll leave you to your paperwork."

"Ok," I said, distracted by my work. "Talk with you later."

CHAPTER TWENTY-ONE

I was ready to make another trip down to pick up the rest of my things, so I took Noah up on his offer to use his truck. I'd talked with David and made arrangements for Saturday, and hopefully he wouldn't be home when we got there. I brought moving blankets and more empty boxes, although I wasn't sure how many more we'd need. When we pulled into the driveway, his car was there.

"Crap!"

"It'll be all right." Noah put his hand on my shoulder. "We'll get in and out, unless you two need to talk a little more."

I knew Noah wasn't looking forward to meeting David.

"Promise me you won't let him get under your skin," I said.

He gave me a quick look. "I'll just be a fly on the wall."

I went in first, and David nonchalantly stood at the kitchen island, unwrapping the morning newspaper. He gave me the beginning of a smile, then took one look at Noah and said "Oh."

His mood changed drastically, and I suspected it was because I'd brought Noah. A perceived threat. No, a genuine threat.

"You'll need to change your mailing address," he said dryly. "Here's your mail."

He then gave Noah the once over. "I see you've found yourself a cowboy." He then returned to the paper.

I could feel myself burn with anger. I glanced at Noah, who thankfully remained in the entry, but there was anger in his eyes. I wasn't sure how he was going to react; inwardly I knew he was as furious as I was, and yet he remained calm; his outward expression never changed.

"Well, aren't you in a mood," was all I could think of to say. "*Fuck you*," was what I wanted to say.

I quickly searched my mind for something more vile, or clever, but I was at a loss. Instead, I picked up my mail and then went outside to grab some of the boxes we'd brought.

Noah followed me out.

"I'm so sorry for that. I can't believe he's acting like an asshole."

Noah took me by the arm and said, "He's just lost the best thing that ever happened to him, and he's taking it out on you. Let's get you packed and out of here."

I led Noah to the bedroom where I still had a few things to put in the boxes, and then I showed him what I was keeping throughout the house. We wrapped the larger pieces in the blankets and we packed the bed of the truck so nothing would move as we climbed the curves of the mountain.

When we finished, I went back in and David was now sitting at the island.

"You have got to be kidding, David," I said sarcastically. "I can't believe you're acting like a total asshole. And it's none of your business if I *have a cowboy*, as you say. I'm done, so the ball's in your court," I called over my shoulder as I left the house. I slammed the door, which made me feel just a little better.

I was furious.

"Want to talk about it?" Noah asked tentatively.

"Not really," I said, my face turning hot again. "He can be such a complete and total ass!"

"I agree," Noah said, but when *he* said it, I became almost defensive.

I glared at him, and when he turned to face me, my reaction had surprised him.

"*Whoa*," he said.

That just made me angrier. "Don't whoa me!"

As much as I tried to fight it, tears filled my eyes, and I tried to hide them by turning towards the passenger window. I desperately tried to stifle a big sniff when my nose stuffed up, but between that and tears, I could not maintain my resolve.

"There are napkins in the glove compartment."

"Thanks," I said, humiliated.

"Why were you so nice to him?" Noah started. "He cheated on you and now he's jealous because he thinks you have someone in your life; someone who can make you happy. And you deserve to be happy."

I looked at him and started to cry again.

It was almost an hour before I spoke. I was so angry with David, almost more so than when I found out he'd been cheating on me, and I wasn't sure how that could be. I'd felt compassion for him when he seemed so resolved the last time I'd seen him. Now, he had humiliated me in front of someone else, and I hated him for it.

I closed my eyes and leaned my head against the car window. I was drained.

The storage yard was behind the one gas station on Highway 18, and when Noah pulled into the yard, I looked at him and felt terrible. "I'm so sorry, Noah."

"We're good," was all he said. It wasn't unkind, but it was distant.

We unloaded the truck in silence.

"I'm hungry," I finally said. "Can we eat before you drop me off?"

"Sure."

No matter how I felt, I never lost my appetite. I could tell the same wasn't true for Noah, for once our meal came, he only picked at his food.

"Sorry," I said again.

Noah just looked at me. I knew I'd disappointed him, but he didn't say a word throughout our meal.

"You okay?" he asked when he dropped me off.

"Yeah."

"Then I'll head for home."

While the sound of the truck on the gravel driveway made me feel like I was home, the lonely silence in the air chilled me.

A week later, I was able to make a withdrawal from my new checking account to give Sam a down payment on the purchase of the cabins. David had only deposited about a quarter of what we'd talked about, and he'd said he'd have the rest in a week or so. I knew that sometimes sorting through finances could get complicated, so I didn't give it much thought. The money would be here in time for me to add to what I'd already given Sam, and I'd also have money to give deposits for the work that needed to be done in the cabins. I had a little time before I had to pay for what I'd ordered.

Escrow would close in another three weeks, but Sam said I could start working on the cabins now. I'd rented an additional storage space so I could accept deliveries when the area rugs, bedding, artwork, and furniture started coming in. I thought a systematic approach to the remodeling would work best, so I started with cabin number one.

The first time I visited the flooring store, I hit it off with the owner and one of the store designers. I told her I'd like to get my design business established up here, and if anyone came in asking about design services, I'd love to meet them.

So when I went back in to place my final order for carpeting and blinds, I was excited to learn there was a potential design client who needed help with his mountain home restoration. The agreement was, I'd make all the flooring and window coverings selections I could from the store, and they would arrange for delivery and installation with the client directly.

I just might have my first client!

When I got back to my cabin, I filed all the cabin flooring and blinds orders, then I was curious who could make enough money to buy a large second home up here on the lake and then afford to furnish it.

When I called Mr. Underwood, he was friendly, but he sounded very official. From the sound of his voice, I placed him at least in his forties, but it was difficult to tell. I'd discovered long ago that names and voices rarely matched the person I imagined in my mind. I explained my fees, and we made an appointment to meet at his home the end of the week.

Could more of the pieces be falling into place?

That Friday I rang at the gate, and I was buzzed in. My instructions were to make the first right, then left, and I wouldn't miss the home.

"Mr. Underwood," I said as I held out my hand. He was older than I'd thought, in his early fifties, and just as distinguished as his name. He reminded me of Robert Redford; thick reddish hair with a touch of gray at the temples, a neatly trimmed mustache and goatee, piercing blue-gray eyes and very fit. The way he dressed reminded me of Ralph Lauren, with a large scale plaid shirt in green tones, and a gray sweater with both sleeves rolled up. He wore well fitting expensive jeans, with what I thought were leather ankle boots. He was quite handsome and distinguished, and I was intrigued! He matched his name! And I was glad I'd dressed appropriately; I wore a taupe top, black pants and a black sweater.

"Please, call me Grayson." He said, taking my hand. For a moment, the way he held it, I thought he was going to kiss it. I had to admit, I was a little disappointed he didn't.

"And, please call me Annie," I said.

"Come in. Come in." Grayson lead me through the doorway into a large entry where I could see that tall windows lined the entire back of the living room, revealing a spectacular view of the lake. Grayson Underwood's home was stunning. Water surrounded it on three sides. It was much grander than *our* lake house; over ten thousand square feet, nine bedrooms, ten bathrooms, a game room, a library, a chef's kitchen with staff bedroom and bath. Plus a double boat dock and elevator!

It would be my largest project to date, but the magnitude didn't frighten me. My first impression was that the job would be more like decorating rather than remodeling, and that was well within my comfort zone. Once I had a chance to talk with Mr. Underwood, he could give me a list of what he'd like to do.

"This is a wonderful home, Grayson." I did my best to sound neutral and unaffected, but I'd never seen anything quite like it. "I'm anxious to see everything and hear what you have in mind."

I set my bag down, but first took out my notebook so I could write down what his thoughts were. We went room by room, and I made copious notes, asking questions, getting answers.

"We don't have to do it all at once. And I don't have a time limit. I would like to start in the master bedroom so that when I come to the mountains, I have one finished room." He put his hand on the small of my back as we came back to the entry.

"Please have a seat." Grayson indicated one of the chairs in the living room, and he sat opposite me.

He swiveled in his chair, all the while studying me. I felt he was estimating my abilities, trying to determine if I could tackle the job. Or possibly more?

"What do you think?" he finally asked. He went to the bar and poured a glass of bourbon. "Care for a drink?"

I never drank hard liquor and didn't drink at all in the middle of the day for fear I'd want a nap an hour later.

"I'm fine, thanks," I said, hoping I wasn't offending him.

"Is this a project you'd like to undertake?" he asked, his compelling blue eyes appraising me.

"Absolutely," I answered, trying not to sound too enthusiastic. "I *do* have a few more questions for you though, if you don't mind."

"Certainly." Grayson came back to the living room and joined me.

"Is there anyone else who would be involved in the decision making?"

Grayson slightly raised an eyebrow. "Meaning, is there a *Mrs.* Underwood?"

It was a question I asked everyone as a way of qualifying them, so it did not take me off guard. "Yes, or a significant other."

"No, just me." He tilted his head and studied me. He had an air of self-confidence I admired.

"How often will you come up to the mountains? And after the master bedroom, which room would you think about working on next?"

"I'm thinking I'd be here once a month, and then I'd like to do the living room, and dining room."

"Do you have any thoughts on a budget?"

"I don't, really. I know I like nice things, and quality is very important to me," he said, looking out to the lake.

"Sounds great to me. I think that's all I need for now," and set my pad and pen down. "I'm very interested and I have some ideas.....would you like to see my portfolio?"

"No, I can tell a lot about people when I meet them; in the way they present themselves."

I was flattered I'd made the cut.

"I'd like to present a design fee, and as I'd said when we first talked, we can do it by the project, or by the hour. Which sounds best to you?"

He'd apparently already thought about it, for he immediately said, "By the hour, I believe. That way you can spend the time you need and not feel rushed."

I hadn't expected instant project approval, and I was ecstatic, but didn't want to show it. "Great," I said. "Do you want me to get back to you?"

"No...I'd like to get started." Grayson stood then, successfully disarming me with his smile. "I'll get you a check, and I'm looking forward to seeing what you put together. I can tell I'll like whatever you do."

"If I can take some basic measurements while I'm here, then I can start with a floor plan and go from there," I said. "I can call you when I have something." When I went to get my tape measure, I knocked my bag off the chair where I'd set and was embarrassed by my clumsiness. I did my best to make a quick comeback by saying, "Let me know when you'll be up here next, and I'll try to work around your schedule."

He said, "Just call me and I'll make sure it works out."

"You're making this very easy," I said, relaxing a little. "I think I'm going to enjoy working with you, Grayson. You'll be very happy." Once I made my way back to the master bedroom suite and started drawing, I felt relief and was back in control of myself until he came into the room.

Aside from the butterflies, I felt comfortable with Grayson as a client, but him standing there and watching my every move made me a little self-conscious again, and I dropped my pad while I was measuring. He came to where I stood, picked it up, then and helped me finish.

As I drove back to my cabin, I was suddenly overwhelmed by what had just happened. Grayson hadn't wanted to see my portfolio, and he assumed he'd be happy with what I could do. *And* it appeared money was no object. What an incredible opportunity ahead of me. I would do my best to make sure he was pleased.

After setting my bag and portfolio on my bed, I called Noah to tell him about my new client, but there was no answer. I could hardly wait to share with someone, so I went down to the office to talk to Sam.

"Hey, there," he said. "Noah left a message for you. Let's see if I remember it correctly. Okay. He got a call this morning about a job he had bid on in Colorado, and they want to start tomorrow before the weather starts turnin'. He said he'd be home in about a week."

"Hmm."

That was really disappointing. Not only did he take the wind out of my sail, but he hadn't even told me about this potential job. I was deeply disappointed, but I had to remind myself, he didn't owe me any explanations about what he had in the works. Even I could realize I was just overreacting. And when I thought about it, it would give me the uninterrupted time I needed to work on Grayson's plan and on the cabins.

"Well, I was hoping to share some great news with him, so I'll tell you instead," I said. And I told him about Grayson and the wonderful opportunity.

"Looks like everything's gonna to work out for you, missy. Good for you," he said.

"Maybe so. In the meantime, I'm hungry. I've *been* hungry since I got up here."

After grabbing a bite at Ginny's, I found a thrift store. I definitely needed a worktable, and I found just what I needed. I took the legs off and put it all in the car, and re-assembled it when I got back. I'd start working on the floor plans this afternoon.

Also tomorrow, a crew was coming in to take out all the furniture and carpet from the first cabin. Then they could start cleaning and oiling the cabin walls. Once the new flooring was in, I needed Noah to build some cabinets and then bedding and furniture would arrive. It was the first of August, so if Noah returned as planned, I was totally optimistic I'd be able to get them all done by the holidays. That was my plan.

CHAPTER TWENTY TWO
Alyce

With Daddy's military pension, the rental income from the small house and apartment brought in enough money for us to live on. The only time money was tight was if a tenant moved out, but Mama was a pretty good saver and it didn't happen often that we had to scrimp. Usually there were people lined up to rent from us if something came available.

I still hung out with the neighbor boys, but as I started developing, my body started changing and one day, one of them accidentally hit me in the chest with the kickball and I winced in pain. Until then I'd been like them, flat chested and wearing cut-off jeans, but once one of them mentioned 'tits' everything changed. They were no longer at my door seeing if I could come out, and when I tried to join them, they didn't let me in. At first, I thought it was because they were afraid of hurting me, but then I realized it was because now there was no way to hide the fact I had always been a girl in a boy's club.

"Well, those boys don't know what they're gonna' miss, now do they?" my grandpa said when I told him.

"But they're shuttin' me out," I cried.

"You and Daisy have always been able to make friends, and this will be no different. It's just another steppin' stone to growing up and becomin' a young lady."

But I didn't want to grow up, and I had no interest in becoming a lady.

Since I suddenly didn't have many neighbor friends, I decided I needed to at least try to find girls I could hang out with. There was a girl I met in my class, Janice, and we started havin' lunch together in the cafeteria. Sometimes we'd both bring a bag lunch and sit outside under one of the big trees in the grassy area of the school grounds. She had red hair and kids used to tease her, calling her carrot top. She'd just give them the finger.

We started goin' to the movies on the weekends, and sometimes after school we'd go to her house and listen to records and dance. That was my favorite thing to do; we'd dance until we dropped, laughin' and singin' to all the current songs. We'd take turns sleeping over at each other's house, and Mama was pretty cool about lettin' us be when it was Janice's turn to stay at our house.

We took the bus to Compton and shopped at Sears, then had an ice cream at the counter in Woolworth's. We'd window shop for things neither of us could afford, sometimes even goin' so far as to try on clothes we never had money to buy.

Janice's mother smoked and had other women over, and one time we went to her house, Janice took a couple of cigarettes out of her mother's pack of Kent's and we smoked. Or I tried to smoke. Janice knew exactly what to do, but I didn't, so I coughed and then when I finally inhaled, I hated the taste it left in my mouth. I was sure Mama would figure it out when I went home, but she never did. She was still smokin' one or two cigarettes a day herself, and the next time I saw her light one, I told her I thought she should quit.

The next year, when we were in high school, I figured out Janice's mother was a lesbian. Janice took me into the master bedroom and opened dresser drawers to show me things I'd never imagined! I didn't totally understand a relationship between a man and a woman, much less two women. I swore her secret was safe with me, for I had no one else to tell, and I'd never be able to tell Mama.

However, I later wondered if everyone else knew, because like me, Janice didn't have many friends. I didn't care, and Janice didn't seem to care either.

With Daddy gone, there was no more dinner curfew. Mama still made dinner at five o'clock, but it was usually somethin' we could eat any time. So if I wasn't home, she'd just cover my meal in tin foil and leave it on the counter for me to eat when I came home. Because there were no regular dinner meals at Janice's, sometimes after eating something at her house, we'd come back to my house and eat again. Mama still made cookies, and when they were fresh, we'd each take a handful and either go sit outside if it was nice out, or lie on my bed and eat them.

Around this time, Grandpa met a woman he wanted to marry. I thought he was too old to have sex, but when I said something to Mama about it, I could tell she was not at all comfortable talking about it.

"Everythin's not about sex," she said. "And where did you get those ideas?"

"Everybody knows about that stuff," I said indignantly.

So Grandpa married Marie, who became Granny. They sold the property in Paramount and bought twenty acres in Porterville where they could have animals.

First I lost Daddy, and then I lost Grandpa.

Mama had suffered with her depression for a long time after Daddy died, and now with Grandpa gone, it was just the two of us. She did her best to keep me from seeing her at her worst; if she felt especially weepy, as she referred to it, she'd take a nice hot shower, then go sit in her room and pretend to read one of her many books.

Often I'd find Daisy sitting with her, her head in my mama's lap, and she'd look at me as if to say Mama needed her more right now. At first, I was jealous, for Daisy was my dog, but I quickly realized my selfishness in wanting her all to myself. Daisy needed to be with Mama for now. Sometimes Mama would pat the seat cushion next to her on the divan and I'd go sit with her. Me on one side and Daisy on the other.

"You're both my comfort," she said once, and I didn't know what to say back.

When she quietly cried, I really didn't know what to say, so I just put her arm around me and rested my head on her shoulder.

Sometimes I'd watch the old man who lived across the street from us. He was there every day, sittin' in his rocking chair on the front porch. He'd read the paper, then fold it neatly and keep it on his lap. He'd just sit there, rockin' for the rest of the day, and if a bug came by, he'd swat at it with the paper. He'd acknowledge a neighbor if one walked by, but his favorite pastime seemed to be watchin' leaves fall from the big tree in his yard. The minute one would fall onto the lawn, he'd boost himself up out of his chair and go down the three steps to the yard, reach down, and pick that leaf up. He might look at it for a second or two, but then he'd climb those same three steps back up and put that leaf in a basket he kept near his chair. Every once in a while I wanted to go across the street and say "hey", but I didn't have the guts to do it.

It wasn't more than a year later that he died. When I told my grandpa, he said it was from boredom. "Once he retired," he said, "he didn't have nothin' to do."

Once Grandpa and Granny were settled into their new place, Mama sent me to stay with them for a few weeks during the summer. It was then that she got a part-time job at Buffum's department store in downtown Long Beach, where the newspaper ads were always hand drawn. She worked the elevator, and when she was in a good mood, she'd tell me about all the people she saw during the day; men looking for a bathrobe for their wife, or sexy lingerie they claimed was for their wife or women with unruly children, and once she saw who she swore was Audrey Hepburn.

It became our little joke when she'd say with her fingers pinching her nose "third floor, ladies' lingerie." I've used that line for years to break the silence when I've been on a crowded elevator and most people got a kick out of it. If they didn't, I didn't really care. I got a kick out of it.

About a year later, Daddy's sister wrote telling Mama how Grandma thought her younger husband was cheatin' on her, and how much of a scandal it would be if word got out. The letter went on to say that if she stayed with him, everything would probably be left to him when she died. There was no way I could have asked Mama, or she'd known I'd read the letter.

One afternoon, Mama brought a man home and told me she was going to marry him. He was a salesman at Buffum's, someone she got to know while working there. He was nice enough and treated Mama good. I never could get used to having another man living in our house, though.

He worked in the shoe department. His name was Al, and he made my mother laugh.

CHAPTER TWENTY THREE

It was the end of August, and we'd had an unusually hot spell so I'd done most of my work outside in the shade. We'd watered our gardens outside the cabins every day, to make sure the new flowers and plants stood a chance of surviving until fall and winter rains could nourish them.

A week after our initial meeting, I had my first appointment to show Grayson floor plans and what I'd put together.

"Why don't we meet for lunch?" Grayson suggested.

"Sounds good," I said. "Let's meet at Ginny's coffee shop; they have a large table in the back where we can spread everything out while we wait for our food."

I've remembered what he wore that day; he had on a brown checked shirt, jeans, and the same leather ankle boots. Even though it was hot, he draped a brown tweed sport coat over his shoulder. He certainly made a bold fashion statement, and lunch customers turned and watched as he walked through the front door all the way to the back. I felt my face flush.

I had everything laid out for him when he arrived. We ordered lunch, and then I showed him several options. I had photos of furniture pieces and fabric samples. I'd also brought some wood flooring samples to use as an option for the carpeting that was now in the bedroom.

During the presentation, the butterflies were back, but I could tell Grayson liked everything I'd done. And I was thrilled with the direction we were heading.

While we ate, and to spark conversation, I asked him why he decided to buy a home up here.

"First, it's so peaceful here, and it seems it's one of the few places I can truly relax. I put in a lot of hours during the week."

"What exactly *do* you do?"

"A multitude of things," he said. He played with his glass of iced tea. "I own a company that does a lot of energy efficiency management and development of systems. Most of our work is in Southern California, but we are also licensed in three more states. So it keeps us busy."

Grayson studied me quietly, and I wasn't quite sure what he was thinking. He continued, "I'm also into real estate, and have made a lot of money there, too. Mostly with larger properties."

We ate in silence for a moment.

Then Grayson said, "Tell me a little about *you.*" He rubbed a fabric sample between two fingers and then looked at me. "This is nice."

I thought the short version was best, so I said, "Well, I also came up here because of the peace, and have decided to buy and refurbish a series of cabins and run them as a bed-and-breakfast."

"Very admirable," he said, thoughtfully nodding. "And quite an undertaking, I imagine."

"It is, but I'm really excited about it. "

"And are you tackling this on your own?"

I finished the last bite of my sandwich, and then answered, "Yes, that's another part of the challenge. I'm in the process of getting a divorce and my husband is staying down the hill."

Grayson nodded and hadn't taken his eyes off me. I could sense he was about to ask me something else when Noah appeared at our table.

Surprised, I said, "Hey."

"Hey."

"Oh, Grayson...this is my friend, Noah. I didn't realize you were back," I said to Noah, touching his arm. I was so surprised by his bad timing, I felt like giving him a strong pinch.

"Pleased to meet you, Grayson," Noah said comfortably, as he extended his hand.

"As am I," Grayson replied, acknowledging Noah with his hand and a tilt and nod of his head.

I broke the silence. "Grayson is the new client I told you about. We've been going over floor plans and fabrics." I absently picked up a fabric sample, though Noah didn't look down at it. "Noah is a local contractor and has a job he's working on in Colorado..."

"Well...I don't want to interrupt you," he said. "I didn't realize you had an appointment. I saw your car as I was headed to Sam's. I'm literally on a quick turnaround and will be heading back to Colorado tomorrow." He nodded at us. "So I'll leave you two to it."

Grayson extended his hand to Noah. "Again, very pleased to meet you, Noah," he said, graciously.

"You too." Noah turned to leave, and I watched him for a moment.

"Boyfriend?" Grayson asked. He leaned back in his chair and folded his arms across his chest.

I thought I was going to die.

"Noah? He's a friend. He's really been a big help to me since I moved up here. He knows just about everyone, but I guess that happens when you're from a small town." I wiped the corners of my mouth with my napkin, then folded it and put it back on the table. I glanced at Grayson, and that image of Robert Redford popped into my head again. He hadn't taken his eyes off me since Noah left.

"Well," I said, touching the fabric samples again, "was there anything here that spoke to you?"

"Yes, there was, in fact." Grayson pulled aside one grouping and said, "This is it. Let's get it ordered. And I like your idea about using the hardwood flooring in the bedroom. It'll really change up the room." He studied me again and said, "You've done an outstanding job, Annie. I believe we'll really work well together." Grayson touched my arm, then after a moment, withdrew it.

I could feel myself grow warm, and I hoped I wasn't blushing again.

I said, "I'm glad you decided on this; I'll get everything ordered this afternoon. I can't wait to see the room pulled together."

"Likewise."

"Let me get this," I said when the bill came.

"Absolutely not," Grayson said, as he took out his wallet. "A woman never pays," he added. Grayson stood and watched me put all my presentation materials away in my bags. He pushed my chair in after I started walking away and then followed me to my car.

"I'll let you know when we have a schedule," I said. "We can paint first, then flooring. Then you might be without furniture for about four weeks. Oh, I meant to ask as we move ahead, if you had any ideas about what to do with your old furniture; possibly someone you wanted to give it to? Or if you wanted to use it somewhere else? I'm sure I can arrange to have someone pick it all up."

"I'd like to donate it to a family if I could. Can you find out how to handle that for me?"

"I'm sure I can. Let me call around."

"Great, and don't forget to bill me for your time. I really appreciate having you here." Grayson waited for me to get into my car, and then closed my door.

He certainly is a gentleman, I thought.

I'd forgotten to get an iced tea to go, so after Grayson left, I went back in to the restaurant. A few minutes later, I came back out.

"Hey," Noah said, startling me.

"Sorry, I didn't mean to scare you. I stopped at the grocery store across the street and then saw you were still here, so I waited."

My hand was still on my car door, and he reached for me.

"I feel like we've been strangers," he said.

"I have to say I do too, especially with you leaving. But I've also been really busy, so it's worked out okay." I loved the way Noah's beard had grown out since I'd last seen him. His hair was longer, too.

"Looks like you have a great new client. Just what you need to help you get established up here." Noah paused "I hope he stays just a client."

I looked at Noah incredulously. Why would he say something like that?

"I can tell the way he was looking at you when I came in..."

"Noah, you're kidding me, right?"

He hit a sore spot.

"He's a client. A handsome one, but he's not interested in me."

"I'm just saying.... I'm just watching out for you."

"Like I'm not able to take care of myself?" I sounded defensive, even to my own ears.

"I know you can," he said, touching my arm, but for some reason, I quickly pulled it from his grasp.

"Annie," he started, but I didn't let him finish.

"I need to get back and put this all together so I can get it ordered," I said and got into the car.

"I really came over to tell you I'll be at the Cowboy bar tonight. I'll buy dinner."

"I'll think about it," I said, closing my car door. I pulled out, leaving Noah standing there.

It only took me a few minutes to get back to my cabin, but I was annoyed all the way. How could Noah even think Grayson was interested in me, and I *certainly* wasn't interested in having a relationship with *him*? He was too old, although very sophisticated. *And obviously wealthy.* But that wasn't what I was looking for in a relationship. I'd be dishonest if I didn't admit I'd fantasized about it for a minute, but it was because he reminded me so much of Robert Redford!

The relationship I had with Grayson was strictly platonic, and that's how it had to stay.

Then I realized Noah was jealous! Of course! He had waited for me purposely so he could warn me that another man might be interested in me. My anger at him subsided as I thought about how we'd been together in San Francisco, and how he'd made me feel...

This was all crazy.

I'd get the orders for Grayson together, then shower and change into my "cowboy" clothes so I could apologize to Noah for blowing everything out of proportion. I wasn't angry with him any longer and in fact understood he thought he needed to watch out for me. I'd let him know he could come out of the doghouse!

It was nine when I saw Noah's truck in the packed parking lot. I fluffed my hair and freshened my lipstick, then headed into the bar. It was the busiest I'd seen it since I'd been there, and the music was loud and sounded great. I had a hard time finding Noah for a moment, but then saw his back. He was standing at the bar, drinking his beer.

"Hey there," I said as I approached him.

"Hey, back," he said, turning to face me.

I could tell he wasn't sure if I was going to lash out at him again, for his smile was tentative.

"Are we good?" he asked.

"Yes, we're good. I'm such an idiot. I wanted to apologize for overreacting. I just think you caught me off guard."

"Let's drop it, okay?"

"Sounds good to me."

"Wine?"

"I was thinking we could just go back to my cabin and sit by the fire. I have some beer and wine at home."

"I'm in," he said. His infectious smile got me every time.

I kissed him lightly and said, "See you in a few?"

I got back before he did and opened a beer and poured myself a glass of wine. When I saw him standing there, leaning against the door frame, my heart lurched, and I had to fight the overwhelming feeling of needing him.

"I'm sorry for the way I acted today," he said. "You were with a client and I should have respected that. I was hoping to apologize tonight."

I saw the heart-rending tenderness in his face, but before I could say anything, he pulled me into his arms and kissed me...then he whispered in my ear, "I'm really sorry." His hips pressed firmly into mine, and then his hands sought and covered my breasts for a moment before he started unbuttoning my blouse.

"Annie," he whispered hoarsely, "I need you tonight."

I finished the job of taking my blouse off and then unbuttoned my bra. I slid off my shoes and then my jeans, and stood before him in just my panties. He took me all in with his eyes before he took off his shirt and jeans, then he pulled me down onto the bed. I knew that tonight we would make love, and he would show me what it felt like to be with a man who truly cared about me.

We made love twice before we lay there in each other's arms. And each time, I was too filled with emotion to speak right away. But as I'd done the first time we were together, I felt tears fill my eyes, and Noah gently wiped them away. He knew he'd filled me with desire, and based on what I'd told him about my marriage, he probably knew I'd never felt this way before when I made love with my husband.

I was hoping he could prove to me that he was a different man than what I'd been used to. That old romantic in me thought that by being with the right person, it could make all the difference in the world...

CHAPTER TWENTY FOUR

I felt a sense of contentment after Noah left that morning. My body felt different. I'd responded to him like I'd never done before.

I found it hard to concentrate the entire day.

After my shower, I brought a cup of coffee out into my little garden and Jezebel followed me, nudging me to pet her. Maybe because of last night with Noah, everything felt different. The air was fresher, the trees rustled more in the wind, and the silence totally relaxed me. The endless green was so peaceful, and I tried to imagine how it would look and feel once the snow came.

I realized then I'd never actually seen it snow. When we had the lake house, we purposely didn't make the trip up if it was snowing because we'd never used snow chains and were unfamiliar with driving in bad weather. We'd loved playing in it once a storm had passed, and we all wished it would have snowed at least once while we were snug inside by the fireplace.

I knew I'd continue to have random thoughts about my marriage, but suddenly I went from a heavenly bliss, to feeling my old world crashing down on me. I couldn't help but think back to when I met David...had he ever been a lover? Was he ever sensitive to my needs, and was I the one who changed? I couldn't remember feeling the way Noah made me feel when David and I made love.

David never really touched me, or if he did, it was never deeply; not tender and coaxing. And it rarely brought me to any satisfying end. Of course I'd told him it had. But was that what I'd expected marriage to end up like? Just having sex?

I never would have been able to talk to him about it. How do you tell your husband you're not satisfied, when he is? Then I thought about Noah, how he seemed to know what to do to make me feel the way I do, and it made me wonder if David only thought he was a lover?

I must have pushed David away. I slid into a funk. I was in seventh-heaven, and now my heart felt heavy. I needed to snap out of it. I was blaming myself for the sorry state my marriage was in, when I needed to focus on how liberated I truthfully felt. I needed to take a deep breath and sweep all the 'what ifs' aside so I could think about starting my new life. I had everything going for me now; Noah, the cabins, my design business...

I needed to go back to earlier this morning...to thinking about Noah...and the way he made me feel. The way he touched me, whispered to me, kissed me...there was passion there, like I'd never known.

Even without sex, I knew he cared about me. I loved his handsome and rugged mountain look, and yet he was so kind and thoughtful. An involuntary smile came to my face as I pictured him standing in the doorway to my cabin, and I missed him. Then the realization hit me; I'd never made a doctor's appointment to start birth control! I'd have to do that today.

Noah was leaving for another week, so I filled my time with checking orders, both for my cabins and for Grayson's lake home. I worked on another floor plan for his living room and dining room, and after my doctor's appointment down the hill, I stopped at the design center and found some furniture and fabrics for the next phase. My first cabin restoration was coming along, and when Noah returned, I hoped he'd have time to work on the new vanity and kitchenette I'd designed.

I had another meeting scheduled with Grayson, but this time at the lake house, where I'd show him the floor plan and ideas for the living and dining rooms. We sat at the large kitchen island, which was perfect for laying everything out. Plus, it gave us a wonderful view of the lake.

As before, Grayson liked everything I showed him, and only pulled one piece of furniture he didn't care for from the plan.

Grayson had prepared a light lunch, which was a pleasant surprise.

"So tell me," Grayson said. His eyes were sharp and assessing, while also magnetic. "How's it going with the cabin renovations? And are you happy up here?"

"Well," I started, "the renovations are going well. I'm really in my element. I love the activity, and if nothing is being done, I feel like we're running behind. But we're good. I still have to work on my marketing plan, which I keep postponing. That's not what I enjoy most."

"And how about being happy here? Is it enough for you?"

I thought for only a moment, and then said, "I actually love it up here. It's such a different pace, and while I haven't been through a winter yet, I think I'm going to really enjoy the seasons."

I would have liked to ask him more questions about what he did, but was afraid I wouldn't fully understand. I was curious about the people in his life. He was so proper, and I wondered if he ever let anyone in. All the decisions he'd made were his decorating choices, and he obviously felt comfortable not having someone to run things by. It must be one reason he was so successful. He'd said there was no one, and I wondered if he ever felt it was a high price to pay for having so much. These questions and thoughts were of course all none of my businesses, but I was curious. I liked learning about people.

When we finished lunch, Grayson stood and started clearing our plates. He casually touched my arm and asked, "Would you like to take some leftovers?"

"Oh, no, I'm fine. Thanks, Grayson." I never ate leftovers, so I didn't want to waste the food. I watched him meticulously stack the dishes first on the counter, then rinse them, then put them in the dishwasher. He was very efficient and obviously set in his ways. He really didn't *need* anyone to help him. As if he could tell I was watching him, he turned and asked, "A penny for your thoughts..."

I felt myself flush, but quickly recovered and started packing all my samples, keeping out those we were going to order. I would never share what I was truly thinking, so instead I said, "I was thinking about the pillow choices. Are you ready for me to get started or do you want to wait until you see what your bedroom looks like?"

"I'm good," he said, turning back to the dishes. "Let's get it all ordered."

"Super. I'll let you know when we're ready to install the bedroom then, and thanks for lunch. You sure you don't want me to help finish cleaning up?"

"No, it'll give me something to do."

On my way home, I stopped at the grocery store for more cat food. The kittens would soon be ready to start on soft food, so I picked up something for them, too. When I got back to the cabin, I brought every-thing in, then picked up the kittens and kissed them. I would have loved to keep them all, but that would be impossible. I was going to have to figure out what to do with them.

At the beginning of September, the morning sun was unrelenting. Noah was still out of town, so it was a perfect time to meet with David and to sign the papers he'd had drawn up. I went to his office rather than going to the house; it was more neutral territory, and if truth be told, I really had no desire to see if David had changed anything in the house in my absence.

By the time I got down there, the temperature had climbed, and the heat was like an oven. I checked my lipstick before I got out of the car, then tucked my blouse back into my pants. His glass entry door mirrored me as I watched myself walk up. I felt very self-conscious when I walked into his reception area. Of course, everyone *knew* we were get-ting a divorce. I had never been social with his receptionist, and I felt exposed and uncomfortable. She'd been privy to our personal business, and I hated that.

"Hi, Annie," she said with a knowing smile. "Go ahead in to his office."

When I first saw him, my stomach surged unexpectedly, and the sight of him caught me off guard. It only lasted a minute, but it felt like an eternity. Shadows darkened the skin below his eyes and he looked worn down, however, his demeanor was cool and controlled. Was this harder on him than I'd thought? He'd had the best of both worlds for a long time, and maybe this entire ordeal was a slap in the face. After all, he'd had to tell everyone, including his parents and children, that we were splitting up.

Each time I'd seen him, his frame of mind had been unpredictable, and I found myself reacting empathetically to his moods again.

"Everything going all right for you?" he asked.

I didn't fail to note the sarcasm in his voice. He motioned me to sit at his conference table, distancing himself from me. Was it intentional? I felt as though he was treating me like a client, and I hated it. I was on his turf, and he was the one in control.

"Yes, it is," I finally remarked. I wondered if he thought I hadn't originally heard him, as he was shuffling some papers and I could tell he was off somewhere else. Once I had his attention again, he watched my every movement, and I tried to remain nonchalant.

"Here we go, then," David said, handing me a stack of papers. "We spell everything out, if you want to take some time to review it all. I've blocked out time enough to get this portion completed."

'How accommodating', I thought as I started reading. Everything seemed in order, how we'd written up the preliminary agreement, and how he'd written in my name first. David pushed a pen my way, but I took my own out of my bag and signed two copies everywhere he'd marked with a sticky note. David signed his copy and then gave me a complete set.

"I've also drawn up a Quit Claim to the house if that's still what you agree to," he said, handing me another document.

"Will you let me know when to expect the balance of the cash?" I asked.

"Yes."

"How are your parents? And the children?"

"How do you think they are?"

"I feel like I should have talked to them, to let them know I'll always care about them."

"Don't bother. I told them you left."

This was it.

There was no turning back now. I'd never see Ruth and Ed or the children again. I wondered what they all thought of me. I couldn't handle calling them...I would have to write to them once I figured out what to say.

I'd also never see our house again, and I sadly realized I hadn't missed it while I'd been away.

"Oh, I almost forgot," I said, taking my house key off my key ring and setting it on the table.

Was I mistaken, or did I see just a stab of something in David's eyes? As quickly as it appeared, it was gone. As I watched him gather his papers, I realized there was nothing left for us now. I'd loved him, and I'd wished for the life I had, but it was all gone now.

There was nothing now to keep me from starting a new life, and that felt fresh and exciting. The closer I got to the cabins, the more comfortable I felt about my new life. I knew this was my new home. And I knew I'd made the right decision.

CHAPTER TWENTY FIVE

I was well past due for a trim, so I made an appointment to see Laura the next day. There was also a manicurist in the shop, so splurged and got a mani-pedi too. I hated taking the time to primp, but I had no appointments, so it was a good day to do something for myself for a change. Plus, the salon was air-conditioned, unlike the cabins, and it felt good to be inside.

I brought in some fliers about finding homes for the kittens. As much as I'd fallen in love with them all, there was no way I could keep four cats at the cabins.

"I saw David," I said as Laura draped me.

"And how did *that* go?"

"It was strange. He looked terrible, and I felt his unhappiness."

"Good god, Annie, quit feeling sorry for that jerk. Oops, did I just say that out loud?"

"Yes, you did, and yes, he is one, but I still feel bad when he feels bad. It would be presumptuous of me to think it was because we were ending our marriage; maybe his girlfriend dumped him."

"Whichever it is, he's the loser, and you, my dear friend, have your entire life ahead of you. Speaking of which, how's it goin' with the mountain man?"

"I really like him," I said.

"Are you two an item?"

"I suppose so. He's so easy to be with, and he's been there for me a couple of times when I thought I was falling apart. He helped me move some things from my house and put them into storage. He's been very patient with me, and I can tell he really cares about me, which differs totally from how I used to feel with David."

"Do you think it's a little early for you to get involved with someone?" Laura asked lightly.

"I don't know. It feels right. We'll see how it goes," I said. "Oh, my new client is incredible," I said cheerfully. "I told you he's older; reminds me of Robert Redford with his reddish brown hair. He's great to work with and likes everything I've shown him."

"Good for you, Annie. You're taking off with a jump start." Laura turned me in the chair. "Catching a rich one could make a nice life."

"I've already gone the older man route and I want someone who cares more for me than they do about money."

Laura's next client came in and she called out, "I'll be ready in a couple minutes."

She combed my hair one more time and untied my cape. I'd let it grow long again after Loni's wedding, and Laura had suggested we cut it to shoulder length.

"I like it," I said, turning my head from side to side. "I like the fresh look."

I had to wait a few minutes for the nail gal and I watched Laura sweep the floor and wipe down the chair. Her next client sat, and after Laura turned her to face the mirror, she asked, "What would you like today?"

The woman fluffed her short hair, and then said, "Just a trim is good."

Other than my school friend Sarah, Laura was the only real friend I had. We'd become close in a short time, and I always felt comfortable sharing my thoughts with her. Over the years, I hadn't had friends other than wives of David's friends. And with them, I'd always had my guard up, afraid I'd say something that could get back to David. Maybe something too critical, or too private.

When Laura looked over to see how I was doing, I just smiled. I had so much going on; my cabin restorations, Grayson's home, Noah...I had a full plate, and I loved every minute of it.

The best news was that Noah would be home tomorrow, and I could hardly wait to see him.

Noah called before he headed up the hill to make sure I'd be there, and the minute his truck hit the gravel parking area, I was waiting for him. I opened my door and I could see his eyes take me in. He looked down at the portion of my breasts my open robe exposed. I could tell from the look on his face I'd accomplished what I'd intended.

"God, I've missed you," was all he could say as he pulled me towards him, his mouth starving for mine. I knew he'd waited for this moment and he was almost frantic to have me, but knowing him, he wouldn't rush. He'd want to savor every inch of me.

In between making love, we nibbled on cheese and crackers, had wine and beer, and then I made us each a sandwich. Not the most romantic of meals, but neither of us wanted to leave the cabin. We could eat again tomorrow.

"When we walk into Ginny's in the morning, everyone will know about us," Noah said. "Our faces will be glowing. Shall we show the world we're together?"

"I think everyone knows, anyway. It's not like we haven't walked in together before," I said, applying my lipstick. "It's not a secret. I'll take some fliers in about the kittens too. See if I can find some homes for these babies!"

When we walked into the coffee shop, a few heads turned in our direction, and a couple of people said "Good Morning," but then they quickly went back about their breakfasts. Like I'd said, we were old news.

All Molly the server said was, "Well now," then took our order.

Ginny said, "Well, finally."

CHAPTER TWENTY SIX

Alyce

Mama's husband, Al, turned out to be a creep. He showed one side of himself to her and another to me. He always wanted me to sit by him and watch the television when my mother wasn't home, and at first I did, until my instincts told me to stay away from him. He never touched me in ways he shouldn't have, but he would 'accidentally' come upon me while I was dressing, and I was certain he'd opened the door to the bathroom more than once while I was in the shower.

I didn't want to tell Mama, since this was the first time she'd been reasonably happy since Daddy died, and I was afraid she wouldn't believe me. About six months after they were married, I came home from school, and Al was gone. Poof. Like he'd never been there.

Mama never went into details, just said, "Things weren't working out like I thought they would."

The problem was solved, and we never talked about him again.

When I was sixteen, Mama bought me an old Volkswagen Beetle, but said I could only drive it if I got a job and paid for my own insurance. Along with everyone else I knew, I was dying to have a car, and found a job at the coffee shop working dinner during the week and breakfast on the weekends. I was so nervous at first; I was sure I was going to drop something, but the other waitresses were real friendly and taught me how to balance three dishes on my arm at a time. I knew just about everyone who came in to eat, so all the customers were patient with me too, which helped. The owner, Jack, could bark orders at us all, but I soon learned that was just his way. He always made sure I counted my tips out right, and made sure all of us girls got to our cars at night if it was dark out.

I met my future husband Jim there at that diner. He would come in after school with a couple of his buddies and I could tell he was sweet on me. He'd order a soda and leave me a fifty-cent tip.

We started dating, and Mama liked him well enough. Most of the time he'd come to my house, and we'd watch television. If it was a program she liked, Mama would sit and watch it with us, or if she wanted to go read, she'd go to her room and leave us alone. We never petted at my house; only in Jim's car.

It was almost another year later that Rudy started comin' around to see Mama. Rudy was an insurance adjuster. Mama met him when someone hit her car, and he came out and wrote up the claim. He started callin' to see how she was doin', and to see if she'd found someone to fix her car. And then they started going out.

Rudy was ok, and didn't have any 'touchy feely' issues, but he drank. And when he'd pass out on the couch, Mama would cover him up and let him sleep it off. One time, I opened the door on him when he was in the bathroom throwing up and from then on, I couldn't look at him again without picturin' vomit all over the floor.

This time, I didn't want to see her get hurt again, so I told Mama about the bathroom incident.

"I think you ought to get a new boyfriend."

A few days later, when I came home from school, just like Al, all traces of Rudy were gone.

It took almost another year before Sam came into the picture. He was the most normal man I'd seen her with. He was a teller at our bank and said he'd lost his wife a couple of years past. He didn't smoke or drink, and *for a while, everything seemed like it was working out. He never moved in, which was even better.*

But about six months after Mama started seeing him, he, too, disappeared from our lives. Seems his wife had never passed away, but was happily (or now unhappily) livin' in Long Beach, still thinking good old Sam was on a lot of business trips.

From that point on, Mama swore off men.

I still worked at the diner, and Jim still came in. The owner, Jack, told us all once about givin' food away to our friends.

"It's cause for dismissal," he said.

I always made a point of showin' him Jim's ticket, even though he'd said it wasn't me he'd been concerned about.

Jim wanted to get married when I finished high school, but bein' a little wary of men myself, I wanted to get a couple years of city college behind me first, before we settled down and had children. In those days, women didn't always take their education seriously, and most of the girls I knew got married right out of high school and had kids right away. Or some got pregnant while they were still in school, and even got married before they graduated. I also knew I wanted to have a job so we could afford to buy a house one day. So right after I graduated, I got a job at the utility company as an office worker.

The girls at the diner gave me a wedding shower, and since I'd never been to one, I had no idea what to expect. We played silly games, and I never saw so many gifts, even when it was my birthday. We got almost everything I could imagine we'd need to start married life. We were going to live in the apartment above the garages until we could save enough money to buy our own home, and Mama had said we could use the washer and anything else I needed from the house. Jim's parents bought us a full size bed, so for the shower, his mother got us sheets and pillows. Mama took me to a secondhand store, and I found a dresser and two nightstands. We took our old divan, coffee table and end tables from the living room, and Mama went out and bought new for herself.

"*That's the first new furniture I've ever had,*" *she said, happy as could be.* "*It's too bad Daddy couldn't be here to see it.*"

It looked great in the house.

I wanted a church wedding like my folks had, so I'd have wedding pictures to frame. We found a non-denominational church in the neighborhood, and Jim's dad was who walked me down the aisle when we did finally set a date. I found a printer who would print just a few invitations, mostly so I could keep one for my album, and after the wedding, about twenty of us had sandwiches, chips, beer, punch and cake in the church hall. None of our relatives came out from Kansas. We hadn't seen them since Daddy died anyway, and Mama said we didn't need to ask them to go to the expense of comin' out. I didn't tell her, but I sent them an invitation anyway, hopin' they'd at least send us some money.

I wanted to wait to have children until we had a house, but Jim wanted to start a family right away. I felt like a baby machine, because we had both our children, a boy and a girl about eighteen months apart. I had my hands full and was really lucky Mama watched them for me so I could go back to work.

We scrimped and saved and finally had enough money for a down payment on a small three bedroom, one bath house in Lakewood. An advertisement for it sold me. It said, "*Living in beautiful **Lakewood** is more than owning a home ... it is a new and better way of living.*"

Jim worked in the aerospace industry, and about seven years into our marriage, there were a lot of layoffs. He and some work buddies started goin' out to a local bar to sympathize with each other when someone got their pink slip or was transferred to a different department.

"*I'm just going to stop and have a couple beers,*" *Jim would say.*

Sometimes he never made it home on time for dinner, so I'd leave his plate on the table and cover it. When he started rollin' in around midnight, I quit making enough food for him to eat.

"*Hey, I'm hungry,*" *he'd say as he crawled into bed.*

"*You should be here when we eat,*" *I'd say.* "*And you reek of beer.*"

Now, I'd never been to this bar, so I never knew about the destructive elements within its four walls. One day, Jim came home with a motorcycle in the back of his truck. Not just any motorcycle, but a Harley Davidson. I had no idea where he got the money, and he never would tell me. I also had no idea he even knew how to ride one.

When Jim finally got his layoff notice, he decided he'd had enough of the stress, and he told me he didn't plan to find another job until he had some time to decide what he wanted to do with his life.

I couldn't believe it! We had two children and a mortgage!

Somehow we managed to keep our heads above water; we had some savings set aside, and that carried us through almost six months, until Jim withdrew what was left to work on his Harley. And then one Saturday when I was doing laundry, I found drugs in his pocket.

CHAPTER TWENTY SEVEN

In mid-September, I had a surprise call from John, David's attorney friend, who was acting as the impartial party in our divorce. I'd finally had a phone installed in my cabin, so I wouldn't have to always impose on Sam to find me if I had a call.

He wanted to meet with me. I didn't really want to take a day to drive down the mountain, meet with him, and then drive back again, so I asked if it was something we could discuss over the phone.

I'd been outside raking the never-ending stream of leaves that fell onto the paths to the cabins; Sam had warned me it was a gallant cause, but futile.

"I know I'm David's friend, but I've come across some things I believe we need to discuss," he said.

I braced myself and sat.

"I've come upon two pieces of property David purchased in his own name after your marriage."

My stomach turned.

"*What?*"

"One is a lemon ranch in Fallbrook valued at about eight thousand dollars, and the other is an apartment building, also in Fallbrook, valued at ninety thousand. There are mortgages on both, but they've also sheltered quite a bit of equity for him."

"Are you sure? How did he do that?"

"You mean how *did* he do it? Or how *could* he do it?"

I needed to catch my breath.

"I obviously now see how he *could* have, but how can you do that?"

"By setting up a corporation. Which he did."

I was speechless. I was so angry my throat tightened, but I refused to break down.

"I feel like an idiot," I finally said. "I don't know what to say." Thoughts were racing through my mind, and I was growing more furious by the moment. "How could he do that?" I asked again, and then quickly realized how stupid it sounded.

"Annie, I'm sorry..."

"I just saw him, and I genuinely felt sorry for him. He looked like shit, and I felt bad. Obviously, he's had his own interests in mind the entire time we were married..."

I could feel my head pounding and I stretched my neck to relieve some of the muscle tension. My face was fiery and my hands had turned cold. I literally felt like someone was sitting on my chest. I breathed slowly and eventually pressure everywhere subsided.

I was livid, and I needed time to think this through.

"Can I let you know what I'd like to do?" I asked as calmly as I could.

"Absolutely, Annie. I'll wait for your call. Again, I'm sorry."

We hung up. I closed my eyes. I needed to think. I was furious. Once I could sort through some of my thoughts, and the urge to kill David lessened, it registered that I had some options.

I called John back and told him to stop our divorce proceedings and that I wanted half of everything we had, even if it meant David had to sell the house. I also wanted half of both the newly discovered properties, and I was going to go for blood.

After we hung up again, I tried to cool off and get my heart rate back to normal, but I felt that awful adrenaline rushing through my body. I was going to do everything I could think of to not have another one of those attacks. I focused on the birdbath and feeder like I had before. It seemed to take forever, but I could feel myself start to relax, and I just kept breathing deeply and slowly. I hated the anger I felt, and I hated the reaction I was having.

And I truly hated David!

I didn't sleep that night, and the next day I was still so angry and antsy, I decided to spend some time going through paperwork in Sam's office. I packed up things I wouldn't need in order to run the B&B, and organized everything so I could find things. I wanted to be careful not to change so many things that it would offend Sam. When I came across several old photos of him and his wife Trudy, I asked him if he'd mind if I framed some and hung them.

It surprised him at first, but then he liked the idea.

"Tell me about her, Sam," I said, setting aside the photos. I needed a minute to sit.

Sam sat in his desk chair. "Well," he started, leaning back, "I never could figure out how someone like her would want to marry someone like me." He almost beamed. "We were married over forty years...and I can't think of a day I wasn't happy. When we retired, we made this our home, and we loved every minute of it."

"What did you do before you came up here?"

"We were both teachers. Met in college. She taught grammar school, and I taught high school. What a difference *that* was. She'd come home tellin' me about the cute things her little darlin's did, and I came home tellin' her how I caught some knucklehead ditchin' class."

I wanted to know about her death but wasn't sure how to broach the question. Sam decided on his own to tell me.

"Trudy had cancer, of the lady type, and then when she started that chemo..." he paused and bowed his head, "she had a stroke."

"Oh Sam, that's awful," I said sadly.

"The chemo didn't cause the stroke, but because of the stroke, we never had a chance to see if that damned treatment would've worked. She ended up in one of those homes...I hated going there. She died right after that."

We were both silent. "And my life just hasn't been the same." Sam looked at me and said, "Until you came up here, that is."

I was stunned.

"First, I had Noah when he lost his parents, and now, even though you came up here with your own sadness, you've given me something to look forward to. Watching you work on the cabins, and wishing I had just a sliver of the energy you have, well, it makes my heart happy." I went to him and gave him a big hug.

"Oh, Sam," I said, "You've been perfect for me too. I love this place, and together we can make it thrive again. I've totally enjoyed the process of being able to create for myself, and I keep saying it's so peaceful here, it's been just what I've needed." And I hugged him again.

Sam watched as I finished sorting through the old file cabinets, storing everything but the last ten years in banker's boxes. Then I cleaned out the desk drawers, asking him if he wanted to keep anything that I thought we didn't need. We filled a box of things he *wanted*, and we put it into the storeroom along with everything else we didn't need to have immediate access to.

By the end of the afternoon, I was done, and tired. I stood, stretched, and then wiped the dust from my hands.

"We did it!" I said triumphantly.

"Someone's outside, curious what we've been up to," Sam said, opening the front door. There stood Jezebel. "Itching to get away from those kids, are you?"

"Well, I'm going to wash my hands and go see how Noah's doing."

I hadn't told him about my conversation with John, and when I did, I wished I hadn't. He'd been working on one of the kitchenettes, and he was so furious he reminded me of an angry bull in a ring; he turned beet red, stomped his foot, then threw his hammer. He was ready for battle, and I was relieved David wasn't here.

"You need to take him for everything he has."

"Believe me, I am," I said. "But you need to calm down."

He reacted angrily to my comment, just like I had when David had made me angry and I didn't want to be told what to do.

"Sorry," I said. "I know you're only trying to protect me, but I need to take care of this myself."

He looked at me like I'd wounded him.

"Why is it what when I tell you how shitty he's treated you, you defend him?"

"I'm not defending him. I'm just saying I feel like I can take care of this. I don't want you to get in the middle of it."

I touched his arm. "I'll be fine. I hate him."

Within the week, Noah had finished the bath vanity and kitchenette for the first cabin. I'd given him some ideas for rustic and he'd run with it. Once those were finished, the flooring could go down, and then I'd install the rug, bedding, artwork, and window coverings.

The next week, cabin number one was finished. I'd given each cabin a name and tried not to be too corny. Cabin number one became "Woodhaven". I used artwork and décor that reminded me of the woods.

I'd started working on ideas for my business card and brochure, and my friend from school, Sarah, had become a graphic designer. We hadn't spoken for over a year and it was good to talk to her. She still lived in Las Vegas, and I brought her up to date with what was happening with David. She didn't sound her usual upbeat self, but said she was just feeling restless when I asked her about it. I knew her and also knew there was more to the story, but if she didn't feel like sharing, then I would not press her. When I told her about the cabins, her voice brightened, and we ended the conversation with me promising to send her my ideas.

Noah recommended a woodcarver to make new signs along the highway, and we ordered new exterior light fixtures for each cabin so guests wouldn't need flashlights to make their way around at night.

Cabin number two, now known as Black Bear Cabin, was just getting started, so the process was moving along quickly. The goal was to get everything finished by winter, so we had about two months until deadline. Sam and I brainstormed names for the rest of the cabins and I had the woodcarver make signs for them. We called them Cedar Lodge, Dogwood Cabin, Pinecone Cabin, Majestic Pines, Deer Hollow, Wood Haven and Black Bear Cabin.

Noah had finished a large remodeling job, so he had time to focus on getting the cabins finished, and then his plan was to work on his own cottage. He'd gone with my idea about the black and white diamond painted floor for the kitchen and dining area, and it looked great. Black granite counter tops were just coming available, and they'd gone in; all it needed now was furniture and finishing touches.

He'd had me come out and give him some decorating ideas, and I jumped at the opportunity to help him. I still had my catalogs from the furniture market, so we could sit and go through them. Noah was on a budget, so we needed to order a few things at a time. I also suggested we look for vintage furniture that had character, and he liked that idea too.

I loved going to antique stores and unlike most men, so did he. We found some great anchor pieces along with unique accents, and I felt that in no time we'd have his home furnished.

I'd asked him if at some point he could help me look at four-wheel-drive Jeeps; I didn't need one yet, but I would in a couple of months and I wanted to start thinking about it. Of course, Noah offered to go with me anytime. So one morning, when we both had time, we headed down the hill to the Jeep dealership.

"I'll be the easiest sale of the day," I said. "I don't care what color I end up with, but I do need automatic. You can decide everything else."

I rested my hand on his knee and looked at him, squinting as the sun shone in on his face as he drove. He finally moved the visor to block some of it out. I hummed along to one of the new country songs on the radio, and a couple of times I sang along. I thought back to when I used to do that when I first met David.

"You have a pleasant voice," he'd said. "But I prefer to hear the music itself."

I eventually stopped singing, and then I started preferring *no* music as we drove.

For some reason, the music had come back to life for me.

"Does it bother you when I sing?" I asked.

"No, I actually enjoy it; I don't know the words myself, so when you sing along, I hear them better."

I kept my BMW for special occasions, and with Noah's help, drove away in a new red four-door, four-wheel-drive Wrangler. With my cowboy boots and Jeep, I was quickly becoming a mountain woman. Winter would be the genuine test!

As much as it sounded like a cliché, being with Noah was almost perfect. We spent as much time as we could together, and every time I saw him, my heart raced. He was romantic, sometimes bringing me a red rose, or surprising me with dark chocolate, which I loved.

He also knew how to make me respond to him when we made love, and at first I worried I'd be a little self-conscious. But I knew that when he started kissing me, he knew how to show me he cared. I couldn't imagine the other two women he'd been interested in walking away from him. Sometimes people just don't realize a good thing when they have it.

While the mornings had been brisk, the cloudless sky promised warmer weather later, so on a Saturday, we took a break and went out in Noah's friend's boat. It was still in the water, but would come out around Thanksgiving, way past the official Labor Day end of the season. Since the last winter hadn't brought the much needed rain and snowfall, the water level of the lake was down. Some of the docks weren't located in deep water, and they'd been extended out into the lake so people could still use their boats. We found a parking spot on the highway and then climbed down the hundred or so steps to get to the dock. I thought I was fairly acclimated to the elevation, but I got winded.

"Oh great, I'll have to walk back up these!" I said, huffing and puffing.

"Well, I have a solution for that," Noah said. "We can take the boat out and I'll drop you off at the Village then come get you in the Jeep."

"Let's see how I feel when we're done."

"Here she is," Noah said, stopping at the dock where the boat was. "I'll help you on board so you don't take a tumble," he said, grabbing firmly to my left hand and making sure I was solidly on board before letting go. It shocked me how the warmth of his hand transferred to mine, and I hated to admit I was sorry he had to let me go.

My balance was a little wobbly, and I was grateful when Noah stepped into the boat to steady me. He patted the seat next to him as he sat and started the engine. Once on the lake, he drove slowly around so I could see all the beautiful and expensive homes lining the shores "This is heaven," I said, closing my eyes.

"Hold on to your seat," Noah warned, as he revved the motor and took off. It reminded me of my mother learning to drive our boat, and water sprayed both of us. I couldn't help but laugh as he wiped my face. I could tell he'd been watching me, and I felt my face turn red. He still had that effect on me.

Water had soaked his shirt and I couldn't help but notice the muscles in his chest. A line of water dripped down his arms. Noah took off again, and water sprayed us one more time. He laughed. Being with him was like being with a kid. The next time we went out on the boat, I'd have to bring a hat, some sunglasses and a towel!

I'd been to the Village since I'd come up, but mostly the extent of my shopping there had been the shoe store. We anchored at one of the Village docks and drank in the sun. It was so relaxing. After about an hour, we decided to have margaritas and lunch at a Mexican restaurant there. I was starving, and devoured so many chips I was unable to finish my lunch.

"It's cooling off. I guess all good things must come to an end," Noah said. "Do you want me to leave you here and I can take the boat back and come get you? Or do you want to brave the steps back up to the car?"

"Can you leave me here and come back and get me?" I dreaded climbing so many steps.

I had about twenty minutes to kill while Noah parked the boat and brought the Jeep over to get me, so I found a place in the sun where I could sit and look at the lake. It was such a beautiful day, and I was surprised there weren't many people walking around. I closed my eyes and just absorbed the air and sounds of water splashing the retaining wall in front of me.

I took a deep breath and then let my mind drift and the sounds of the lake took over; a boat coming into the docks, a boat off in the distance. Ducks called, and a family gathered for a picture. The lake was so tranquil.

Then a shadow blocked the sun, and a hand took mine to help me up. Noah was back.

I'd found homes for two of the kittens and had them and Jezebel spayed. I couldn't resist, so I kept one of them for myself. I named her Socks, since she had four white paws that reminded me of booties. I missed having them all in bed with me, but I had to admit I slept much better with only Socks and Jezebel. They say that people with pets don't sleep as well as people who don't have them, and I had to agree, especially when the kittens felt like playing in the middle of the night.

The fall weather was still warm enough during the day, so we took the boat out several more times before it came out of the water. We also took a Saturday to take the tour at Wildhaven Ranch in Arrowhead/ Cedar Glen, where injured animals that can't make it back into the wild have been nursed and protected. After seeing and hearing about the animals, I was hooked, and I offered to revamp their gift shop by teaching the volunteers tricks of display, and helping them buy products wholesale so they could make a profit. They already had a t-shirt with a great drawing of their raccoon, and I asked my friend Sarah to help them do mailings requesting donations.

In mid-October, the last of Grayson's bedroom furniture arrived, and I made arrangements to have it all delivered. Grayson wouldn't be back for another two weeks, so that gave me plenty of time to add the finishing touches. I preferred to do a complete installation rather than piece by piece, so that the entire room would come together at one time, making it more impressive to the client.

I also coordinated a pickup from the local shelter to take his old furniture, and they were delighted, for there were plenty of families up there who could use nice furniture. I left the donation receipts on the kitchen counter.

I heard from our attorney again and he let me know he'd halted the divorce proceedings like I'd asked. He told me he'd get back to me when he had something drawn up that I could see. Just talking to John made my anger flare, but I was glad I didn't harbor as much hatred for David as I had a month ago. It would take me years to learn that hatred and dwelling on revenge were not the solution to all things. In the meantime, I tried to picture David hearing from his friend that I now knew about the properties, and I took pleasure in knowing it must have driven him crazy.

Obviously, John would no longer be his friend.

CHAPTER TWENTY EIGHT

I didn't tell Noah about my last conversation with my attorney. Truthfully, I wanted to stop thinking about it all, and by telling Noah, I'd just be reliving the whole thing and we'd both end up being upset.

I scheduled a time to meet Grayson, and I was a bundle of nerves. The completed bedroom looked great, and even though he'd given me the freedom to pull it all together, I was on pins and needles, waiting to hear what he thought. I'd gone with a little more contemporary lake look, with wide plank hardwood floors, a taupe-brown upholstered headboard, tan bedding with dark brown fur pillows, and dark leather accent reading chairs in front of the fireplace. The night stands were oiled wood on rust colored metal stands. New lamps really added the right amount of ambient lighting.

"It's absolutely spectacular, Annie," He said upon entering the room, the warmth of his smile reflecting in his eyes.

I felt like a child standing there beaming, but I couldn't help it. I hoped my face hadn't colored as usual. His eyes took in everything; the bedding, window coverings, accents. Then he looked at me with a faint glimmer of humor. *He'd seen me turn red!*

"It's exactly as I'd envisioned," he said graciously, looking away. "Excellent." He continued to nod his head. "I'm delighted. I only wish everyone did as good a job for me as you've done."

Then he motioned me to follow him back into the kitchen.

"This calls for a celebration. Care for some wine?"

"Oh, no thanks," I said to his offer; he'd already poured himself a glass and nodded towards me, reaching for the bottle.

"You have a lot of talent, Annie, and I think you could be very successful in L.A. Have you thought about re-inventing yourself down there? I could use you on some of my projects."

I thought about how to answer him diplomatically. "I don't really want to go back down right now. I feel I've found something up here and it feels right."

"Some*thing* or some*one*?"

I didn't think I needed to share my personal life with him, so I said, "Something. It's a whole new beginning for me here, and it feels good. I've just gotten started with the cabins and I'm excited to get them finished."

"I see," he said, but he kept his eyes on me. Then he changed the subject. "I'd like to continue with decorating the kitchen after the living room and dining room. I don't need too much, but I'd like to have some accents. Add some color. What do you think?"

By being happy with my work, he'd inadvertently made me the most confident I'd felt in a long time. I wanted to bask in it for a while longer, and then I realized the time. I hated to break the spell.

"Oh," I said again, looking at my watch. "I hate to run, but I have to get back to the cabins; carpet is being installed in two of them, and I'm eager to see how it's coming. I'll bring some things for you to look at the next time we meet then."

"So I take it the project is coming along well?"

"It is," I said, gathering my things. "I'm really glad you're happy, Grayson. You've been super to work with. And I want you to know how much I've appreciated having you as a client."

"I've truly enjoyed it." Grayson toasted me. He was a hard man to read sometimes. He could be very cool and formal, or allow a slight crack to show in his armor; he was also just a man, and most men didn't wear their emotions on their sleeve.

I left there floating on air and on top of the world. As I took the winding roads back to the cabins, I couldn't help but notice how the trees were turning orange and brown, which was breathtaking. Down the hill, only one or two trees in our neighborhood changed colors, almost jarring the senses as they stood amongst all the other evergreen trees. In the mountains, at least a third of the trees were changing, and I'd never seen fall quite like it. It was the first change of seasons I would experience, and I felt like it was also the first change of seasons in my life.

However, when I got to the cabins, I realized that with the change, we'd also had an overabundance of leaves that would need to be raked to keep the grounds looking neat. I was determined to keep them under control, and my intentions had been good, for I'd thought I could tackle the maintenance myself. It was a totally unrealistic undertaking, and I was hoping Sam knew a handyman with a truck.

Laura and I met for dinner at the Cowboy bar to get caught up on life. The last time I'd seen her, she was with someone I'd not seen before.

"His name is Jason," she said. "He and a few of his buddies came up for the weekend and we just connected. He'd come back again when I saw you. I really like him."

"Oh my god, you sound like me when I first met Noah."

"Yeah, I do, don't I? It's way too soon to tell if he's Mr. Right, but I feel different when I'm with him."

"Just when I'm getting settled, you're not going to be moving down the hill, are you?" I was thrilled for her, but I didn't want to lose the only female friend I had up here.

"Let's wait and see how it goes before you start missing me," Laura said. "Although so far, he's really great. He has two small children, whom I've met. They're very sweet, and they let me hold them while we were watching T.V."

"Where's the mom?"

"Well, she died a couple of years ago."

"My god, Laura. That's terrible!"

"It is. He's just beginning to think about starting a new life, so we're taking it nice and slow."

"Holy cow. A built in family," I said thoughtfully. "You'd make a great Mom."

"I don't know about that. I still need more time to get used to the possibility."

"What does he do?"

"He's a marine mechanic and has his own shop in Newport Beach."

"That's a great area," I said.

"He loves it, and he stays really busy."

I pouted. "I want it to work out for you, but I don't want to lose you," I said selfishly.

Laura deserved a happy life with someone who loved her. She'd been a hairdresser for almost ten years and had worked hard. She rented a small cabin in Cedar Glen by her shop and had made the mountains her home. If this was indeed to turn into something serious, she'd obviously have to consider moving back down.

She seemed relaxed, and I told her she looked happy. I tried not to think more about it, so I brought her up to date with the goings on in my world. We didn't stay long after dinner, and when we stood to leave, I gave her a big hug and said, "I'm behind you with whatever you decide to do." I thought she was going to cry. It was how I felt, too.

The next day, I managed to catch Ginny at a quiet time so I could talk to her about providing something for the breakfasts at the cabins. Since I was at her place just about every morning myself, I knew I'd eventually catch her and this morning had been perfect timing. When I saw her, I waved her over.

"Do you have a minute to talk about the B&B?"

"Since it's not too busy, I deserve a break. I'll sit and have a cup of coffee, if you don't mind?" Ginny asked, coming back to the table, coffee in hand.

"Not at all," I said, finishing my notes. We talked about the different muffins they always served, and I asked about the cinnamon rolls.

"Obviously, when we get closer to opening, we can order what we think...and I can get all the butter, creamer and sugar," I said. "Or can I buy the packets from you?"

Out of the blue, Ginny said, "I'm getting old," more to herself than to me. She stretched her back muscles. "Being on my feet so much is taking its toll."

"How long have you been up here?"

Ginny sighed, "Oh, about twenty years." She closed her eyes and slowly rolled her head from side to side to stretch her neck muscles.

"Did your husband come up with you?" I always felt like I was prying when I asked people questions about their private lives, but I was curious; I knew Ginny had been married.

"No, sadly, he never made it up here."

"Oh," I said, wondering if I should have pushed.

"Oh, it's okay. It's been over twenty years. He was killed in a car crash on the freeway; crushed between two semi trucks. Killed him in an instant."

"Oh my God." My hand unconsciously went to my mouth. "I'm so sorry, Ginny. That's just awful." My mind conjured up images that made me wince.

"It was pretty bad all right. Thank goodness we didn't have any children, although now it would be nice to have someone around to take care of me. When I decide to get older, of course," she said and laughed.

"So you came up here yourself?"

"Yes. I wanted to start all over, and I thought this was as good a place as any." Ginny looked around then added, "You can see I don't move around a lot."

"Well," I said, "I'm glad you made it up here. It gives me courage to keep trying." I started getting up from the table. "Now that I've stirred up a hornet's nest..."

"It's fine, Annie. I've worked my butt off, but this place has been really good to me."

"Well, I need to get going. When we get another cabin done, we can figure out what to order."

"Sounds good to me. You know where to find me. I think I'll just sit a minute more while I can."

I left thinking what an idiot I'd been. Like the story Noah told me about the bat on the woman's face, I knew it would take a while to get the image of Ginny's husband out of my mind.

CHAPTER TWENTY NINE

I knew once David found out John told me about his secret properties, I'd be hearing from him, but I never expected him to show up on my doorstep. I'd just brought the last grocery bag in and had set it on the counter. Jezebel and socks were out of dry food, so I started cutting the bag open to feed them.

"*What the hell, Annie,*" he said, standing in my doorway. He was rattled, and he had something in his hand.

I'd never been afraid of David, but seeing him made my skin crawl. I dropped the bag of food and cat chow went everywhere.

"Shit! *What the hell yourself, David,*" I said defiantly, looking down at the mess I'd made.

"I thought we had everything worked out, and now *my* friend John says everything's changed!" He was furious now, and I wondered if he'd been drinking. No doubt the stress of the drive, especially if there was traffic, must have added to his aggravation.

"How did you find me?" I asked, leaving the mess on the floor and going to him, determined to not let him into my cabin. I'd never seen David violent before, but I didn't like the way he was acting. I stepped past him, outside into my garden. Just the fact he was there invading my space made me more anxious.

He turned to look at me. "*It's easy to find someone when you want to,*" he said sarcastically, then added, "This *is* a small town, remember."

He'd violated my privacy, and I was getting more angry as we both stood there.

"What do you want?" I asked, coolly.

"Why are you doing this to me?" his face had really reddened, and I wondered if he was going to give himself a stroke. I saw loathing in his eyes, and I caught my breath.

"Why am I doing this to *you*? You threw away our marriage. Not only did you betray me, but you bought property that I never knew about. Why would you *do* that?"

"It was for me," he said simply.

I couldn't believe he said that.

"The fact you even did something like that just proves what a shit you are. If you bought it, it should have been for both of us. And now it will be!"

"It was so I'd have something..." he was almost pleading.

Then I realized he was making sure he'd have something if our marriage ever ended. Something he wouldn't lose.

"You repulse me!" I said, and I could feel my heart pounding.

For the first time, I looked at him and detested everything about him. His face was ugly and distorted. He'd had time to work his way up to the hostility he now felt towards me. And the frightening thing was that if I'd had a gun, I could have killed him, and I don't think I would have cared.

I decided the best way to fight him was to stand there and remain as calm as I could. I'd let him try in his attorney's voice to convince me I was being unjust to him; that all this was unfair. That it was his right to insist we set this aside and continue with the original divorce agreement.

And then, like in a movie where the hero suddenly arrives, Noah's truck pulled in to the parking area.

"What the fuck is he doing here?" David's face was so red now I actually hoped he'd drop dead.

Noah rushed over to us and took my arm. "Are you alright?" he said, panicked.

"Fuck off, *cowboy*," David said.

"Hold off now," Noah tried to calm him down with both hands.

"*Did you hear me? This is not your business!*"

"I don't know what you two are talking about, but it looks like it's getting out of hand," Noah started, and then David lunged for him.

What had just happened?

Noah fell down, then David went after him, but Noah's age and strength worked in his favor as he pushed David off him.

"*Stop it, both of you,*" I screamed.

But David tried to lunge for Noah again, and this time Noah jumped away and David went down. He stayed there for a moment, and I thought he might actually cry. This was unbelievable! I could see how people were murdered in passion and outrage.

Noah bent over, with hands on his knees, just to catch his breath. David was still down on the ground and had his hands over his face.

Then Sam came out with his rifle, as if he was going to make everything right by shooting someone. If it wasn't so serious, it would be comical. The headline would read, "Old mountain man shoots soon to be ex-husband while he fights with wife's boyfriend!"

I let out a sarcastic cry at the image.

"For god's sake, David, *get up*," I said. I was so disgusted, it took everything I had to not kick him. "And how did *you* get here?" I asked Noah. For some reason, I was now angry with him, too.

For a minute he looked at me like I was the one who was crazy, and then Sam piped up, "I called him."

"*Get up*, David," I said, "and go home before I report you to the Bar. Your behavior is appalling. And it will change nothing. In fact, it makes me wonder what else you've lied about...but I want to get this over with as soon as possible, so I'm not going to look any further."

Was there anything else I could say to him while I had his attention?

"And I need my money, now."

David stood and brushed himself off. His hair was disheveled, and he looked dreadful. He rubbed his hand on his shoulder. Good. I hoped he hurt himself.

We watched as he despondently made his way back to his car, all traces of rage left behind. Sam followed him back, I'm sure to be certain he truly left.

I, on the other hand, stood there, trembling. It could have gone much worse.

Noah came to my side and touched my arm. "Are you okay?"

I stepped back from him, like he'd been the one who'd gotten out of control, and he winced. I didn't know why I did that to him, and I knew it hurt him.

"Jesus, Annie," was all he could say before he stomped off.

I didn't hear from Noah for a few days, and at first, I thought he might have gone back to Colorado to work. At least he could work off some steam there.

In the meantime, it gave me some time alone to try to put things in their proper perspective. I tried to focus on the cabins and felt we were coming along quickly now. I had a few bookings lined up, which was encouraging, since we'd only had one weekend stay since I took over. My marketing materials were being printed, and I was anxious to start distributing brochures and get an ad in the paper. I wanted to have a couple more cabins ready before I pushed harder.

A few of days after David's display of whatever we wanted to call it, I had a terrible case of indigestion. I knew I'd been stressed, so I attributed it to that, but around two in the morning, I threw up my undigested dinner. I don't get sick, and in fact, the last time I'd thrown up was right after I'd turned twenty-one; it was the day after an evening I'd drank way too much.

Once I got everything out of my system, I felt much better and was able to go back to sleep. The next morning, I slept in, and when I finally got up, I made a quick list of everything I hoped to accomplish that day.

I wasn't very hungry, but knew I needed to eat something, so I just had toast for breakfast. And I ate some Tums. They seemed to settle my stomach.

That afternoon, I was exhausted, and took a nap; I was hoping I wasn't coming down with the flu. That night, I just sat in front of the fireplace, with my two cats by my side, and read.

The next morning, I felt much better and had to do some errands down the hill. I felt like I was having menstrual cramps, so I packed my period paraphernalia and I ate a quick breakfast before heading down. One thing I needed to do was pick up more cat food and litter again for my little angels.

CHAPTER THIRTY

Alyce

It took about a year of dealing with the marijuana and the drinkin' for me to get to where I wasn't gonna put up with it any longer.

I was so naïve. Even after Daddy died, I'd always hoped that once you got married, you could live happily ever after. I also wanted what every parent wanted for their children; to have a normal, stable life until they were grown and married themselves.

I knew that what I was about to do would at least temporarily burst that imaginary bubble I'd always held close, and I knew Jim didn't have anywhere to go.

I was makin' enough money to keep up with the house payment and to support us, so we didn't need him for the money. And I, for sure, didn't need him actin' out in front of the kids. He'd never been physically abusive towards me, but when he was high or drunk, he started calling me fat, or lazy, or a bitch, no matter who was there. I asked him to try to turn his life around, but he wasn't interested.

So one day, I told him to find some place else to live, and I changed the locks on the house. I knew if he really wanted to get in he could always break in, but I was hopin' he'd leave us alone. And he did.

At first, he didn't tell his parents, but every time they called the house, he wasn't there. God knows what he told them when he talked to them, and when he eventually told them about us, they were heartbroken.

"You two don't have nothing to do with this," I said when they finally came over. "I promise you'll always be a part of their lives. They deserve grandparents."

I thought his mother was going to cry her eyes out.

I did eventually divorce Jim, and while I prayed I didn't have the same bad luck with men that Mama had, I knew I wasn't going to be happy bein' by myself. When one of my co-workers introduced me to a man named Jerry, I started thinking of a new life.

He worked at the telephone company and had lost his wife about five years before. He'd never had children and was shy and very quiet. He had a great sense of humor once he felt comfortable around you. From the Midwest originally, he loved livin' in California, and he loved my kids. It filled my heart to watch him pretend to pull a coin out of their ear, or cup his hand over his mouth when they told him a silly story. Plus, he had a dog. I looked for any signs of strange behavior or weird habits, and I didn't see any.

I even asked my kids how they felt about him; did they feel comfortable? Did he do anything weird around them? Kids have a good sense of people.

He had a little beer belly, but he didn't drink beer, so he didn't mind that I was chubby. He called me buttercup.

I was still old-fashioned and never let him spend the night at the house unless the kids went with their grandparents or my mother. We dated for about a year before we got married, and I thought we made a good couple. He had his own house, and when we decided the kids would feel more comfortable living in my house, he gladly moved in with us. We rented his house out, which brought us a little extra income.

We were married a little over five years when Grandpa's wife, Marie, called Mama.

"I've put him in a rest home," she said, her voice quivering. "He fell and needs someone to take care of him."

"I'm coming up to see him," Mama told her.

"You don't have to," Marie said.

"Of course I do," she'd said.

That next Saturday, I wrote down directions on how to get there, and Mama and I drove up. Grandpa was in terrible shape. He didn't recognize either of us, and he looked like he'd fallen more than once, what with bruises all over him. Marie didn't look much better; her bony arms dangled from the sleeves of her soiled housedress and her fingernails were dirty. She constantly fidgeted with her out of control wiry hair, and wouldn't make eye contact with either of us.

"My daughter took care of it all," she whispered.

"What does that mean?" I asked.

"She said it was the best thing to do. To put him in a home."

Marie's daughter refused to come to the rest home to talk to us, and we had no idea where she lived.

"You tell your daughter she needs to call me," I said harshly. "We need to be kept up to date with what's goin' on with him." I was fit to be tied.

I checked with the administrator, and all the paperwork was in order. Grandpa had been admitted two weeks ago, and there was nothin' we could do about it. Marie was his wife, and she'd signed the forms.

"You might want to see this," the administrator said, handing me another set of papers. "Looks like his wife has divorced him."

The divorce was final just after Grandpa had been admitted. I rushed back into his room, and Marie was still there, sittin' quietly in a chair.

"What have you done?"

I wrote my phone number down on a pad of paper and gave it to Marie.

"Have her call me or there'll be hell to pay."

"What was that all about," Mama asked once we got back into the car.

"They put Grandpa in that home. Didn't you hear Marie?"

"I did, but it didn't make sense. Grandpa looks bad."

"Mama, they've put him in that home. Don't you understand?"

"Well, I guess not really."

Grandpa died not long after that, and we only found out after his funeral. Marie called to let us know.

"What about the farm?" I asked.

"Oh, I think I signed it over to my daughter."

When Jerry made me call a lawyer, he said there was nothin' we could do about any of it if they were divorced. He said he was sorry.

And that was that.

Three years later, Mama was told she had congestive heart failure. Her breathing had become labored, and even when she was sittin' quietly, I could hear her wheezing.

"I've been tuckin' away money all these years," she said one day. "And I'm thinkin' about goin' into one of those old folk's places."

"You're not old," I said. "You'll live forever."

"I figure my life would be easier, and so would yours. They have activities and there'll always be someone to look after me."

I hated the idea. But even the kids said they'd noticed she was slowin' down something terrible. When she brought it up again, we looked at several homes before she made a decision on one. I went through the house with her, and she decided what she wanted to take with her. Some days she was surprisingly matter of fact about it all, and sometimes when she found somethin' tucked away in a drawer, she'd say somethin' like, "Now why on earth would I have kept this?"

Some days, she couldn't hardly make a decision. When she was that way, I'd tell her we could stop and come back to it later.

I wasn't sure Mama would like it, bein' in a home, and since she didn't need the income, we left most of her things in the house and didn't put it up for rent. That way, if she ever changed her mind, all we'd have to move back was the few things she'd taken with her. Turns out, she sometimes asked about some of those things we left behind. If I could find it in the house, I'd bring it to her and more often than not, she'd look at me and say, "Now where has that been?"

When Mama used to talk about Daddy, she didn't always make sense. She'd start by saying things like "after Daddy's heart attack," then end with statements like "he never thought about us when he did it."

Or she'd say, "He'd never talk about it, but your father really had a hard time after he came back from the war. He had nightmares. Then I did too, after he took his life. I wondered if I should have been able to see it coming."

I knew she'd soon forget our mixed-up conversations, so I didn't think much of them. When she mentioned the police comin' to our house after Smitty's family was murdered, I started wonderin' what was going on in her mind. All she'd ever told me was they were still trying to figure out what had happened.

Of course, I know now they'd already put the pieces together, and were trying to figure out why Daddy did it. But there'd be nothing they could do about it, because he was dead.

On one of my visits to her in the home, Mama pulled out a box of our old local newspaper clippings and finally showed them to me. I hadn't seen them when I was helpin' her pack up, so at first I didn't understand how she had them.

"Unsolved Mystery of Family Killed in Their Cabin!"

It was the story about Smitty and his family!

"When the Smiths didn't return home Sunday afternoon, the family became worried. Because no one answered the phone in the cabin, Smitty's brother called the Sheriff who, after visiting the mountain home, made the grisly discovery. Smitty's brother drove up and identified the bodies."

And the next clipping was:

"Murder and Suicide Connected!"
"At first it appeared these were two random occurrences; one an unfortunate suicide and one a multiple murder. The Sheriff's department finally linked the two men together when it was discovered they were business partners. 'It appears John Murphy committed the murders and then took his own life.' "

Who had gone up to identify Daddy's body? Obviously, it had been Mama.

I now knew Daddy took his own life, but there was nothin' else in the photo box that could answer the lingerin' question...why had he killed Smitty and his family?

I felt the blood drain from my face and had to put my head between my legs so I wouldn't faint. Mama just watched me, confused by my reaction.

"I've been tryin' to tell you," she said.

"Mama," I started, once I could gather my wits. "I thought you were just imaginin' all this."

"I'm sorry you had to find out. I wondered all these years if I should have ever told you, but I've carried this mess in my head all this time."

The only thing I could think of saying was, "Why are you telling me this now?"

As I watched her put the papers back into her box, all I could think of was, 'Why didn't you say something? I watched as you tried to put your life back together so many times, and I couldn't do anythin' about it.'

Daddy had caused all her unhappiness, not because he died of a natural death, but because he'd killed someone.

Without thinking about how she might be feeling at that moment, I knew I had to get out of there. I left the bag of groceries I'd brought on the counter of her small kitchen; her caregiver could put everything away when she checked in on her. In fact, I saw one of them go into another room as I hurried to the elevator, so I knew they'd be in to see her soon.

It took forever for the elevator to come, and then it seemed to take even more time than usual to get to the ground floor. I was grateful no one else wanted to go down. I had a minute to myself. I rushed by the sign out desk and it was only when I was outside that I stopped to take a breath.

I could feel my heartbeat rushing through my ears and while I knew it was only stress, it scared me.

What Daddy had done was unforgivable. He ruined so many lives. But what Mama knew had to have been unbearable for her. My mind raced back to feeling helpless when she cried, how she cuddled with Daisy, and how she was repeatedly let down by deadbeat men. She deserved so much more, and I'd had no idea how to help her.

I couldn't go back in time, but I could go back upstairs to see her and apologize for running away like I did.

"I thought you just left," one of the staff said as I walked back in.

"I did. But I forgot somethin'."

When I got to my mother's room, her door was closed, and I gently knocked.

"Oh, hey, Alyce," her caregiver whispered. "She's down for her afternoon nap."

"Was she okay?"

"Oh, sure. She seemed surprised you'd left, but said something about probably forgetting you told her you were leaving. She's fine, though, so don't you worry."

Like a cowardly lump, I stood there for a few minutes, wondering if I should go in and wake her, but then thought I might confuse her even more if I did. I eventually turned to leave.

"Tell her I'll call her later tonight then."

"Will do, dear."

CHAPTER THIRTY ONE

As I started down the hill, I had another indigestion attack and, thankfully, had some antacid in my console. I chewed on a couple of tablets and felt better, but by the time I was halfway down, I felt like I was going to throw up again. I pulled into a small turnout, and I proceeded to lose my breakfast! Within a few minutes, I felt much better.

My day was full, so I decided to continue my trip, and thought I'd feel well enough to get everything done. But within minutes, I broke out into a sweat and found another turnoff. My body grew clammy then, and as I eventually cooled off, I got a chill. I sat in my warm car until my body returned to normal, and thankfully I didn't throw up again.

I had a long enough reprieve to get everything on my list taken care of and then headed back up the hill. I was making the first turn when I my empty stomach turned and I felt nauseous. *"Please tell me this isn't happening again,"* I said aloud, rolling down my window. I made myself take deep breaths. I turned off where there was a honey stand to let traffic pass. I knew I was going to throw up again, but there was nothing left in my stomach. Pain shot through my abdomen, and I knew something was wrong. I got out of the car, turned, and then let myself fall face down on my hood.

The woman behind the honey stand rushed to keep me from sliding down to the ground.

"*Are you alright?*" she shouted above the noise of the cars driving by.

"Something's wrong," I said. "I'm definitely sick, and I need to go to the emergency room. But I don't know where it is. I've never felt this bad ever!" I was frantic, and I started crying. I felt like a big baby.

"You'll be alright," she said soothingly. "I'll call an ambulance."

"No, don't," I said foolishly. "Call my friend. She'll come get me."

I gave her Laura's phone number at the salon.

"I think I'm going to fall asleep..."

"Your friend is going to meet you at the hospital. I've called an ambulance."

Somehow, she helped me back into my car, and I laid my head back. With the doors closed, the warmth of the car enveloped me, seeping into my bones. I did not know how much time had passed, but at some point someone was knocking on my window. I felt like I could hardly stay awake.

"My God, you look like death warmed over," Laura said when she saw me.

"That makes me feel even worse," I said, crying.

"I didn't mean it that way. You look like you feel awful. But you'll be fine in a couple of minutes. Hang on. You're on an IV. Your pants were soaked in blood."

Within minutes, an ultrasound technician was checking my abdomen.

The emergency room doctor was in soon after and started asking me some medical history questions. I asked if Laura could come be with me and I reached for her hand.

"You've lost a bit of blood. Are you on the pill?" he asked.

"Yes."

"When did you start taking it?"

I tried to think back in time and calculated it'd been about eight to ten weeks.

"I'm in a new relationship, and we had sex right before I started the pill. I'd spotted that first couple of weeks, which I thought was just my period regulating to the medication."

"Tenderness in the breasts?"

"Yes."

I was having a miscarriage. It most likely happened after the first time Noah and I had been intimate, and before I started taking the pill. I'd had no full menstrual cycle.

"There are two ways we can deal with this," the doctor said, setting his chart down. "One is to let the miscarriage continue to happen naturally, which could take some time, and you could be uncomfortable. Or, we can perform a medical procedure where we dilate and open the cervix to remove tissue from its inner lining. That's the simplest option."

"That's what I'd like to do then."

"I need to call Noah," I said after I awoke from the anesthesia. "I'm not sure how to tell him, but I have to."

"I agree, Annie. He's probably worried about you anyway, and he has a right to know. You can call him and tell him when you can be released." Laura handed me the phone by my bed, then said, "I'll step outside. But I'm here." She then squeezed my hand.

I called Noah. If I had to leave a message, would he even call me back? I hadn't spoken with him since the confrontation with David. But he hadn't called me either...maybe he'd finally given up on me and decided life without me would be much easier for him.

The moment I heard his voice, I could hardly talk.

"Hey," I said, and then burst into tears again.

"Are you okay?"

"Not really. I'm in the hospital...and I've just lost our baby..." I hadn't meant to blurt it out, but it there it was.

There was a long stretch of silence and I knew Noah was digesting what I'd said. I couldn't help it, but I cried harder.

He finally said, "I'll be there as soon as I can..."

"I'll be here for a few more hours, and then I can go home."

"Noah's on his way here," I told Laura. Crying had caused me to hiccup, and I tried hard to calm down.

Laura embraced me. "Just try to relax and get some rest. You'll be fine, and up and around in no time." Laura stayed with me until I exhausted myself and finally slept.

When I awoke, Noah was sitting by my bed, eyes red from grief. He pulled me to him and encircled me with his strong but gentle arms, and of course I started crying again.

"I'm so sorry, Noah. I had no idea," was all I could think of to say.

They finally released me and I could hardly wait to get home to my own bed. The nurse reminded me to take it easy for a couple of days but also made sure I knew there had been no complications, so my recovery time would most likely be short.

The minute Noah opened the door to my cabin, Jezebel and Socks were there and just seeing them lifted my spirits. "Hi, my girls," I said.

I changed into my PJs and climbed into bed. It wasn't cold, but Noah started the fire anyway, and just listening to the crackling sounds the wood made, relaxed me as it always did. Noah said he and Sam would go pick up my car and get it back on to the grounds. He offered to bring something to eat when I had rested more.

"Oh, god, Sam will know I was pregnant. That's so embarrassing!"

"I just told him you had female problems. Nothing serious. Are you okay?" he asked again. His face was drawn, and I could tell this whole mess overwhelmed him.

"I am...I haven't really digested it all yet. I didn't know I was pregnant, so I'm still unable to think clearly. I know I dropped a bomb on you, Noah. And I can't believe I'm crying again." I took a few minutes to compose myself. "I'll be fine. And I'll be hungry when you get back."

The cats climbed on my bed and lay next to me. I petted them, then went back to sleep.

Noah was back in a couple of hours and knocked quietly on my door.

"I'm up...come in." I was sitting in one of the chairs by the fire.

"I brought nourishment," he said, setting turkey sandwiches and iced tea down on the small coffee table.

"I'm famished," I said. It felt like I hadn't eaten in days.

"Will you stay with me tonight?" I asked.

"I wouldn't leave you for anything."

"Even though I can be annoying?"

"Yes, even though."

CHAPTER THIRTY TWO

During the night, I woke a few times unsure of where I was, but each time, I reached out to make sure Noah was there, and then quickly fell back asleep. We slept until almost nine the next morning, and it surprised me how good I felt. I cuddled with Noah, my back against the curve of his body, which not only kept me warm, but made me feel secure. When we finally decided to face the day, we were both hungry, so after showers, we dressed and left for Ginny's.

"Are you okay?" Noah asked as we parked.

"I feel really good. I'm surprised. And since we're speaking again," I said somewhat sheepishly, "can we get back to work on the cabins? I need to do something to fill my time."

"But I think you need to rest," Noah said, stopping me as we walked.

"I can rest and work. I'll just take it easy if I get tired. I can't really say I feel like they did anything, which is weird. I should feel something," I said pensively. I'd just lost a baby, but in my mind, it hadn't been real. As hard as I tried, I just couldn't think of it that way.

"Are you sure you're ready to get back to work?" Noah looked at me like I was a madwoman for even thinking about anything but what had just happened. I could see the toll it'd had taken on him.

"I'm good. I just need to slow down for a couple of days, but the guys do all the hard work. I just supervise," I answered with a timid smile.

"You just never stop, do you?"

During breakfast, I could tell he was not happy with me, and I knew he was just upset. From across the table, he took my hand and shook his head.

"I was hoping to have an open house and ribbon cutting before Christmas, but I don't think we'll be finished in time," I said.

"When are the new signs going to be ready?" he asked, trying to shift his mood.

"Next week, so once those are up, people driving the highway will be able to see where we are. That itself should help our bookings a lot."

I played with my straw wrapper for a few minutes, and then said, "I'm ok to stop by the grocery store on our way back to the cabin. We need something we can make sandwiches with and I could use more water. I'm still totally dehydrated. I do know I'll want to take a nap today, so if you have something else to do, you won't offend me," I said.

After shopping, Noah carried the groceries in and put them away while I changed back into my pajamas and climbed under the covers. He used the wood in the basket to add to the fire, then went outside and gathered more. Soon I was sleeping.

Noah left to check on a few jobs, but came right back. I could tell he hated to leave me, although I knew I was fine; I was just tired. We hadn't talked about the miscarriage all day, and I tried not to dwell on it. After dinner, though, sitting in front of the lit fireplace, Noah brought it up.

"How are you feeling about all this?" he finally asked.

"Honestly, I'm trying *not* to think, but when I do, my thoughts are mixed." I tried not to, but I sighed. "Part of me says that since I didn't even know I was pregnant, having a baby was not on my mind. And *that* part of me says this definitely isn't a good time to even think about it. *And* I strongly believe that if there was a miscarriage, then there was something wrong with the baby, and the pregnancy needed to end."

I stopped to think and asked for a glass of wine. Noah brought it to me, along with a beer for himself.

"I do eventually want children...I think...but for so long, they weren't in the equation. So I'm not even sure how I feel about that either. My mind hasn't gotten to that point yet." I didn't want Noah to think I was against having children, but knowing I'd never have them with David meant they were never in my overall plan.

I watched Noah's face as I said all this, hoping he wouldn't think I was uncaring, and I could tell he remained lost in thought. What was he thinking about me?

"What about you, Noah? Do you want a family?" I finally asked.

He seemed to study me for a minute, then said, "Down deep I've always thought, or wished, I'd find the right person to settle down with. And I guess that means having a family. In a perfect world, I think that if it's meant to be then, it'll happen and it'll be the right time too."

His eyes were beautiful in the fire's light, and I watched them as he traced my face with his fingers.

I said, "Even though this whole thing has made me sad, I'm pretty practical, and I know I'll be fine. It almost doesn't feel that it was a pregnancy, if that makes any sense."

Jezebel wove her way around my legs and I reached down to pet her.

"I know everyone deals with miscarriage in their own way. I think I'd feel differently if we were planning on having a baby. I may still be in shock, but I'm not sure what I feel. I feel detached; like it hasn't really happened. Does this make me a terrible person?" I asked, hoping I hadn't disappointed him.

He pulled me up so we could lie on the sofa and watch the fire. "I don't think you're a terrible person, Annie. I think this all needs to settle in. And I think you're the strongest person I know. *And* I think you'll be just fine."

Noah turned to look at me with mischief in his eyes. "If I could, I'd love to show you how much I care about you by making love to you all night.... but I'll just have to wait and show you when you're ready."

"I'd love that too, Noah. And I'll let you know just as soon as I know myself." Then I kissed him.

The next morning, a couple from Los Angeles checked in, and I showed them to their cabin. We gave them number one, Woodhaven, which had been the first to be renovated. I was dying to hear what they thought about it. When I opened the door to the cabin and walked them in, the wife said, "This is perfect! Oh, my gosh...I could stay here forever..."

It was just what I needed to hear. I showed them how to light the fireplace, and then I said, "If you need anything, let me or Sam know. We'll have muffins, coffee and OJ in the lobby tomorrow morning," I said, and turned to leave.

I felt unsinkable, and I was grateful for such a breathlessly beautiful mountain day. I loved it when the wind blew through the trees so that the sun could peek through, and I just stood there for a moment and took it all in.

I stopped in my cabin to give Laura a call. I'd expected to hear from her earlier, but I knew she would have wanted me to have my private time to deal with all this.

"Hey," I said. "Busy?"

"Hey. Are you doing okay?"

"I'm really good. And Noah has barely left my side. It feels good to know someone cares about me like that."

"We all do. I've worried about you, Annie."

"I'm fine."

"But how do you feel about all this?"

I knew at some point I'd have to tell her, so I did.

"Physically, I feel great. I have no side effects from the procedure. Mentally, I feel alert, content, and okay with it all."

"But don't you feel like you lost something? That something changed?"

"I thought I would, and I'm sure I'll have moments where I'm able to reflect on it all more clearly, but I didn't even know I was pregnant. So I wasn't happy or unhappy about it. It's obviously not a good time for me to have a baby, and I don't want one right now. I feel there'll be a time later, and then I'll feel differently about it."

"And how does Noah feel?" Laura asked.

"I think he's a little numb as well. He knows it's not the time for us to have a child. We're not ready for that yet. But I know it hurts him. Noah's funny though, in case you didn't know by now. He doesn't always let you know how he's feeling," I said. "We've promised each other we'd keep talking about it if we feel like it, and we both agree it's the healthy thing to do."

"Well, I'm glad you two are talking. And I get it. I'm not sure how I'd deal with it, but I feel for you."

"And I appreciate it. You've become a good friend, Laura, and I care about you, too. Oh, we also got our first guests and they love the new cabin."

Aside from Noah, Laura was the only person I was going to talk to about the miscarriage. And I felt a sense of relief when we hung up.

I went to the office, and as I walked in, Sam came around the counter and I gave him a high five.

"This is just the beginning," I said. I could feel it.

"You're in a good mood this morning," he said.

"I am. For a while there, I've felt my life was just a gigantic puzzle, and I finally feel the pieces are all fitting together." I nodded, confirming my feeling. "There's still a way to go, but it's getting there."

"So it seems to be."

"Sam, I talked to Ginny about being our vendor for breakfasts... she can provide us with muffins and coffeecake. We could make coffee and stock orange juice in the refrigerator. Would you call her and ask if I could pick something up this afternoon? I'm thinking we could get enough for a couple of days and then freeze the rest for the next guests. Once we get up and running, we can get regular deliveries from her."

"Will do, Boss," Sam said, saluting me but smiling.

I'd noticed Ginny was stopping by more frequently, bringing Sam lunch and spending an hour or so with him. Now and then, I'd see or hear her leave in the morning. They were great friends and I could sense how they felt comfortable with each other. I'd secretly wondered if they spent intimate time together, then laughed to myself for even thinking about that. It wasn't like they were ancient! And they both deserved the companionship!

"And I'll stop at the store today to get plates, utensils, and napkins," I said. I'd set out some current brochures of things to do, and I was glad the new sofa and chairs were already in to spruce up the lobby.

The week before Thanksgiving, we had a last-minute reservation for the long weekend and I was so excited I could hardly stand it. We'd planned on a quiet dinner with Sam and Ginny on Thursday, and my parents wanted us to come to Arizona for the rest of the weekend, so I was beginning to feel stressed.

"I can handle it," Sam assured me when I told him. "You two go have a good time with your folks."

On Wednesday, I had a hair appointment with Laura.

"I'm going down to Jason's," she said. "I've never done it before, but we're going to cook a turkey. His mother and mother-in-law will be there to supervise, so I can't do too much damage."

"So things are going well?"

"He's talked about me moving in with him....."

I looked at her in the mirror. She stopped working on my hair.

"So you thought you'd just drop the bomb on me, eh? Sounds like you're going to have to make some big decisions soon. How do the families feel?"

"To tell you the truth, they're actually good with it. They think it'll give the kids stability. And I like both sets of parents."

"Have you looked at local salons to see if there are any that appeal to you?" I asked.

"I've checked out a few, and the rent is definitely a lot more than it is up here. But I found one that looked really nice, and the owner said she had extra walk-ins I could take to start out with. I think this is the one, Annie. He's terrific and the kids and I really get along. They actually want a mom, which is a bonus."

"Instant motherhood," I mused again. I'd been there.

"I'm a little stressed."

"Well, if I can do anything, all you have to do is let me know. I can't thank you enough for being there for me when I needed you."

226

"That's what friends are for, silly," she said. "What are you two doing for Thanksgiving?"

"Ginny's making a turkey, and we'll eat at the restaurant. Then we're going to see my parents."

"They'll love Noah. I know it."

"It'll be a little awkward. But I'm sure it'll be fine."

"Just try to enjoy yourselves."

"Thanks for the advice; I'll leave you a huge tip!" And we both laughed.

Ginny assured me she had everything under control for dinner, so when we got to the restaurant, Noah opened the bottle of wine we'd brought. He poured us all a glass while Ginny and I brought everything to the table.

"To the cabins," I toasted once we were seated.

"To the cabins," everyone chimed in.

CHAPTER THIRTY THREE

In the five years since they'd moved to Prescott, I'd only visited my parents three times, and those were all without David. Prescott and my parents weren't on his 'to do list.' They knew when they moved there they were moving away from me and Long Beach, and I fully supported their decision. They wanted a different way of life than the hustle and bustle that was growing more hectic for them. I respected that. It wasn't as though Loni was near; she'd moved several times since her marriage.

There really wasn't anything for them to do if they came to visit me, and the one time they came out didn't work out well. The problem was that David made them feel uncomfortable in our home. He'd try to find out what they were going to do by saying things like, "Well, I'm busy today." Or "Where are you off to? It's not like there's anything new to do here," instead of saying something like, "What do you feel like doing today?" He could have *acted* like he was genuinely interested. They thought he was trying to find out when they planned on leaving.

After their first trip out, they started making subtle comments about the fact that no one wanted to come visit them. Eventually, I sensed the resentment on both our sides growing, so I was the one who was nominated to travel. And I honestly didn't look forward to making the trip out there. There were only so many times you can tour a town and surrounding areas, so mostly it was just sitting around and doing nothing. Most people might consider that relaxing. To me, it was stressful. I usually brought something to work on, since I could think of a hundred things I needed to do at home. Unlike David, I always kept a smile on my face and tried to never let on I was restless.

But now I truly missed them, and even though I called them frequently, I looked forward to seeing them for a couple of days.

My parents lived in a charming mobile home park, whose entrance was off the road just enough that if you weren't looking for it, you'd miss the sign and the road leading in. Nestled deep within the park, which was surrounded by gigantic pine trees, was a mini forest.

"I never expected this," Noah said as we slowed to the five mile an hour speed limit to cross over a small bridge.

Mostly filled with full-time residents, occasionally temporary spaces were available. Motor homes filled most of them for the holiday, and they'd decorated their areas with fall florals and pumpkins.

About half way into the park there was a small town square with western-style buildings with hand-painted signs. The Post Office, where residents could pick up and drop off their mail, was the smallest. Then next to it was the park office, disguised as the General Store, a Jail, and the Saloon complete with western style shutter doors. The owner of the park lived there year round, and their home was built like a log cabin. Outside on their front lawn was a large painted green wagon filled with fall flowers to add some color.

"There's even a creek," Noah said.

Until he said that, I hadn't given the park much thought. I suddenly realized why my parents had been so attracted to it; in a way, it was recreating the feeling of being in the mountains.

When I introduced them to David, I never thought about how they felt; I just assumed they'd like who I liked. But now, I had to admit; I felt a little nervous about how my parents would receive Noah. The moment we got there, though, I could immediately tell they liked him, and I could see Noah was relaxed and comfortable around them, too.

After initial introductions and hugs, I saved my mother, and us, the embarrassment of mentioning sleeping arrangements.

"Which room is Noah's?" I asked.

My mother had laid out a small lunch and she and my father acted like normal parents, making small talk trying to get to know a new person. They asked Noah a hundred questions about himself, and how he came to live in the mountains.

My mother had sworn she'd never color her hair, but I could tell she'd started getting it done, for even the small amount of gray she'd had, had disappeared. She wore new glasses but most of the time she forgot to put them on so I could tell the squint lines had deepened between her brows. On the other hand, my father's face was still smooth as a baby's skin. He'd never had much of a beard, and only his temples were showing some gray. He looked very distinguished.

After declining a need for a nap, we cleaned up, and my parents took us on the first of several tours of Prescott.

Because of the holiday weekend, the museum itself was closed, but we walked the grounds of the Sharlot Hall Museum, which was the restored governor's mansion.

"She lived in the attic while she built the museum," my mother said.

It was growing darker and the Courthouse Square was starting to light up for the holiday season. I'd never seen how pretty it was during this time of year.

We ended up in the dining room at the Hassayampa Inn. Built in the late twenties, I could appreciate the Spanish Colonial Revival décor with the hand painted ceiling and beams in the lobby. I would have loved to have had a project with such character.

The next day we visited antique shops, and I found treasures both for Noah's cabin and mine. We stopped in the Peregrine Book Co., and while my mother and I looked for new novels, Noah bought a book about Prescott. Then we went to Willow Lake. It reminded me of Lake Arrowhead, without all the homes built around it. Noah and my father walked the loop around the lake while my mother and I just sat on one of the picnic benches and enjoyed the calm.

"I didn't realize how beautiful it was here," I said.

"It's always been beautiful, but I wonder if you're seeing it through fresh eyes now. I believe you like Noah."

"I do, and he's very sweet. I feel like I can talk to him, although I think I frighten him a little with all my ideas."

"You can do that to someone."

"I should probably tell you now that I've bought some cabins and I've been restoring them." I knew if I waited any longer to tell my parents, they would consider it to be an insult, especially my father.

"Oh," was all my mother said.

We were quiet awhile longer, then she said, "Sounds like you're going to stay up there?"

"I want to, for now," I answered, closing my eyes and taking in the sun. It was surprisingly warm for the end of November.

"I think you're happy," my mother said, patting my hand.

We had dinner at the Palace Saloon, across the street from the Courthouse on what's known as Whiskey Row. Noah's eyes lit up the moment we walked in. On one wall was a huge carved bar, and they filled the opposite wall with mounted deer heads and old photos.

We ordered, then Noah and my father went back to look at the glass cases of memorabilia.

I heard my father say as they made their way back to the table, "We didn't have cowboys and Indians where I came from."

I could tell it took Noah a moment to register the comment before he smiled.

"No cowboys, eh?"

I knew then my father approved of him.

"It says here," Noah said, reading the brochure on our table, "there have been several major fires here, but in 1900, patrons of the saloon actually picked up the bar and carried it out of the burning building. They set it down across the street, continued drinking, and watched the other side of the street burn. They rebuilt it at a cost of $50,000."

"Here's our food," my father soon said, and we ate like we were starving.

When I had some quiet time alone with my parents, I shared more of the details about the divorce, and I could tell my parents were concerned for me and disappointed I was facing this set back. It would have been a perfect opportunity to tell them they'd been right about my choices, but the stubborn streak in me held me back.

I tried to remember when I'd last seen my parents; was it Loni's wedding? When you don't see someone for a while, all the changes in a person are more noticeable. I'd seen them in my parents, and I wondered what they thought of seeing me. Had I changed in their eyes? Was I still a child? I could tell they were encouraged by meeting Noah and hearing about all the changes in my lifestyle. I knew they felt I was taking on more projects than I should, but as usual, they kept their comments to themselves.

My father hugged me and said, "I think you made the right decision; life is too short to spend it being unhappy. Right?" Then he fondly kissed my mother on the cheek, and for the first time I could see their relationship from a more adult point of view. It was what I one day hoped for, for myself; being with someone I loved, and with someone who loved me back.

On Sunday morning, after an enormous home cooked breakfast, my parents and I stood outside as Noah packed up the car.

"Put the snacks so we can reach them," I reminded him.

A small dog was barking, and I noticed a man in one of the temporary spaces next to them was unloading his car using a small shopping cart he'd obviously taken from the store. He was filling an outside cabinet with some of the groceries he'd bought, and he set the rest inside the open door of the motor home. It looked somewhat permanently fixed, and I asked my mother about him.

"That's George. This used to be their second home, but his wife had Alzheimer's and he had to sell their big house to be able to put her in a home. She died last year, so he lives here now."

"What does he do all day?" I whispered.

"He reads and enjoys the park."

We waved goodbye as we drove away. For some reason, it reminded me of the last time we drove away from the lake house, only this time I wasn't unhappy.

The first thing I said when we got in the car was, "My parents like you."

"But of course. What did you expect?"

"They're growing older," I said thoughtfully.

Noah turned to look at me and said, "Of course they are. You're lucky you still have them."

I hadn't thought about his parent's deaths when I said that, and I immediately regretted it.

"I'm sorry, Noah. I didn't think."

"You didn't do anything. I thought about my parents when we were with yours, and I wished they were still here. I always will. But they're not, and that's something I've just had to live with."

He put his hand on my knee and I patted it.

"Your sunglasses make you look cool," I said, giving him a quick smile.

"Thanks, that's what I wanted; to be cool."

I touched his face, and his stubble was rough. He'd shaved his beard off a few weeks ago, and he hadn't shaved while we were in Arizona. I wondered if he was going to grow it back. Whatever he did, he always looked handsome to me.

It wasn't until we were partially up the mountain that we could see we'd missed the first snow of the season. I was totally disappointed. I wanted to watch the snow falling and to see it gradually covering the roads and trees.

The roads had been plowed, and the berms were still beautifully white and not discolored by mud. When we got to the cabins, it looked like a white blanket had covered the ground. It was about four inches thick, and tree boughs were heavy with the new snow. The parking area and grounds looked clean and white. I loved it!

Noah cleared the walkways to the office and the cabins while I brought in our bags. The cats were hungry, and I let them out. I couldn't help but laugh as I watched them jump in the snow, trying to avoid getting their paws wet.

Finishing my own cabin was next, so that Monday I went into the floor covering store to order my blinds. I saw Melissa and the owner Wendy, and I mentioned I was going to be looking for another client if anyone happened to mention they needed a designer.

"I was hoping you'd stop in soon," Wendy said. "We're actually looking for someone to work maybe one day a week if you're interested. You're good with colors, and style, and if you sell the job, we'll take care of measuring and installation."

"Really? I'm flattered," I replied. I was.

"You can work with our window coverings and all flooring and we can even advertise we have a designer if you're open to that."

"Let me think about it for a minute..." I said. I put my forefinger to my lips and pretended to think. "Sounds great!" I quickly said, smiling. It could be a perfect way to get into some new projects, and to meet more new people. "Let me know what day you think you'll need me and I'm sure I can make it work."

I was finally beginning to blossom again. I sensed a lightness in my step as I left the store, and was feeling very optimistic. It also felt like another piece of the puzzle had fallen into place.

When I told Noah about the job offer, he was excited to tell me he was starting a new remodeling project and his customer was interested in having me help them with the remodeling design along with decorating. This would be our first project together.

There had been three new reservations at the cabins, and I couldn't help but sigh in relief. I'd made arrangements with the town furniture store to provide the mattresses for the cabins, and I put their cards where visitors could see them. They'd already called to let me know someone had come in and ordered not only mattresses but a complete bedroom set for their home up here. They'd stayed in one of the cabins while their house was being painted and fell in love with the store.

And then a young couple had come in to talk to me about booking the cabins for their wedding guests next summer. It would be a perfect place for them to stay before the wedding since they were all from down the hill. Sam and I worked out a group rate, and I hoped they'd be calling us back.

I heard from our attorney that David had agreed to the new settlement agreement and that he was going to sell our house after all. I found I didn't have the least bit of compassion for him now, and while part of me felt relief that my feelings for him were growing indifferent, another part of me was concerned I was seeing a side of me that I'd not known was there; that of becoming unforgiving and coldhearted. And I didn't particularly like it.

Before Christmas, we had our first big rain storm.

"I haven't seen clouds so low and dark in a long time. We're in for a good one." Sam said.

Thunder crashed as clouds collided. I loved hearing it and seeing the sky burst. I wanted it to rain. I was ready to cleanse the trees and land—and myself.

Wind blew leaves from the trees, and then moved them along the ground. Even though it rained hard, I loved the sound it made on the roof of my cabin. I hoped all our roofs would make it through the season..

Everyone I came across commented on how they loved the rain, but within a few days, most people were over it and complained, wishing it would go away.

"When it's hot, I wish it was cold," Sam said. "And when it's cold, I wish it was warmer. Just can't win, can we?"

It stayed cold enough that the rain turned into snow and a few days before Christmas, we had our first major snowfall. And since I didn't know what to expect as far as people coming up to stay with us for the Christmas holiday, so I was pleasantly surprised when two families booked the week between Christmas and New Year. I made sure we had Christmas wrapped chocolates on their pillows and cookies and lots of hot cider and cocoa in the lobby next to the small tree I'd decorated.

My parents invited us to spend some time with them again, but I really wanted to stay up in the mountains. It was my first Christmas there, and I thought it would be romantic to spend time with Noah. We'd decided not to spend a lot of money on each other; I still had a lot of expenses with the cabins and he was saving to finish a few major things around his property.

On Christmas Eve we stayed at Noah's, sitting by his fire with his dog Rufus, opening our small gifts, drinking wine, then making love. On Christmas Day, we slept in, and then had muffins and orange juice before heading over to Ginny's, where she made a wonderful brunch before we exchanged gifts.

I'd heard Noah mention wanting a knife, and I enjoyed watching him open his buck knife in a leather shield.

"Thanks, Babe," he said.

I got Sam a Swiss pocket knife, since he was always working on projects, and since Ginny always wore aprons, I had two of them personalized with the coffee shop's name and logo. Noah, Ginny and Sam had chipped in and bought me a metal branch coat rack that we could keep in the office.

While there was still plenty of snow on the ground, I was disappointed we didn't have a fresh dusting for our guests to wake up to. No matter what they say, everyone wants to come up to the mountains for a white Christmas.

I wanted one as well, and my wish came true.

CHAPTER THIRTY FOUR

Alyce

When Mama went into the home, I took over all the bookkeeping. I'd made up a sheet for the two tenants, listing their rent, if they'd paid a deposit when they moved in, and I discovered Mama had been paying all the utilities and not charging anyone for them. I didn't raise any rents, but I let them know they needed to pay their share of everythin'. I added that information to their sheet and told them that when the bills came in, I'd pay them, but I'd split each one in half, and they could pay me back. I also hired a gardener. There was more dirt than lawn or flowers, and the yard needed sprucing up.

Two years later, Mama died.

Mostly, I didn't want anythin' from her house, but we had to clear it out so we could get it rented. Jerry and the kids went with me, and I figured I could take a quick look at everythin' and set aside what I thought we could donate. I'd always wanted a hope chest when I was growing up, so I suggested my daughter take the blanket chest Mama kept at the foot of her bed. We went through all the kitchen things so see what was worth keepin'.

I went through her clothin' first, and there wasn't anythin' there I wanted to keep. I gave my son the job to toss all the underwear in Mama's dresser, but to leave me anything else. I filled boxes with trinkets, her jewelry box and photo albums so I could look through them when I felt like it.

We had a yard sale, and someone bought her vases of fake flowers and her porta-potty and all the old towels she had. Goodwill came and got everythin' that didn't sell.

We painted and put in new linoleum and carpet, and I put a FOR RENT sign out in the front yard. I must have had twenty calls from people driving by. We found a nice family to rent Mama's house, and I let them bring their cat. I told them this was the house I'd grown up in, and I expected them to take care of it and treat it like their home.

About a month later, when I found a few minutes to start sortin' through the things I'd brought home, I started with Mama's jewelry box. Inside it, she'd kept Daddy's Purple Heart Medal, along with the others he'd received. He only had one tie pin, but I found all his pocket knives and his weddin' ring. He hadn't worn it much that I remembered; he always worried he might get it caught in the tools he used throughout his life. I kept all his things, but only a few pieces of jewelry that I remembered Mama wearin'. I gave the rest to my daughter and then donated what she didn't want to a local thrift store.

Then I started with the photos. I sorted them into four stacks; one for what I wanted to keep, one each for the two kids, and one of people I didn't recognize. I couldn't see any reason to keep those, so I tossed them.

I went through Mama's souvenirs from different places that had meant something to her, and then I came across the old newspaper articles about Daddy and Smitty. I didn't know what I expected, for I knew she still had them. They still took still took my breath away.

I wasn't angry anymore; I just felt like an old wound had been picked at, and it was startin' to bleed again.

I was still sittin' in my chair when Jerry came home that day. I told him I'd found the newspaper clippins', and how it'd opened everythin' up again. I held up the newspapers; he'd never seen them.

"I don't know what to do," I said.

"I don't think there's anything you can do."

"I don't want to tell the kids," I finally said. "Anyway, everyone's dead now. There's no one else who knows."

"I know it isn't what you want to hear, Alyce, but I think you should just quit trying to figure it out. You don't know why he did it, and what you do know, is that your mother thought she was making the best decision to keep it from you. That's what you just said you wanted to do with the kids. You're trying to protect them, aren't you?"

I tried to show him the newspapers, but he just shrugged.

"I wish you would burn them," he said gently.

But I couldn't quit thinkin' about it. I thought about it to the point I couldn't sleep at night. I was used up, it eatin' at me like it did. I'd lived so many years believin' my world was one way, only to find out it had all been a lie. I was furious with Daddy because he'd taken his life, but I couldn't figure out why he had to kill Smitty and his family. What had they done? What was it that it had to end so bad?

I was also fiery mad at Mama again, too. I know she was tryin' to protect me from the truth, but knowin' and understandin' that, didn't seem to make me feel better. But then, wasn't that what I was wantin' to do with my own kids? Keepin' this secret? Isn't that what Jerry said?

I really wasn't sure why I felt that if I saw where Daddy committed suicide, I'd find some sort of closin'. Of course nothin' would be as it was almost thirty years ago, but if the cabin was still there, maybe I could see it firsthand.

Then, I finally had the nerve to make the call.

"We don't have much snow left," the lady on the phone said, I'm sure, thinking that's why I was calling.

"I'm callin' about cabin number five."

"Cabin number five hasn't been restored yet and isn't in use at this time," she'd also said. "But we have others open."

"I'd actually like to see it before it's restored if I could."

I was even more determined now to go up.

When Jerry asked if he could go with me, I understood he thought I was crazy and that I needed someone to be with me. I tried to be as nice as possible with my response, but the answer was still 'No.'

I'd go on my own. I felt I needed this time to myself.

I would make the trip when she called me back. I'd probably only be gone for a day or so.

CHAPTER THIRTY FIVE

Right after Christmas, I had a call from a woman who was interested in coming up, but wanted to know if cabin number five was available. I explained that we were in the process of restoring all the cabins and we hadn't gotten to that one yet, but that she was welcome to stay in any of the other ones.

She wanted that one in particular, which I thought was interesting.

"I'd actually like to see it before it's restored if I could," she said. She left her number and asked if I'd call her when I thought I was getting close to working on it.

Her name was Alyce Murphy.

On the third Wednesday in January, Alyce Murphy checked in. She looked to be in her mid-forties. It was hard to tell. She was attractive, although her skin was splotchy, and she wore a heavy coat and black boots. I wondered if she'd always worn her hair pulled tightly back into a ponytail because the hair around her face had noticeably thinned. Although she had red lipstick on, her face was drawn and she had dark circles under her eyes.

As Alyce filled in her registration, I was curious to find out why cabin number five was so important to our newest guest, but I kept my interest in check. She *seemed* to be genuine when she said, "I love this setting. The cabins look comfortable...and very charming." But she was remote, and I could tell she was a little apprehensive.

"Thanks, I just bought them this last summer, mostly because I felt so relaxed up here. And it's turned out to be a positive change for me." I didn't feel the need to share my life story with her, so I left it at that.

"Where are you from?" Alyce asked.

"From Long Beach."

"*Oh my gosh*, I'm originally from Paramount." She momentarily let her defenses down, and she smiled.

"I went to Jordan High School," I said, which was about a mile south of there. "I can't believe how many people I've run into who are from near where I lived. My father used to remind me to behave when I was young, because when I grew older, I might run into those people again and have to apologize for something I'd done. It was his Chinese superstition, I think, but it's true."

I watched her as she took in her surroundings, her eyes focusing from one section of the lobby to another. I wondered what she thought.

"Have you been to the mountains before?" I asked.

"I've never been here...but my father has..."

"*Really.*" I waited for more and when Alyce offered nothing, I asked, "and when was that?"

"Oh, over almost thirty years ago."

Thirty years? I tried to hide my astonishment.

"Wow. That's a long time ago. From what I understand, they only used cabin number five for storage. Do you know for sure it's number five?"

"Yes."

I'd never find out what her story was unless I came right out and asked, but I sensed she wasn't ready to tell me. So, instead, I said, "I can take you to your cabin if you'd like."

Alyce picked up her one bag, and followed me, our footsteps on the gravel echoing loudly in the silence.

"I can't believe how quiet it is up here," she said, looking up at the trees. She sounded a little more relaxed.

"It's the same way I felt when I first came up here."

I unlocked cabin three and turned on the light, and was disappointed when she didn't comment on the way it looked. So I just said, "Here you go. We've named this one Cedar Lodge."

Still pre-occupied, Alyce asked, "Even though you said it's a mess, I'm grateful to you for lettin' me see it." She set her bag down on the bed and looked around the room. "This is very *charming*," she finally said. "Did you do this?"

I was immediately unhappy with myself for placing so much emphasis on myself instead of focusing on Alyce's obvious issues.

"This is great," Alyce sighed loudly. "I'm starving; is there a place where I can get somethin' to eat?"

I told her about Ginny's and the Sports Bar and said she'd be happy with either.

"I have a map in the office."

"See you in a few minutes," Alyce said, taking the few things she'd brought out of her bag and setting them all on the dresser.

I poked my head back in and said, "I almost forgot. Let me show you how to start the fire; you'll want one. It really warms up the cabin and, personally, I love snuggling under the covers when the fire's lit."

When she came back into the office, I gave her a map and showed her where Ginny's was. I thought she'd be more comfortable with the atmosphere there.

"We also have muffins, coffee and orange juice for morning. So when you're ready, just come into the lobby."

"Our guest, Alyce Murphy, is interesting," I said to Noah. "She's the one who insisted on seeing cabin number five; she called just after Christmas. The guys are coming in the morning to move everything out of the cabin, and I'm dying to know what she's looking for."

"Five's the one that had the bats, right?"

"Ugh. Don't remind me. But yes. Hopefully she'll talk to me tomorrow."

The next morning, I sat with Alyce while she had juice and muffins in the lobby. I'd pulled my hair back into a ponytail and forgone makeup. Alyce wasn't wearing any either, and she looked like she had gotten little sleep. By the way she bounced her leg while she ate, I could sense her apprehension with the morning's events. The men were due any minute, and in no time, I heard their truck pull in. When I told her they were here, she leaped from the chair and, in doing so, caught her foot in her purse strap. She made a heavy landing on the hardwood flooring, and while she recovered quickly, I could see her face had turned almost crimson. She'd be sore in the morning.

"Why don't you lock that in your cabin?" I suggested, pointing to her purse. "You won't really need it while we're checking everything out."

"Good idea." She brushed herself off. "What a dork."

Most of the pungent odor of the bats had dissipated, but the cabin still smelled musty when I opened the door. I could immediately see her spirits sink.

"Let's just start," I said as we opened the folding table I'd left near the door. "This can be our staging area. It'll be a lot easier than bending over."

We each grabbed a box from inside and set it down.

"Should I just open it?" Alyce asked hesitantly.

"Go for it," I said lightly.

They were both filled with old business records that dated back over thirty years, so we could likely toss them.

"Let's put these to the side and I'll ask Sam if he wants to keep anything."

Then we each grabbed an end of a dresser and brought it out. I pulled out the drawers and checked inside and under them for anything of interest. There was nothing, so I asked Alyce to help me set it aside. There would be four areas; one for "keep", one for "consignment" and one each for "toss" and "donate". I'd already arranged with the consignment thrift store in town to take anything that would be in good enough shape to sell.

I asked the two young men to start bringing out the rest of the furniture so we could see what, if anything, could give us any clues to the past. Everything got the once over, and like any treasure hunter, I was hopeful there would be *something* of interest, whether it had to do with what Alyce was looking for or just a surprise. Other than old drawer lining paper, so far there had been little. As we inspected each piece, I had the men put it in its respective pile.

I could tell Alyce was interested in seeing everything inside, so I told her to go ahead and look at whatever she wanted to.

"I'm dying to know, though," I finally said "what it is about this cabin that interests you?"

Alyce stiffened, then relaxed. "Daddy died here."

I came to an abrupt stop. "*What?*"

"He hung himself."

"*Oh my God!*" I'd said it aloud before I realized it. I'd never heard anything so awful, and I tried to disguise my shock.

"I was just thirteen."

"Oh, my god...I'm so sorry for you." I could still hardly believe it. Just thinking about it made me shudder. "I'm sure you don't want my butting in. I'm sorry."

Alyce tried to camouflage her desperation, but tears filled her eyes, anyway.

"Do you want to stop?" I asked.

"No. I know I'm not gonna' find anythin' here, and part of me accepts that. My mama just died, and she'd been tryin' to tell me for several years that my father committed suicide. When I was young, she told me he'd had a heart attack."

For once in my life, I was without words. I took Alyce's arm and said, "Are you going to be okay?"

"I don't know."

"Well, let's keep looking and see if we can find something. If you feel like it, you can talk to me."

As we made our way into the cabin, we stepped through clumps of dust and we both sneezed. An old moth-eaten handmade quilt I could imagine was lovely in its day, was draped over a dresser. I asked the men to take out the old mattresses.

"These definitely need to be tossed," I said, pinching my nose. "And these old threadbare broken chairs. I don't know why anyone would have kept them."

Once all the furniture was out and thoroughly examined, I decided not to keep any of it. I asked the guys if they'd take a load to the dump to make a dent in the yard.

To Alyce I said, "Do you want to take a break?"

"No, I'm good," she said.

"Then, let's look in these boxes next."

Mostly we found more bookkeeping records. The next group of boxes were dated and filled with old photographs and guest registers. The mood changed instantly as we found more boxes, dating back to 1928, approximately when the cabins were built!

Alyce looked at me in anticipation, and even I had to admit, I felt a flutter of excitement.

"Let's take these to the office. We can sort through them later, if you can stand it." I looked at Alyce. "Let's keep looking."

We found a couple of shoe boxes; one with a tortoise shell mirror with hazy glass and tarnished silver, and the other with old letters. But there was nothing left of real interest that could shed any light on our mystery; only some old women's clothing in the closet, some extra musty blankets, some old books (that I would keep and try to de-odorize), some old paintings (that I would also keep), two mantel clocks, a set of bronze bear bookends, and some old crystal ash trays.

Alyce said, once again resigned, "I think the guest book might be the only thing of interest, and maybe even then he could have checked in under a different name."

"Well, let's get these into the office and get ourselves cleaned up. I'll make us some sandwiches. Then we can see if we can find something of interest. The guys can finish cleaning out the cabin," I said.

With boxes in hand, we made a few trips back to the office and left them in a stack on the floor.

"I'll be back in a few minutes." Alyce said. I could tell she wanted to be by herself for a while, which was understandable.

I made turkey sandwiches and set them, along with sodas and some chips, on the coffee table.

"There's something about the mountain air," I said. "Since I've come up here, I'm always hungry."

"This looks good. Thanks."

We ate in comfortable silence for a few minutes, then I couldn't help myself.

"I've noticed a slight accent," I said. "Were you originally from the South somewhere?"

"Ah, no. Everyone asks me that. It's just me talkin' like my folks did. They were from the Midwest, and I haven't been able to shake the habit. My husband has tried, but after a while it gets annoyin' when he points it out. I've at least made sure my kids pronounce their words correctly."

"So," I ventured, "do you work?"

"At the gas company in Long Beach." Alyce looked at the painting over the fireplace. "Besides this, are you a decorator?"

"I am."

"Well, you're pretty talented."

"Thanks."

I shared the short version of how I ended up here, not wanting to bore her with the details.

"I've been divorced, too. My husband now, Jerry, is really good to me and my kids. Daddy died a while ago, and Mama just died last year. That's when I found out he killed a man and his family. And then he killed himself. Here."

She looked down at her sandwich and set it down.

"Kinda' takes my appetite away."

About ten minutes later, Alyce picked up her sandwich and said, "Well, let's get back at it."

I decided to start with the box marked 1960-70. I'd let Alyce go through the registers.

"Let me know if you recognize anyone famous," I said. "We could keep the page and frame it."

She carefully read each name while I sorted through paperwork and photos. They were of people and places I'd never be able to identify; a couple photos of town, with snow-covered cars and trees, looked like something the museum might want, so I set those aside.

I brought out two more sodas and started on another box.

"This might be it," Alyce finally said, nervously handing me the book. "It says John Smith, which is not his name; he was John Murphy, and the man he killed was Ralph Smith."

A chill went through me, and I involuntarily shuddered.

"The heck with this Coke," I said "I need some wine."

"I'll have some too."

I poured two glasses and then sat back down.

"You don't owe me any explanations, but since we've come this far... what are you going to do?"

Alyce scratched her head in thought. "I've thought about nothin' but that for months. My husband says I need to understand I just might not figure it out, and I need to resign myself to that. Of course, when someone else can be logical with you, it doesn't make you feel like being more logical yourself. I know Daddy loved me, and I think I just need to forgive him for what he did, and leave it at that. Mama protected me for all these years, and I don't know how she was able to go on with her life the way she did."

"Well, I've certainly had nothing like that happen to me, so I can't say that I've had to live through something like this, but I'm going with your husband on this. You don't have enough information to figure out what happened, or more, why. It must have been something so overwhelming to him, that he felt he had no choice. I have to admit, that's just awful to think about..."

"It is." She shrugged. "I'd like to stay tonight, if that's okay with you. I'll leave in the morning."

"That's fine with me. Take all the time you need."

We finished our wine in silence, then Alyce went back to her cabin.

Even though a chill was in the air, Alyce sat outside bundled up in her heavy coat and a blanket and watched the activity as the cabin was beginning its path to renovation. Strips of old carpet and padding were outside, along with an old vanity and toilet. The guys needed to make at least one more load to the dump.

I watched her from the office, and couldn't help but think how easy it was to bring new life to something like the cabins. After all, they were just material things, and all you had to do was tear out what you didn't want, and replace it with what would fix the problem. If only we could do that with our lives; cut out the mistakes and bad spots, and replace them with something better.

When Sam pulled in, I helped him unload his groceries, and then walked back toward cabin five. I'd let the girls out and Socks decided to check Alyce out. I watched as she first sniffed the blanket at her feet, and when she decided it was okay, she jumped onto her lap.

"Hey, kitty," Alyce said softly, making a kissing sound with her lips.

Socks took that as an invitation to sniff Alyce's lips, and once satisfied, she curled into a ball and made herself comfortable. I could visibly see the tension in Alyce's body release. I knew she was hurting, and I wished there was something I could do to help her. I had my own issues, but unlike hers, so far they'd been ones I could face head on, and with *living* people. It didn't make the problems any easier, but at least I could fight back.

"Hey," I said, as I came up to her. "I see you have a friend."

"Hey," she replied. "I do. And it's sort of mindless to watch them work. They're making a lot of progress."

With everything now out of there, a lot of the mustiness was gone, and I knew cleaning and oiling the pine walls would make an enormous improvement. It wouldn't be long before this cabin was finished, and I was looking forward to it.

I stayed in my own cabin that night, hoping that if Alyce felt like talking, she could come to me. But after a quick dinner from Ginny's, I came home, fell into bed, and never heard another thing.

Alyce left that next morning without saying goodbye.

Part Four

As it Turns Out

It's been almost a year since it all began. The part of the journey that alternated between humiliation and unhappiness is now mostly behind me. Enough time has passed that many of the sharp edges have grown smoother. The ten pounds I'd gained over the years have fallen off because I've been so active, and I feel attractive again.

Where I'd momentarily lost my confidence, I've quickly recovered it. I feel myself continue to blossom. And I believe I can do almost anything.

When I see a baby now, I'm drawn to it, and I always make a point to comment on how beautiful he or she is. I never used to do that, and I'm sure it's because I think about losing *my* baby. But then I sometimes wonder if I'm still untouched by the loss because I've never wept. Maybe I never will. When Noah and I talk about it, I see the pain in his eyes, and I'm sure he feels this was a child for us. I fight back tears of my own to see him this way.

But for some reason, it still doesn't feel real to me. And I wonder how long the thought of having children is going to remain an open one for me.

My divorce is final and I'm satisfied with the outcome. David decided against buying me out of the house, and he sold the property in Fallbrook. I imagine him at some point buying something else, a bachelor pad, which would suit his needs better.

The last time I was down in Long Beach visiting an old client, I drove by our old house. Since I'd loved this one with all my heart, I'd wondered if I could ever be happy with another house. I felt an initial mix of affection and apprehension as I got closer. I pulled over and sat across the street. My heart fluttered, but within minutes two children ran out on to the front yard and tumbled down the slope to the sidewalk. They stepped on the flowers I'd planted so long ago while chasing each other.

I realized someone else loves this house as much as I did. I also understood there were so many other places I could live and be happy; up here in the mountains, being one.

While sometimes I try to banish them, thoughts of David continue to come out of nowhere, penetrating my unconscious mind. I'm still angry with him for what he did to me, and I'm trying to forgive him. I hate the way I feel when something so negative consumes me and tries to take over my life. Sometimes, though, I had to admit I relished watching him, normally so sure of himself, losing the upper hand and being cut down for his deceit.

Mostly, though, my anger has been replaced with energy and believing the pieces of my life's puzzle will eventually all fall into place again. And they have begun to.

I know it takes two in any relationship, and while I didn't deserve the way he treated me, I've come to realize it wasn't just him...I didn't pay attention to our lives together, either. I've vowed to never repeat the mistakes I made.

I thought our marriage would end up happily ever after, whatever that truly means. And sometimes when I look at Noah, lying in our bed, tangled in our sheets, I'm in love with him; his face, his hair, his person. I know he would move mountains for me, and just knowing that, makes me care for him even more.

I know my impulsiveness sometimes frightens him, and yet I feel he is the one for me. I'm going to do my best to keep my part of the relationship going. This will be my second chance.

I see the sun more.

Life has a way of moving on. A woman who managed one of the three gas stations up here realized a lifelong dream of having a restaurant. She re-opened a favorite family-style restaurant on the main highway after her father died, leaving her some money. I'd only heard the locals talk about it, for it'd closed before I came up. The original owner had suffered a stroke. Everyone who drove by watched as they updated the interior with new flooring and upholstery, and they were still painting the exterior when they finally re-opened. The day the front door opened, there was a waiting line to get in.

Grayson's living room and dining room projects are finished, and he wants to start on the game room next. Someone must have been looking out for me when he arrived, for even with the financial complications the divorce brought on, I could finally give Sam the balance of the down payment I owed him, plus I started making payments on the loan itself. I finished paying for all the work we did in the cabins, and I've been able to set aside what was left, to live on while we build our bookings.

My friend Sarah designed and printed two brochures for me; one to use for the cabins, listing them each by name and showing their décor. And one for me as a designer up here, using the cabins plus adding the work I'd done for Grayson.

It was perfect timing when they came in, for I met a new client; a woman who is going to restore her mother's lake house cabin. Her name is Carrie Davis, and she spent her childhood up here. She eventually went down to Los Angeles for college, but wants to live here. Her mother, Elizabeth, had been up here since 1929, during prohibition, and I can only imagine how interesting her life would have been.

I think the *most* significant ending to this part of my story is that Sam started working on the mantel clocks we found in cabin number five, now the Pinecone Cabin. He got the first one cleaned and restored, keeping the aged patina of the wood. We decided to put it on the mantel in the office.

When he started working on the second one, inside the mechanism, he found a folded note that had, at the time, stopped the clock from working. We figured this must have been the clock in number five when John Murphy hung himself.

He rushed to get me and showed it to me. All it said was,

> *"When you find this, time has stopped for me.*
> *I am desperate and I can think of no other way to*
> *end this. I didn't mean to destroy their family. And*
> *now I'm destroying mine. I'm a terrible person. A*
> *monster. I can never forgive myself for what I've done.*
> *I love you both,"*
> *John*

"What will you do now?" Sam asked, watching me refold the note.

I was so taken by surprise, I was momentarily at a loss for words. I reached for his arm, as though I needed his support, but I did it more to think...to try to put my thoughts together. Obviously, this was what Alyce was looking for, and while it didn't answer her questions, it would show her how he felt. And that he was sorry.

I'm not sure why exactly, but my first thought was to let it be; to not tell Alyce about the note. She'd left here knowing she would probably *never* find any real closure to what led up to what her father did, and this note wouldn't give her any answers. All it would possibly do was open those wounds again, making her unhappy.

"I'll think on it." I said.

Spring brought out the daffodils that had lain dormant, and new buds sprouted on the trees that had lost their leaves in the fall. Spring also brought with it warmer temperatures and a long sigh of contentment.

And that's when I sent Alyce a note.

Dear Alyce,

I think of you often and hope this finds you at a point where you've found some peace. Rain and then snow fell after you left, covering the ground with water to cleanse and feed the soil. A rejuvenation of sorts. Crisp new leaves are covering all the bare trees, and tulips have begun to shine in the sun again.

When I think of all that, I think of you.

Sam found this folded and tucked into a mantle clock. It seems to have stopped the clock at 9.

I hope you have found forgiveness in your heart.

Fondly,
Annie Parker

It had all started under the warm skies of summer, when I first arrived in the mountains. It was incredible how slowly time passed, yet how quickly it swept by when I wasn't paying attention.

John Murphy

I originally came from Kansas where, like most families in the thirties, farmin' was what we did. We were one of the few farms raising cotton, while others around us raised wheat and corn. That's where I met and married Doris.

She was seventeen, and I was eighteen. It was one of those things you hear about, bein' love at first sight. She worked at the little general store in town where I'd go to pick up our supplies, and I knew the minute I saw her she was the one for me. I could tell she liked me, too, even though she was modest and bashful. She'd shift her eyes down and turn red when I looked her way.

Neither of our families had any money, so our weddin' was just a small town church one, with our Mamas and their friends makin' the food for afterwards. We got lots of handmade things, like sewn and embroidered flour sack towels, crocheted blankets and doilies, jars of canned jams and fruits, and a pair of knitted stockings for our first Christmas. It always amazed Doris how I'd remembered all that, but I reminded her she made me help address the dang thank-you notes to everyone afterwards..

I had only been with one gal before Doris. Kind of what you'd call a one-night stand. A couple of buddies talked me into going into a bar out of town so no one would recognize us, and after drinking too much, we each left with a girl. There were plenty of them there, looking for a good time. I was so clumsy, it was embarrassin'.

The next day, I not only felt like dung from drinkin' too much, but I was ashamed for what I'd done. I carried those dirty memories with me for many years.

Doris had never kissed anyone but me, and I loved her more for that.

I knew I didn't want to stay on the family farm—I had brothers who were determined to keep workin' the land, certain they could turn things around. But it was 1932 and things were bad everywhere; we'd had no rain for several years, and the land was dust.

When Doris' mama died, her daddy decided to move to California. We packed up everythin' we had into his pickup truck, and traded off the drivin'. I'd heard there was plenty of work out there and I was sure we could have a better life than what we'd have if we stayed. I went to a trade school and took a class on weldin' and got a job at the shipyards in Los Angeles Harbor, near San Pedro. Doris found a job at a department store, and every week we'd sit at the kitchen table of our little apartment and pool our money. After paying our rent, we'd deposit what we had left into our savins' account.

We were married almost two years before Doris got pregnant, and while I was happy to hear the news, it scared the devil out of me. Doris lost her job at the department store, so we moved in with her daddy. I found a second job doin' body and fender work for a shop in town, and worked weekends to make extra money. Doris worked cleanin' houses for a few of the dairy farmers in town. Her daddy would drive her and pick her up so I could take our one car to work. When she was seven months pregnant, the swelling in her ankles and feet was so bad, her doctor told her to stop workin' and keep her feet up. We were both afraid somethin' would happen to the baby if she didn't quit her job, so that's what she did.

There was no room for a baby in the house, so we took the service porch and made it into a bedroom. It was only big enough for a crib and Doris hated the idea, but I reasoned with her that a baby wouldn't know the difference, and that in no time, we'd buy somethin' of our own and have more room.

On the day Alyce was born, I was scared shitless. This beautiful baby girl was mine, and when I first set eyes on her, I didn't know what to do. Panic was an option, but I reasoned with myself that we'd be just fine, and I assured myself I'd be able to provide for my family.

I bought us a Kodak box camera, and we must have took pictures every day. I loved seeing Doris with the baby, and we gave thanks she was so good natured. I loved to hold her high above my head, but stopped doin' that when one day, I had spit up all over my face. You wonder what a baby thinks, always bein' cleaned and fed and held. I figured out soon enough; they think the world revolves around them, and I guess it does.

About a year later, we bought the house next door to Doris's daddy, which made them both happy, and that's all I ever wanted; was for her to be happy. It was such a tiny house, only one bedroom and one bathroom, but we both felt it was worth it to have something of our own.

While I never planned on ditchin' my responsibility to serve my country, I would have been lyin' if I said I wanted to serve when the war broke out. On my little girl's birthday, my letter from good ole' Uncle Sam was in the mailbox. I was being drafted!

It was the worst feelin' I'd ever had leavin' my wife and daughter, but I did it. They visited me once while I was in boot camp, and Doris told me she'd made me cookies but had given them all to the soldiers on the train. When they left, I could hardly watch them go, but I raised my hand and kept a cheerful face as I waved to them on the train. I knew my life was goin' to change for the worst, and when we eventually made it to France, it did.

I had a buddy while we were on the front lines; Ralph Smith, but we called him Smitty. We shared responsibility for using the bazooka. One day he'd carry it, and I'd shoot it, and the next day, I'd carry it and he'd shoot it. I saw injury and death everywhere, and I didn't think I'd ever make it back alive. I lived with a constant knot in my gut, and a ringin' in my ears.

In France, I was wounded and shipped to a military hospital to mend. I spent weeks in bed, first feelin' sorry for myself, then when I saw how bad some of the other soldiers were, I was ashamed of myself. Some not only had missin' arms and legs, but some had terrible damages to their faces and heads.

When I finally came home, I could hardly wait to see Doris and my sweet little Alyce, and I'll never forget them both crying when I held them. Doris just hugged and hugged me, but I could tell Alyce was a little scared of me. Except for a slight limp, I looked like him, but I was definitely not the same man who'd left them there at home three years ago.

For years I'd wake up in a panic, certain I was back on the battlefield, and preparing to die. When I did that, it frightened Doris, but she wasn't afraid of me; just of the nightmares.

"You're okay, John. Go back to sleep," she'd say.

Every time I heard loud noises, I'd have to fight my first reaction, which was to drop to the floor. I did that once in a public place and everyone turned to stare at me. Alyce was with us, and it scared her, but good. But once Doris realized what had happened, she rushed to help me get back on my feet.

"He's all right," she said first to our little girl, then to the people who'd gathered around me.

I found that after the war, I had very little tolerance for some fairly ordinary things. Noise was one of them, but things not goin' as I'd expected, seem to rile me up fairly easy. Doris would kindly (and sometimes unkindly) point out that I'd go from zero to a hundred in a split second, reactin' and overreactin' to whatever it was that had just happened. I promised I'd work on that, but I'd forget to until it happened again.

Smitty looked me up when he got out of the service. I was working for a local auto body shop, and since he was thinking of relocating to California, we decided to open a shop together. I was good with repairs, and Smitty could paint, and we both wanted to be in control of our lives. Plus, it was great having a friend I could talk to and who understood what I was going through.

Smitty had two boys who were a little older than Alyce, so we had friends we could spend holidays with. This worked to fill the empty space we felt because we never saw our families in Kansas. And all they saw of us were some of the pictures Doris sent home.

Doris and me finally saved some more money, and we got a loan so we could build another house on our property. We built a two bedroom, one bath house next to our small one, and that would be our new home. We also built a two bedroom, one bath apartment over three new garages in the front. The way we figured, the rental income would cover the cost of the loan and we could eventually make some money.

Smitty and me worked well together, and the repair shop did pretty good. A lot of guys couldn't afford new cars, so we ended up fixin' and repaintin' them. They started referrin' their friends, and then their friends started referrin' their friends. Smitty and I struggled to keep up with the amount of business we had, but we didn't want to hire anyone and give away any of our profits.

Meanwhile, a really good job offer came in to do body and paint work at the Fort MacArthur Air Force Base back in San Pedro, and we couldn't pass up the opportunity. We kept our shop open, but only on the weekends, *which meant our customers had to wait a little longer for us to get the job done; but they didn't seem to mind.*

If I ever had any spare time, I loved watchin' Alyce play with the neighbor kids. I'd been working on a boat in the garage and she turned out to be a pretty good helper. I know there were times when I should have held my temper with her when she got underfoot, but she quickly learned to sense my moods and would steer clear of me if I made a mountain out of a molehill.

One time, though, I got upset with her for not being able to figure out the tool I needed, and I yelled, "Dammit, Alyce!"

For a minute she looked like I'd hit her with a ton of bricks, but then quickly asked, "Is it this one, Daddy?" as she handed me the tool I was looking for. The last thing I'd ever do was hurt her, and I was ashamed of myself for my reaction.

Bein' my stubborn self, instead of just apologizing, I said, "Yes, it is. Good girl."

Around this same time, I came upon an opportunity to invest in some land. It was a place called the Salton Sea, in Imperial and Riverside counties, just about sixty miles south east of Palm Springs.

The sea was actually a lake, created by accident in 1905 when the Colorado River flooded into the desert; it was the largest lake in California. In the 1950s, it was a thriving resort community and growin'. You could golf, swim, water ski and party. They claimed it would be the next Palm Springs, but with water.

The idea was to buy some land where new homes were planned, then once the homes were built, sell them for a nice profit. My accountant, Phil, is who told me about this investment. He had already purchased ten lots and was lookin' to start a partnership of people who had a little extra money to invest. Doris and I had about ten thousand dollars saved up, and after talkin' it over, we decided to take the leap of faith. We knew we'd miss an opportunity of a lifetime to be a part of somethin' really big if we let this slip away.

We gave Phil five thousand dollars, and he made arrangements to have plans drawn up for the buildin' of the houses. He said he'd let us know as soon as he had somethin' for us to look at. In a couple of months, he showed us some floor plans, and they looked really good. Construction could start a couple of months after the utilities went in.

He said if all the partners chipped in a little more money, we could be well on our way, so we withdrew more from our savings and gave him the money. Doris and I took a trip down there to see how things were goin' and the lake was full of water and there were people everywhere. Our lots were one block from the water, so we thought for sure we couldn't lose. We both knew this was goin' to be the best investment we'd ever made.

Phil had told us when we first started investin', that things always took longer and cost more than figured, and so when he told us there might be times when we needed to invest a little more, we weren't worried. We tucked all our extra money away so's we'd be prepared. A couple of months after we withdrew the last of our original savings, we'd managed to save almost two thousand dollars more.

When the next request came in, we had the money, but we were surprised. Phil thought we should upgrade the plumbin'. Then the next request was because we decided to upgrade the roofin'. He guaranteed these upgrades would bring us more money for the houses.

We could not set aside enough to keep up with any more requests, and we told Phil that.

"I'm sure we'll be good," he said.

But another couple a months went by and he asked us for more. This one was for the upgraded appliances.

I'm not sure why I decided to not tell Doris about this one; I think I was worried she'd think I'd let us get into a money pit investment. But I knew we'd be okay once the houses were done.

I knew Smitty and I had some extra money in our repair shop account. We'd usually go over the books every six months and split the profits. I didn't think there would be any problem if I went ahead and took mine early, so I wrote a check and gave it to Phil.

In the end, there was over forty thousand dollars in extra requests for everythin' from floor coverin's to front and back yard landscapin'. And I'd taken it all from the shop account.

I didn't sleep most nights, and I found I couldn't hardly eat. Doris tried to talk to me, but I couldn't tell her what I'd done.

"I already told you to stop askin' me questions. I'm fine. Just tired," I told her every time she asked. "So just quit askin'. You're making it worse. I'm fine. It'll all work out."

I knew I was lockin' her out, and it was the first time I think I'd ever lost my temper with her. I knew when I did that, I was hurtin' her feelings, and like a jerk, I just couldn't say I was sorry. Walkin' away was all I could think to do. I knew I'd eventually have to tell her. I was gonna to have to tell her what I'd done and then tell Smitty.

I decided to make another trip down to see how the houses were actually coming along, and when I drove up to our property, I was immediately relieved to see such beautiful homes! The additional charges would more than make up for what we could sell the homes for! I was so relieved, I was almost light-headed. It was so hot outside, I immediately broke into a sweat.

There was a man outside one house, and he looked like he was in charge of something, so I stopped to talk to him.

"Oh, my gosh. Great houses," I started. "I'm John Murphy."

"Well, glad to meet you, John," the man said, reaching for my hand. He was smart and had a hat on to protect him from the sun. "You interested in buying one of our houses?"

"They for sure turned out great, didn't they? I'm so relieved."

"About what, sir, if I might ask?"

"I'm John Murphy," I repeated, but the man didn't seem to recognize me. "I'm a partner in these houses."

The man seemed confused because he stood there with a blank look on his face, and then he met my eyes.

"Sir, I think you're mistaken." He gave me the strangest look.

"What?"

"I think you're mistaken. These are my houses." He stiffened.

"I'm in partnership with Phil? I thought there might be another partner?" It came out as a question.

"Sir, I know of no Phil. I'm a major home builder in this area, and I have no partners. Are you certain you have the right parcels?"

I did think ahead to bring my paperwork along and opened my folder. I pulled out the plots, and the man looked at them, completely surprised.

"Well, these are the plots, but they're mine."

All I could do was stand there. There must have been some mistake, but from the look on the other man's face, it didn't seem likely.

"I figure you need to talk to this fellow Phil," he said.

I was sweating profusely by this point and could hardly make it back to my car. I needed to find a phone to call Phil. There had to be some explanation for this mix up.

I had a raging headache. The air conditioning I'd installed in my '49 Chevy wasn't working fast enough, and I was dumbstruck and not able to think clearly.

When I finally found a pay phone, a recording told me Phil's phone had been disconnected. I tried again, thinkin' it was just me being worked up, but I got the same message.

All the way home, I beat myself up, and I couldn't come up with enough words to explain how I felt. I was a fool. I'd wasted all our savings, and I'd taken my money and Smitty's money. Thoughts kept rushin' in to my mind, and yet I couldn't think straight. I was so unfocused, I don't know how I even made it home.

I couldn't face Doris. Instead, I went to the shop and Smitty was there. I'd have to tell him what I'd done.

I was messed up, and he could tell by the look on my face that something was terribly wrong.

"What's going on, John?" he asked.

Then I told him what I'd done. And when I was finished, I crumpled to the floor and cried like I was a baby.

Smitty stood there for what seemed like forever and didn't say anythin'. Then I could see realization hit him smack in the face and he lunged towards me. "What the fuck, John?" and he grabbed me by my collar, pulling me up. "God damn it! You son of a bitch!"

He had a mean punch, and he bloodied my nose. I deserved everything he said and did to me.

His last words to me were "I'm going up to the cabin this weekend to finish moving in and when I get back Monday, I'm gonna kick the shit out of you!"

I couldn't go home. I knew it'd worry Doris bad, but I not only couldn't face her, I couldn't go home bloodied. I don't know why I did it, but I went back in to the shop and got the revolver I kept in my locker. I knew where Smitty's cabin was, and I needed to get this straightened out. I headed straight there.

I parked outside his cabin and waited. He hadn't shown up yet, and truthfully, I was waitin' for both of us to cool down. I knew havin' the gun was goin' to come to no good. After about an hour, I realized I'd dozed, but when I woke up, they still weren't here.

I decided to find a place for the night, to hopefully calm myself down more. I found some cabins along the highway and pulled in. Worried they might wonder why I had blood on my shirt, I put on a sweatshirt I kept in the car.

When the woman at the counter looked at me, I could tell she was shocked at my face.

"I had to brake for a deer and I hit my face on the steering wheel. I'm still a little shaken," I said. It amazed me how quickly the lie came out.

"I'm glad you're ok," she said, handin' me a key. "One night or two?"

"Two." I wasn't sure how long I'd be here; it all depended on how quickly I could get this resolved with Smitty.

I found the cabin and went immediately to the bathroom to see what my face looked like. I was surprised I didn't scare that lady more than I did. I gently washed my face, then laid down on the top of the bed. I was exhausted, but wired up. As I was drifting off to sleep, I prayed I wouldn't do anything more to regret.

By mornin', I was beside myself with guilt. I would go to Smitty's and try to talk to him. I only remembered the gun when I pulled across the street from his cabin and saw his car. For insurance, I took it with me.

269

The minute Smitty's wife answered the door, I knew I was going to be in worse trouble if Smitty and I got into it. She asked me if I wanted coffee. Obviously, Smitty hadn't told her about our brawl yesterday afternoon.

"What did you do to your face?" she asked.

"I had to swerve to avoid hitting a deer and my face hit the steering wheel," I said, again.

"Oh, my."

"What the hell are you doing here?" Smitty yelled.

His outcry unleashed something in me...a warnin' we were not going to be able to work this out. I pulled out my gun and fired at him. The flash of the gun brought me back to another time, when my job was to kill the enemy, and as he fell to the floor, his wife rushed to his side. It was then I realized I'd have to shoot her too, or they'd know who did it.

I was hoping she wouldn't be looking at me when I did it, but she was. The image of her face in anguish was more than I could take, and I shot her in the face.

Their two boys and their dog came rushing into the room screaming, and all I could think about was my Alyce; then I realized they'd be able to identify me as the killer. I had to shoot them, too.

I vomited.

I was out of control.

I left their cabin and somehow made my way back to the cabin I'd rented.

I needed to decide what to do next.

I had definitely gone past the point of no return. And as I tried to think of ways to get out of this mess, only one solution kept coming to my mind. And that was, I was goin' to have to take my own life.

No one would know what I did. And no one would put two and two together.

There would be a murder, and then there would be a suicide.

When I got back to the cabin, I took my wallet out of my pocket and set it down on the table, and then I went back to the car to grab some rope. Shooting myself would be too messy after seeing what I'd done at Smitty's. So hanging myself was the only alternative.

I tried to think of what to write as a note to Doris and Alyce, but what-ever I said would mean I had to tell them what I fool I'd been. My only thought was knowin' Doris would have enough money to live on.

Once all was said and done, she could sell the shop, and she'd be ok.

I tied the rope around my neck and threw it over an open beam in the cabin. I stood on a chair and, like I'd seen in the movies, I kicked the chair out from under myself, and then I hung there.

All I could see in the darkness was Doris' face when I first met her.

I loved that woman.

Annie's Pine Cone Lake House

The Cabins

The Cabin Lobby and Office

The Fireplace in the Lobby

Newly Decorated Cabins

Newly Decorated Cabins

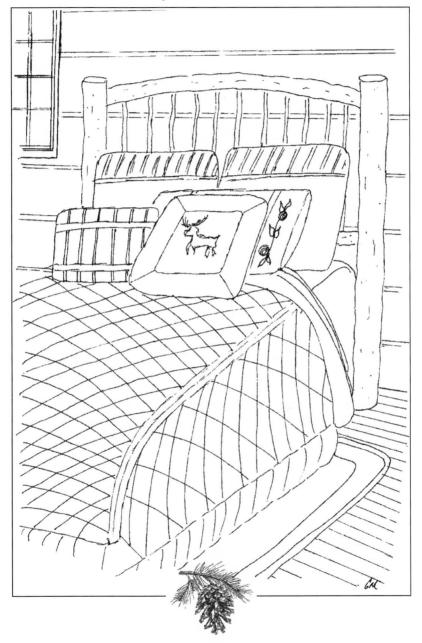

Grayson's Master Bedroom

Grayson's Living Room

AUTHOR'S NOTES

First, I need to thank my husband **Larry Braun**, who is, as Bette Midler sings, the wind beneath my wings. Throughout our marriage, he's been the most encouraging and positive influence in my life. When he asks, "Are you going to work on your book today?" it's never with question or criticism, but with encouragement. Whenever I doubted myself, which was often, he'd say, "Just write it. Write what you want to." And I came to believe him.

In all three books, **Gary Marsh** sketched the cabins and the rooms Annie worked in so you'll get a glimpse of mountain life. Graphic Designer **Susan Newman Harrison** painted a cabin in the woods, and Graphic Designer **Susan Leinen** formatted the images in the books, and does all my website updates and emails.

I also want to thank my best IT friend, **Tim Novak**, for not picking on me when I had dumb questions about downloading or saving my work. My editor, **Pam Sheppard**, is the best; her critiques have always been kind and true. And I want to thank my early readers, **Myrt Perisho**, **Susan Denley** and **Pat Aldridge**. I came to them first, a little nervous, but left with what I needed to know, albeit in gentle wrapping. And my proofreader, **Susan Jorgenson**, did her best to find all my typos and grammatical errors.

And last but not least, I'd like to thank *you* for reading my book. If you enjoyed it, visit my website at www.chrysteenbraun.com, and sign up for my newsletter. You'll be the first to know when the second and third books in the trilogy are available for order.

Like most authors, I always wanted to write, but life, teenagers and being self employed took all my creative juices. For several years, I wrote decorating articles for our local newspaper; my husband and I were remodeling contractors, and for many years we had a design store filled with furniture and accessories. Our philosophy was that everyone deserved a beautiful home, and no matter what your budget was, our interior designers did their best to make that happen.

We'd always wanted a second home, and found a wonderful old cabin in Lake Arrowhead, (which turns out to be Noah's cabin in book two) and then I couldn't resist opening a store selling mountain décor called At The Cabin. We eventually bought another home, with tall built-in bookcases filled with almost a thousand books, and twenty foot tall windows in the living room that looked out to a forest of trees.

You can find photos of both homes at chrysteenbraun.com

When we were getting close to retiring, I decided I still had enough good summers left to write my books if I set my mind to it. I believe I was sixty-eight.

I'd read a newspaper story about an unsolved murder in a town next to Lake Arrowhead, and I wanted to use that somehow in a story; the problem was, I wasn't a mystery writer. So, with a little help from a friend, I came up with the idea of a series of restored cabins that have their own stories to tell.

I'd originally set this story in 2020 working backwards, but when I decided to have Annie narrate the beginning of the story, she's just turned 80. So my entire timeline changed. The story now is in the 1980s and I had to eliminate all our conveniences; cell phones, Google, color copies, and the Las Vegas Furniture Market, which didn't open until 2007-2008. Until then, the furniture market was in San Francisco.

I also had to start over and work backwards again to make sure I had dates and events as accurate as I could. At first, it was a little mind-boggling to have to make these changes, but then I realized it didn't really *change* my story at all. Hopefully, I did a good enough job covering my bases.

All three books in the trilogy take place in Lake Arrowhead, California, and I've taken the liberty of changing a few names and dates to make them suit my story.

Wildhaven Ranch is real, established in 1994, by Diane Dragatto Williams. It's a wildlife sanctuary for native animals that cannot be released back into the wild. All their animals, such as their raccoons, bobcat, bears, and birds of prey, were rescued with the hope of rehabilitation, but were un-releasable.

Wildhaven depends solely on public donations. (I'm a Wildlife Patron.) Annie never worked with them on their gift store, although it was an idea I'd had for several years. If you love animals, please look them up and help support them.

www.wildhavenranch.org

If you ever visit Lake Arrowhead, don't forget to stop in to some of my favorite places:

Timberline in the Glen, Cedar Glen, is one of my favorite stops. It always has the most wonderfully displayed décor and collections, both vintage and new. They totally transform the store for the Christmas Holidays and create a truly winter wonderland.

Cedar Glen Inn, Cedar Glen, is a favorite family-owned restaurant.

Bill's Villager, in Blue Jay, is also family-owned. Spoiler alert; it was my inspiration for Ginny's.

Peter Baker, who is also an author (Earth's Call: Journey to Paradise), wrote his first book, a timely middle age book about climate change, while he stayed in our home in the mountains. Thanks, Peter, for brain-storming with me about The Cabin Trilogy series.

Peregrine Book Co., a wonderful independent book store in Prescott, Arizona, opened in 2012, and is nestled among the many antique stores lining North Cortez Street . We stopped in there while doing research for the Guest Book Trilogy.

"We carry a wide selection of new and used books, as well as stuffed animals, green toys, innovative games, handmade cards and cool indie magazines. Peregrine also hosts national, regional and local authors and poets as well as book clubs and workshops."

If I've made any errors or omissions, I take full responsibility.

Book Two, The Girls in Cabin Number Three, is about Annie and a woman named Carrie, who inherits her mother's beloved lake house. She and her mother have both stayed in Annie's cabins, one in 1930 and one in the present. Carrie eventually learns more about the secrets her mother kept.

Book Three, The Starlet in Cabin Number Seven, follows Annie and a man whose actress mother stayed in cabin number seven in 1929 while filming a movie up in the mountains. She carries her secret until her death.

> If you ever want to chat, just email me at chrysteenbraun@gmail.com I'd love to hear from you!

One of the best things a reader can do to help an author be successful, is to give a review of their books. Here's what you need to do:

- Log in to your Amazon account.
- Go to the product page for the book you want to review, then select the book format.

- Scroll down to the Customer Reviews section and click on "Write a Customer Review"
- Rate the book (hopefully with 4 to 5 stars)
- Write your review, and then press "Submit"
- You'll see a message "Thanks for your review."

Chrysteen Braun